# PLANTATION

## A Novel

## J.L. WHITEHEAD

Plantation

# PLANTATION

A Novel

## J.L. WHITEHEAD

This book is dedicated to my husband,
Scott Whitefleet, who has always been my rock.

To Karen Heenan, my editor and mentor.
K, I could not have done this work without you.

To my mother...I miss you more than I can say.

To every reader who purchased my work.
Thank you!

# Prologue

She raced through the waist high brush, arms pumping, sweat streaming down her face and back. The sun rode high in the cloudless sky, beating mercilessly on her dark skin. How did it come to this?

Her breath came in short gasps as she ran, the weeds slicing at her legs like invisible fingers tearing at what was left of the faded yellow house dress that draped her shoulders like a weathered sheet. Her long hair—once elegantly styled—hung, mangled and knotted, above her shoulders.

She stopped, looking around wildly for any recognizable landmark. Nothing registered. All she could see was grass and trees. She couldn't guess how far she was from the nearest road. She had to get out of the sun and find some shade so she could think.

On impulse, she looked behind her, silently praying that no one was there. The only thing she could see were bees humming drunkenly in the air above the grass…air that was windless, still, and oppressive.

Then, in the distance, she heard them. Dogs, accompanied by the sounds of engines revving. They weren't close but they were close enough.

She broke into a run again, racing towards the trees. In the open, under the blazing sun, she was a moving target. The woods would obscure her, but they would also slow her down. She sprinted, unaware of the pebbles that tore the soles of her bare feet.

The dogs were coming! She had to run faster. If she were caught, they would do things to her. Unspeakable things. Things that had been done in the dark, far away from prying eyes.

She couldn't let that happen. Not again.

Sweat trickled into her eyes, blurring her vision. She wiped it away and ran until she reached the grove of trees that would provide temporary shelter.

Tears sprung to her eyes. If they caught her, there would be punishment. There always was…always would be.

# PLANTATION

Once, she had been educated. She had gone to college. None of those things mattered now. They were less consequential than the potatoes that she had been forced to harvest or the meals she had been forced to prepare.

And then there was what happened after the sun went down.

The dogs were nearer now, but she couldn't tell from which direction they were coming. Inside the shelter of the trees, she collapsed momentarily to try and get her bearings. Everything was unfamiliar. She wasn't even sure if she was running in the right direction. If she could just get to the road, she would be safe.

A sob escaped and a silent flood of tears began to fall. A memory: her man holding her tightly in his arms, saying he would always be there to protect her. A man long gone.

She wiped the tears away with the palms of her hands and pushed on, her legs screaming in protest. She needed to rest. She needed to sleep. She needed to be home, but she wasn't sure where home was anymore.

All she knew was that it wasn't where she was running from.

Vines hung from the branches and snaked across the ground, tangling around her ankles and causing her to stumble. She teetered forward, bracing herself against the trunk of a tree before pushing on. It was at least ten degrees cooler in the woods.

All she could see were leaves and vines as she struggled to get through the dense woods. Her nostrils filled with the thick scent of earth and vegetation. Something skittered off her right shoulder and down her arm, but she paid no attention. In the distance, a crow cawed. She could no longer hear the dogs.

Just as quickly as she entered the dense growth of trees, she burst onto short grass…recently mowed grass. There in front of her was the road she'd been seeking. She could follow it to the nearest town and find help. She looked for traffic, hoping to flag down a passing car that would take her to safety.

She tripped, regained her footing and lurched towards the two-lane highway. Taking a deep breath, she made a mad dash for the road, then suddenly flew backwards as if pushed by an invisible hand. She landed on her back; her limbs locked. She lay on the dark green grass unable to move…unable to think.

She took a shallow breath and smelled burning flesh, singed hair. Her heart fluttered erratically inside her chest, and then it stopped; her eyes staring lifelessly at the blue sky above.

# The Farm

# PLANTATION

# Tarek

When Drake called me three weeks ago to tell me they were going to tear down our grandfather's home, I knew we had to go back. Drake, my sister Indigo, and I had spent so many childhood summers there with our mother's side of the family and my fondest memories of when I was a little took place there. The family barbeques, music playing, and running in the woods with my cousins and the trips to the beach. There were other memories as well, but I don't think about those. I wouldn't allow those memories to interfere with the good ones.

The Farm, as we called it, was a one-story, five-bedroom home, seated on two acres of land in Darcy County, Georgia. At one time it included a chicken coop and four hog pens. Back in the early seventies, people drove out to the Farm to buy fresh eggs straight out of the coop. My grandfather had extreme planting skills and sold his watermelons, peaches and cantaloupes locally. People used to say they could always tell when Otis Robeson had visited the general store because he had the best fruit this side of Darcy County if not the entire state of Georgia.

It was a happy time for us; a time that seemed to stand still locked away in nostalgia so sweet it almost hurts to think about it.

When I told Zach he cancelled his business plans for the week to make the drive with me. He wanted to see the place where I had spent my summers as a kid.

The drive is going to be long, but it'll be worth it. It will take two days, stopping in North Carolina for an overnight stay at the Hampton Inn.

In so many ways, I was glad he was making this trip with me. I couldn't believe it was going to be torn down, the memories it held cast to the wind like fine dust.

I glanced at the clock just above the fireplace.

3:15.

Zach would be leaving his office soon. In my mind, I went over the list of things that I had done as well as those that were left to do.

Bags were packed. Reservations had been made. Relatives had been called so that we could enjoy a good visit while were down there. I wondered how my Aunt Pearl would take meeting Zach. She was one of two remaining aunts, and she was old school.

It wasn't that Zach was gay. Gay was old news in my family. I wasn't sure whether she would accept that one of her favorite nephews had a white partner. Aunt Pearl had never been keen on white people, and from what I understood about her upbringing, she had good reason to feel the way she did.

But Zachary D'Angelis wasn't your typical white man. He was loving and kind and embodied everything decent. Honestly, when we first met, I didn't see his race. I just saw him.

His athletic build was complemented by tousled dark brown hair, gray-blue eyes and a short cut beard that he had to take a razor to every day, otherwise it grew out of control. He said that he loved me before we met. I used to tease him, saying he must've confused me with one of his other boyfriends. He assured me that he hadn't.

When we met ten years ago, we were both in our late thirties. Two cars, one condo and a dog later, we were living the dream as an interracial couple who agreed on most major issues…especially if politics, religion or just about anything socially related.

When we met, Zach took me by surprise and there has never been a dull moment with him. He started out as a friend, then a close friend, then my best friend. Eventually, he became the man that I would wind up sharing my life with.

It didn't hurt that he got along well with my brother and sister, as well as Drake's kids. The very idea of going south made me feel like a child again. It was all about the drive, eating out, laughing with Zach and later with the rest of my family. When I was about eight or nine, my mother packed huge suitcases, cumbersome with clothes for the months we would spend at the Farm. She made sure there was enough money so we could do the things we wanted once we were down there.

One thing I always remember is what she told us each year, the day before we left. She would sit each of us down and tell us to always behave and mind our manners. We were always to say "yes, sir" and "yes, ma'am" and act as if we had the common sense that God had given us. We were never to talk back to anyone older than us and we were always supposed to watch out for each other.

She was adamant about it and for the life of me, I didn't understand why. It didn't make sense until I got a little older and Indigo explained what our mother was really trying to say. She wanted us to behave not just within our immediate family but with everyone that we met. She didn't want us to get in trouble with white people.

I didn't understand that, either…even after my sister broke it down. She told me about the injustices that black people still endured in the South. She made me aware of the circumstances our relatives in Darcy County had to deal with, which explained why there weren't many left down there. Most of them had packed up and moved to Chicago, New York, or Philadelphia.

You would think that if they lived in Philadelphia, I would see them on a regular basis, but the simple truth of the matter was when they left Darcy County, they also left the family. It was as if leaving the South meant leaving everything behind, as if it was the only way to erase all traces of the injustices they had endured over the years.

The last to leave was Aunt Merline. She was the youngest of my mother's sisters and the kindest woman I had ever known. She always had something good to say about everyone she met…even the white people who subjected her family to generations of hardship. To my knowledge, she moved to Chicago without so much as a goodbye. No one has heard from her since; not a single letter or phone call.

I didn't blame her. Her husband, my Uncle Shucky, used to beat her mercilessly. I didn't find this out until I got into my teens; once we knew what he had done, my brother, sister and I avoided him like the plague.

My Aunt Macy, Aunt Pearl and her daughter Latrice were the only ones left in Georgia now. They lived in the Atlanta suburbs, although I wasn't sure where. Drake kept in contact with Aunt Pearl and our cousin, and it was through her that we found out the Farm had been sold and the house was going to be torn down.

Initially, I was afraid of losing a piece of my childhood if the house was torn down, but nobody else in the family seemed interested in saving it or keeping the chunk of land that my grandfather had tended to with his own two hands.

AJ trotted out of the dining room holding a rubber bone in his mouth. He plopped his big body down beside me and began to chew on it. I smiled at the golden retriever that we had rescued from a no-kill shelter five years ago and reached down to scratch his head. He looked up with deep brown eyes, wagged his tail in acknowledgement and went back to chewing on the bone.

My cell phone went off in my pocket. I reached into my jeans and pulled it out, glancing at the caller id momentarily before answering.

"What's up, Indie?" I asked with a smile.

"You!" my sister's voice came out sweet and low, like a fine merlot. She must be at the law office. "Are you ready for this last trip to the Farm?"

"As ready as I'll ever be." I reclined onto the leather couch and stretched my legs, so my bare feet rested on the edge of the coffee table. "When are you coming down, since I know you're not riding with Drake and August."

"What's today? Tuesday?"

"It's Monday."

"Then I'll be flying down on Thursday. I'll rent a car and drive to Aunt Pearl's. We can all meet up for dinner on Friday and take a tour of the house on Saturday, unless you have other plans."

"That sounds good."

"It just ought to. I'm springing for dinner." She chuckled lightly.

"Sounds even better. Not necessary, but better." I smiled to myself. "Okay so here's the elephant in the room. What's the real reason you think they're selling the Farm?"

Indigo paused. thinking of just the right answer. I hoped it would make sense.

"I think there are memories attached to that property. And I think the bad memories outweigh the good."

"All *my* memories were good. Well, most of them anyway."

"That doesn't mean that all the memories surrounding that house were good, T. You know that. Granddad and Grandmom lost their lives near that property. And don't forget that the land used to be five acres, until Carmichael bought them out piece by piece."

I had forgotten about John Carmichael and his family. They owned at least half of Darcy County and parts of neighboring Edison County. Carmichael was known as a ruthless businessman, and there were rumors that some members of his family were part of the KKK.

I never met him, but Drake and Indigo both said there was something slimy about him.

"In the end, it really came down to what Pearl wanted to do with the land," Indigo continued. "It was easier for her to take the payout than to fight. And you know how long and how hard she fought. She just got tired."

"Maybe," I said quietly. "But she never asked the rest of the family to help her. She could have at least called you. You're an attorney."

"True. But when you're tired, you're tired. And when you're that kind of tired, the only thing that can cure it is giving up. Besides, there wasn't much left of the Farm. The chickens and the hogs are gone. The house is falling to pieces and Granddad's field had all but shriveled up. There's nobody to take care of the property and honestly, no one wanted to."

"I still think someone could have done something."

"Would you move to Darcy County to care for a piece of property that no one really wants?"

"It's not about wanting to move down there. It's about preserving something that was in our family for three generations."

"So once again, would you move down there to be the caretaker for what's left of the Farm? And if you wouldn't, how is it fair to expect someone else to?"

She was right. I was just sad that we were losing something that held so many wonderful memories. But I still had unanswered questions. At the rate that things were going, those questions would remain unanswered.

"Tarek let's just make the trip and enjoy our family. It doesn't matter why the Farm was sold. Let's be thankful that we can see it one last time together, share some laughs and then let the memories be exactly that…memories."

"Okay." I took a deep breath. "We need to pay Aunt Macy a visit."

"We will. I already talked to Drake about her. She's still at Millview Nursing Home. We can roll through there on Saturday if you want."

I allowed my mind to wander back to 1975, to one of those summer vacations when I first met Aunt Macy. She was a heavy woman with short hair who reminded me of Florida Evans from the television show, *Good Times*. What I remembered most about her was her infectious laugh…that, and the way she could cook. At every family barbecue on the Farm, Aunt Macy would take charge of Grandma's

Grandma's kitchen and soon enough, it would be filled with the familiar smells of frying chicken, pork chops and catfish.

But time has a way of stealing bits and pieces of a person as it rolled by. Aunt Macy lost weight and then her mind, although many of us didn't know what started first. She used to always tell me I was her favorite, but I suspect she said to all of us at different times to make us feel special.

The door to the condo opened and AJ bounded off the couch. That was my cue to end the call.

"All right, Indie...I gotta go. Zach just came in."

"Well, you tell my man I said hello and I will see him in the deep, deep South." She chuckled again, and I could almost see her at her desk with her pumps slung to the side, long beautiful locs pulled away from her face and cascading down her back.

"All right. I'll see you on Thursday. Have a safe flight. Are you riding back with us or flying?"

"Flying. You know how busy my schedule is. I barely had enough time to get away for this. You just be careful driving and I'll see you in Atlanta."

"Not if I see you first," I said with a smile as Zach crossed the room with AJ in tow.

"Kiss my ass."

I burst out laughing. "I'd be there all day."

"Must be Indie," Zach said as he pecked me on the forehead. "Hey, girl."

"Just remember he could have been mine," she warned playfully.

"I'll let you dream," I said. "Talk to you later."

"Bye. Love you."

"Love you more." Ending the call, I slid my phone into my pocket. "So, how're you doing? Good day at work?"

"Fair day at work." Zach kicked off his shoes. "I'm glad it's over. I'm ready for this trip to the Farm."

I smiled at him as he made his way to the wine chiller and pulled out a bottle of white zinfandel.

"Yeah. Me too." I stood and started towards the huge walk-through kitchen, reaching into one of the smoked cherrywood cabinets for wine glasses.

"So, are you ready to say goodbye?" Zach uncorked the bottle.

I shook my head slowly. "I wish I could say I was. I mean, it's the Farm. The main staple in our family. After this weekend it'll be gone."

"You haven't reconciled yourself to the sale. Did you talk to Indie about it?"

"Yep." I handed him the stemless glasses.

"And?" he prodded.

"She thinks I should accept it and move on. It doesn't matter why the Farm was sold. We should just enjoy family, reminisce and be grateful."

"Do you agree with her?"

"I don't *not* agree with her."

Zach poured the wine and stared at me with those piercing eyes. For a moment, neither of us spoke. He took a sip and then smiled slightly at me. "Something else may be bothering you about the sale of the property. When you're ready to talk, I'll be here to listen."

I nodded solemnly.

"Are you all packed?" I asked, changing the subject.

"Yep." His smile widened, enhancing the dimples on his cheeks. "I'm gonna go take a shower." He started towards the master bedroom, AJ trotting behind him. "You coming?" he asked.

"In a bit." I took another sip of wine. "Enjoy…and don't use up all the hot water."

"I make no promises."

# Indigo

I put the phone down and looked across my desk at the wooden frame next to my name plate. It was a picture of me, Tarek, Drake and his kids, Madison and Autumn. Drake's wife, August, had taken the picture at their family Christmas dinner two years ago.

Memories of my family were wonderful…at least most of them. Tarek's memories of our family were awesome, and I meant to keep it that way. He was too young to know about the squabbles over Granddad's farm. He didn't know about the shady dealings of the Carmichael family. And why would he? Nothing that happened back then affected him directly.

Losing the Farm was always going to upset him. And he's upset with Aunt Pearl for not fighting to keep the property in the family. But truth be told, the Farm stopped being a farm years ago. We watched silently as the years rolled by and the land got sold off piece by piece. The animals were the first to go, and then slowly, the Farm fell into disrepair, and no one seemed to want to step up to the plate to be the caretaker and preserve the memories that had been made over the years.

I acted like Tarek was this innocent little boy who can't manage disappointment but that's just my version of him. Tarek was a dreamer. He tended to look at the world through rose-colored glasses and I couldn't take that from him. As his older sister, it was my responsibility to watch over him, whether he liked it or not. I know he's grown and in a stable relationship with someone who loves him, but he will always be the little brother that I would fight fiercely to defend and protect.

Drake was always self-sufficient, the intellectual in the family. He was decisive; strong…everything I thought an older brother should be. Since our parents were long gone, he watched out for me and Tarek.

"Ms. Robeson?" Lucille Benton stood in the doorway.

"Hey, Lucille." I stood slowly, feeling my lower back crack as I stretched.

"Will you be needing anything else this afternoon?"

I smiled and shook my head, remembering that she had a doctor's appointment. "No. You can take off for the day. I have a few more things to do and then I'll be leaving, too. I hope everything goes well."

Lucille was an amazing assistant. She was also suffering from breast cancer but even with her diagnosis she always managed to carry herself with head held high and with the grace and dignity of a woman that clearly came from an era where it was more important to be a lady than anything else.

"Thank you. And when are you leaving for your trip?"

"Thursday."

"Well, enjoy the time with your family. And for once, leave this place behind and have some fun."

I gave a quick laugh. Lucille knew that I worked too much. She was always on me about that. "I promise to have fun. But I will also have my work cell on me just in case something comes up."

"I'll only call if I have to." She gave me the smile that always managed to warm my spirit and then disappeared, closing the door behind her.

I slipped into my high heels just as my cell phone rang. Reaching for it, I gave the face a quick glance before bringing it to my ear. "Hello."

"Indie?" It was my cousin Latrice.

"What's up, girl?" I said with a smile.

"Waiting on you to get here so I can kick back with my favorite cousin. Plus, I need you to tighten up my braids for me."

I started to laugh. "For fifty dollars I'll tighten your braids." I chuckled. "How are you and how's Aunt Macy?"

"She's fine. I went to see her today. Told her you were coming down and she's looking forward to seeing all of you."

"And how's she managing the sale of the property?"

"Not too well. But she's managing."

I nodded slowly. Aunt Macy was the one who always put together the family barbecues when we visited down south. She was the one who would cook and bake. God, I remembered her red velvet cake and chocolate pie. Latrice was her only niece. Even though it wore on her, she never let Aunt Macy feel as if she were just put away in a home, forgotten by her family.

"Well, when I get down there, I want to take her out to lunch. Or even better yet to the dinner we're having on Friday before we head back on Sunday."

"She'll be thrilled."

"No doubt." I said. "I'm looking forward to seeing you. Have you talked to your mom?"

"No." Latrice paused. "And she doesn't seem like she wants to talk to any of us. I think she's feeling guilty about selling the Farm."

"She had her reasons. We don't hold her no ill will."

"Well, onto another subject. Shucky wants to see ya'll."

"Shucky? What the hell for?"

"He thinks this will be the last time he'll see the family in one spot."

"Well, good luck with that."

"No matter what he did, he's still our uncle."

"I don't have time for abusers even if they're related to me." Blood rose to my cheeks as I shook my head.

I remembered Uncle Shucky too well. He was indirectly responsible for Aunt Merline moving to Chicago and not talking to any of us anymore. I couldn't forgive him for that. I had heard him berate her on more than once occasion…accusing her of everything except the one thing I knew she was doing, which was being a decent human being. I didn't understand it then, but I do now: Shucky did what most men do when they're doing wrong and projected his infidelities onto his wife, trying to make her out to be guilty of the very sin he was committing.

"Even if he's wrong, Indie, you got to forgive him and move on. He's still family."

"None of his blood runs in my veins, so fuck him!" I said with more anger than I had intended.

Latrice sighed. She was big on family relations regardless of the past of the family member in question. "Well, I look forward to you coming down. And I guess the reason why I brought Uncle Shucky up is because he's throwing a fish fry at my mother's."

I rolled my eyes to the ceiling.

"He's trying to show that he's changed, Indie. You, Drake, and Tarek need to at least meet him halfway."

"We don't have to do anything." I took a pause. "But I'll pass the message on to Drake and Tarek."

"I appreciate that."

"So, tell me something, Latrice…what do you think is going to come out of this fish fry dinner that Shucky is throwing?"

"Maybe it'll undo some of the things that have happened in this family. Maybe it'll bring about the healing this family needs."

"Is anyone else coming down for this event?"

"I've reached out to our family in Chicago and DC. I only heard back from one of our cousins who said that he might come."

She paused and I could tell that she wanted to add something to her last statement.

"I know you think that I'm being stupid for wanting to hold onto the family like I do," she began hesitantly. "I know that you don't understand it, but…Indie, you don't know what it's like.

"There's nothing down here. There're no jobs…unless I want to be a nurse, work in hospitality or retail, and honestly, that's not what I want." She paused again. "I'm thinking about coming up to Philadelphia to live."

"What about Aunt Macy?"

"I'll send for her just as soon as I'm settled. I can't leave her down here. If there's nothing left for me, there's nothing left for her."

"Do you need my help?"

"I need your guidance. I've never done anything like this before, but I have to. Things aren't right down here."

She was right. I was surprised that she hadn't made this decision a long time ago. Darcy County was a tiny dot in the outback of Georgia. It might have been possible for her to carve out a living if she moved further north to Atlanta, but not in Darcy County.

"Of course, I'll help you, Latrice. We can talk more about it when I get down there."

I heard her release a breath; almost as if she had been expecting me to say "no."

"Thank you," she said in a low voice.

"No need to thank me. We're family. That's what we do."

"Well, I owe you. Maybe we can go to The Orchard and have lunch."

"The Orchard?"

"It's a new restaurant that just opened right off I-85. It's a really nice place. I'll be happy to treat you."

"That's appreciated but not necessary."

"I don't want to impose."

"No imposition." Something told me there was more Latrice wanted to tell me. I listened for a moment waiting for her to say something. "Latrice?"

"There's something going on down here. Indie." she blurted out. "I can't put my finger on it, but it doesn't feel right."

"Something like what?" I leaned back in my leather chair and crossed my legs.

"I can't explain it but…I just can't wait to leave from here. As a matter of fact, the sooner I get out of Georgia…the better."

"Is it that bad?"

She took a deep breath. "Yes."

# Drake

"Maddie! Autumn! Come on!" August called to the girls. "We're getting ready to leave."

I smiled to myself as I heard them running around upstairs. We would be leaving for Georgia in about thirty minutes. I looked at my computer screen and then began to shut it down. While I was looking forward to the trip, it was more for the girls than for me. If I never saw my grandfather's farm again, it wouldn't make a bit of difference.

Not all the memories were bad. As a matter of fact, most of them were good. But there was a lot of pain in that house. It ran just beneath the surface of the façade of a happy family.

My father used to tell me stories of how my grandfather raised them with a heavy hand. I knew my grandfather had an explosive temper and at times I had seen it up close and personal. Don't get me wrong, Granddad never hit me, Indie or Tarek even though he was brutally old school. In his mind, everyone had their place and if you strayed from that place, punishment was swift and severe. And of course, his love affair with corn liquor didn't help. But he grew up in a different time…a repressed time, when men ruled their homes and their families paid the price for the father's failures and injustices that had been inflicted on him.

"Drake?" August poked her head through the doorway of my home office. She looked just as beautiful as the day we married ten years ago. She was deliciously full figured, filling out her dark blue jeans and red blouse in all the ways that I loved. Her naturally thick hair was tied back with a silk scarf I had given her for Christmas a year ago.

"Yeah babe?"

"I'm getting the kids ready to go. Is the car loaded up?"

I came out from behind my desk and made my way over to her. I couldn't resist. "All loaded." I pulled her close.

She wore little makeup…eyeliner and some nude lipstick. August was naturally beautiful without all the extras.

"Drake?" She smiled as I placed a gentle kiss on her lips.

"You know what?" I murmured.

"What?"

"I think you're amazing. How the hell did I get so lucky?"

She giggled girlishly just as our nine-year-old poked her head into the office.

"Daddy, Autumn's trying to pack all of her stuffed animals in her school backpack."

Madison looked so much like August, her long hair styled in five long braids that cascaded just past her shoulders.

August looked down at her and brushed her fingers over one of her braids. "I'll be up in a minute."

"Okay." Her eyes took in both of us and then she smiled in the way that most nine-year-olds do, then turned and raced out of the office and up the stairs. "Autumn, mommy's coming to get you!"

I smiled while pulling August to me. She kissed me gently on the mouth while running her hands over my arms.

"You were saying?" The way she looked at me made me weak.

"I was saying"—I paused— "how did I get so lucky?"

"That's easy." She ran well-manicured fingertips over my chest. "You just have good taste in women."

Her smile made me want her in every way, and yet we had time for none of it. It was going to be a long drive.

"I'm going to check on the girls." She turned to walk out of the room. "And did you pack your inhaler?"

I nodded. "Yeah, I got it. Can't go anywhere without that."

"And your laptop?"

"We're only going away for a few days."

"Sweetie, I know you." She paused in the doorway, half turning to face me. "You'll go crazy if you can't be in touch with work. Pack your laptop."

"Wow," I half mumbled, smiling.

"I'm just stayin' on top of you."

"Not in the way that I want, but I'll take it," I said with a smirk.

"Okay girls! Let's get your stuff out in the car!" she called to them, padding up the steps.

I smiled to myself. This moment was bittersweet. We were saying goodbye to family cookouts, summer vacations and reunions. We were saying goodbye to a piece of our history.

I understood the reason, even though I didn't agree with it. Aunt Pearl didn't want the responsibility of the family homestead. She couldn't keep up the house which was only held together by hopes and prayers. I couldn't blame her for selling it and I couldn't blame her for who she sold it to.

She got a sweet deal. John Carmichael bought the homestead for three times what we all thought the property was worth. He wanted to tear down the house at once and begin developing a housing project. Rumor had it that would give him a monopoly for equitable housing for the residents of Darcy County.

The sale gave Pearl added income, enabling her to change her circumstances. I knew she didn't want to stay in Atlanta and figured she would use those funds to move to Philly or Chicago and call it a day. And maybe that was for the best.

No one went down south anymore. Family reunions, while still being held, didn't take place in Darcy County. We would meet up at Disney World or Virginia Beach for old times' sake, but much of the family didn't attend these events. Correction: the older family members didn't attend, which was weird because they should minimally want to see the kids.

"Daddy?" Madison stood in the doorway.

"Yeah, baby girl. What's up?"

Her smile always melted my heart. My little girl was going to be tall, but right now, she was all arms and legs…and honestly, if I could keep her as my sweet little girl forever, I would do it in a heartbeat.

"Are we going to see any of our relatives or is it going to be just us?"

"I think it's going to be just us this time, sweetie. Why?"

"Well, this will be our last time going down south for a while, right?"

I nodded. "Probably."

"Then we need to make this visit special."

"Did you have something in mind?" I slid my arm around her shoulders and guided her out of the room.

"Well, I wanted to leave a picture of great Grandmom and Granddad at the place where they were buried."

"You did?"

She smiled. It was the type of smile that daughters had been giving their fathers for generations. I was suddenly aware of my heart beating inside my chest.

"Yep. Autumn and I have been working on it for a couple of days now. We're going to finish it in the hotel tonight. Do you think we can do it, Daddy? I mean, leave it at their grave?"

"I don't think they would mind."

She smiled again and it was like the sun bursting through an overcast sky.

"Good. I'll go get the picture and put it in the car." She rushed out of my office.

This would be a good trip. We would close this chapter of our lives and I was okay with this. After all, we were still writing our story.

# Tarek

When my family in Darcy County had a barbecue, it was more than just a small party. It was an event.

Uncle Shucky would do most of the grilling. Aunt Macy stationed herself in the kitchen and served up potato salad, macaroni salad, fried catfish, and cornbread. Uncle Shucky moved the living room speakers to the windows and music blared from the stereo over the backyard. Aretha Franklin, The Isley Brothers, The O'Jays, Earth, Wind and Fire and The Dells flooded the air as Aunt Pearl served plate after plate of delicious, home cooked, southern soul food. Aunt Merline stayed in the yard and sometimes in the kitchen. Mostly she stayed near Uncle Shucky, until he started working on the second pint of rum.

Uncle Shucky also took us to the gator pond in a sectioned off part of a Georgia State National Park. It wasn't fun. I wanted to see the gators eat something…anything. But most of the time they were floating motionless on the surface or sitting near the banks or in the reeds waiting for something to devour.

I was bored with these visits except for the one time we saw a gator grab a duck. We would have missed it had Uncle Shucky not spied the reptile swim slowly towards the unsuspecting fowl. The six-foot gator had been dark green or black. It seized upon the unsuspecting duck so fast that all we heard was a splash and a quick squawk, and then it was gone. The gator slipped soundlessly under the water.

Later, Uncle Shucky told us that they drown their food so they could eat it. That stuck with me and for the life of me, I didn't know why.

We were well on our way to Georgia when I woke up. The car stereo was playing softly. Zach stared straight ahead, saying nothing when he heard me stir. He looked over and gave me a quick smile. His smile had a way of speaking volumes.

"You okay?" he asked. "You were rocked out for quite some time."

"Yeah." I stretched. "How far are we?"

"Virginia."

I watched him, then I turned my attention to the trees flying past the car at seventy miles an hour. The sun was slowly starting to ebb.

"I'm going to stop at the next rest area so I can take a leak," he said as if he read my mind. "Would you mind taking over driving until we get to the hotel?"

"Not at all."

We were in Virginia. We still had North Carolina to get through and that was a long ride unto itself. But after that we could bunk down for the night. We would reach the Farm tomorrow and I was glad about that. I was filled with a nostalgia that I couldn't explain.

It had been years since I had been down there. When you don't go to a place for years, time seems to slip away almost as if it had a life of its own. I expected the white fence that surrounded the property to be gone. I knew there would be no more chickens, which meant no fresh eggs from the chicken coop. Those were the things that made my visits south memorable.

But memory can play tricks on you. And when you get older, sometimes things you thought you knew could prove to be an outright lie.

The next day we pulled up in front of what remained of the Farm and I looked in awe at the house that held so many memories. It was in worse shape than I had imagined. I turned off the engine and slowly got out, pulling my sunglasses over my eyes. The fence that had once surrounded the whole property was crumbling in some places, completely gone in others. Standing by the car, I took in the full scope of the place. It was as large as I remembered, which surprised me. Four acres of beautiful land; land that I had run barefoot through, listening to my grandmother yelling at me to put my sneakers on before the snakes got me.

Zach didn't say anything as I walked slowly up the unpaved driveway. The first thing I noticed was that most of the windows facing the road had been broken. Someone had spray painted a giant X on the front door.

The roof sloped to one side. Leaves and pine needles had accumulated in the pockets of where the roof dipped but had not caved in. At least not yet. The curve sat directly over the kitchen and two of the bedrooms. One of those bedrooms was mine. Well, mine and Drake's.

"Do you want to…" Zach began.

I held up a finger.

"Shh." I was still taking all this in.

I took a deep breath. I could almost smell the non-existent scent of sizzling meat on the grill. Laughter from family members echoed in my ears, drifting away on the lazy afternoon breeze.

I approached the porch and stood perfectly still. There were no holes in the floor. The oak trimmed front door was still in place, shut firmly on its hinges. I approached cautiously, not sure why I was so hesitant in placing my hand on the knob.

The air was warm…not as hot as the beginning of August but cooler than November. The breeze rustled the leaves in the nearby trees and once again, I was struck by the size of the house and its current state. I wondered how Aunt Pearl could have let it slip into such decay. Without realizing it, I was blaming her.

Not knowing what to expect, I turned the knob slowly and pushed the door open. Instantly my nose was assaulted by the scents of mold and un-lived-in house, intermingled with the ghosts of the seventies. I put my shades on top of my head and looked around the living room. Most of the old furniture was still in place but had decayed to the point that it was unusable; the floor model color television set was long gone but the stereo on the corner shelf remained. The tinted dust cover had accumulated several years' worth of dirt. I peered through it and could barely make out a forty-five still on the turntable.

"Tarek?" Zach said from just behind me.

I barely heard him. Memories of Uncle Shucky with his white shoes, matching socks, and a seersucker suit filled my mind like it paid rent to live there. He always had a drink in his hand. When he talked to you, he always wanted to get up in your face, bathing you in vodka or rum fumes. There were times when the tidal wave of alcohol almost took off my eyebrows.

"Yeah?" I looked through the house. I could see through to the backyard; the outside wall had collapsed a long time ago.

"Are you okay?"

I nodded, turning slowly to face him. The pain must have resonated on my face because without saying a word, he enveloped me in a strong, tight embrace. I hugged him back with equal intensity, involuntarily flexing my muscles against him. The memories hit me relentlessly. Aunt Merline seated quietly in the kitchen as Uncle Shucky got drunk in the back yard. Now I knew that she was preparing herself for the abuse she was going to receive when she got home, but I didn't understand it then.

Aunt Macy was too busy playing hostess to see what was going on, or at least that's what I thought. Everyone knew Uncle Shucky was a drunk, but we kids were completely oblivious to the physical abuse Aunt Merline received at his hands. I think she deliberately shielded us from anything that could have left us emotionally scarred.

I remember Aunt Pearl taking a stand against Shucky; but she did it firmly and behind closed doors. I didn't see it, but I heard it.

Zach's hand slid against the side of my face, caressing my cheek. That spoke volumes of what he was trying to do, but it didn't stop the flood of emotions that threatened to overtake me. I shrugged him off, heading into the dining room. The stink of mold assaulted my nose as I took in the peeling light green paint, shattered table, and broken chairs.

The kitchen was to my left. I walked in and was immediately struck with images of my grandmother and aunts baking, cooking, chattering, their laughter floating through the room. The refrigerator door was open, hanging drunkenly on one hinge. The oversized sink was empty. Instinctively, I reached for the light switch and flicked it upwards. Nothing happened. I shook my head absently, realizing that no electricity had run through this house in years.

I took a deep breath and immediately regretted it. The house smelled awful.

"What room did you sleep in?" Zach asked softly.

I pointed towards the back of the house. The kitchen separated the first bedroom from the guest rooms that sat towards the rear of the house. My grandparents' master bedroom was to the right of the dining room.

We walked out of the kitchen together and turned to the left, entering the first bedroom. The room smelled wet…damp. The room Drake and I had shared was small…smaller than I remembered.

Tattered blue curtains hung at the windows, while flakes of light blue paint littered the floor. My grandfather had built a makeshift closet to hold our things. It was empty. The full-sized mattress that my brother and I shared was soaking wet. I didn't want to touch it.

"This is it." I turned around to look at Zach. "Was it."

He looked over the room and then back at me.

"Are you ready to go to the hotel?" he asked.

I nodded reluctantly. I didn't want to leave but I didn't want to stay, not in this place so different from my memories. But being here was a stark reminder of all that I was losing.

I couldn't blame Aunt Pearl for not wanting to take on responsibility for the Farm. It was a lot of land to take care of, even with a riding mower. There were no animals. The chicken coop, the hog pen and the stable that housed the cows had been replaced by crumbling outlines of what had been. I remembered when those semi-buildings housed animals, when my grandmother went out to the chicken coop to retrieve eggs, when my grandfather took me out to slop the hogs and milk the cows. The memories turned in my head like a carousel. It was beautiful in its intimacy and warmth. And it no longer existed.

"I figured I find you here."

I turned to see Aunt Pearl in the doorway between the living room and dining room. She had gotten noticeably heavier over the years, but she had never allowed her weight to give her a reason not to carry herself with pride. Her hair fell just above her shoulders in a stylish bob. I never remembered her wearing a weave, but it looked as if she just had her hair done.

For a moment I stood still, then I rushed to her and wrapped my arms around her bountiful body, flooded with emotions. She hugged me back with a hard strength. I could've sworn that I felt her shudder, but when I pulled back, there were no signs of tears in her eyes.

She pulled a piece of tissue from her pocket and wiped her nose. "How ya doin', baby?"

"I'm good."

"You look it." She turned her attention to Zach. "Zach?"

He smiled disarmingly, flashing white teeth and beard-covered dimples.

"Well, don't just stand there. Come give your aunt a hug." She reached for him, and he stepped into her arms.

That was unexpected. I thought she would have strong feelings about meeting Zach. She knew he existed, and she harbored opinions about gay life. I knew she didn't have a warm spot for us, so her taking Zach into her arms was a surprise.

"You are so much more handsome than what I pictured." she said, taking a step back from him. Her smile was warm and inviting; her makeup was flawless. She was making her late seventies look great. "Let's get out of this broken-down shell of a house and go grab some dinner."

She led us out of my grandparents' house and away from my memories. As we followed her to the gravel driveway, I noticed she was wearing flat shoes. I didn't remember her ever wearing sensible shoes before, but time had done its thing.

"Follow me," she said with a luminous smile, clutching her purse to her ample hip. "Try and keep up."

Zach got into the passenger side of our car, and I got behind the wheel. I had just started the engine when my aunt pulled out of the driveway leaving a trail of dust behind her. We followed close behind her...barely. I forgot how fast she drove. The woods were a green blur as we rolled through Darcy County. In some ways, the area looked the same and in other ways it was completely different.

We flew past a park lined with trailer homes. My grandmother had a friend there that she visited with from time to time. Her name escaped me, but I remembered that her home always smelled like a mixture of Mr. Clean and lavender.

"So that was good," Zach said, pulling me out of my thoughts.

I flashed a smile. "Better than I thought." I looked up at the road as it curved to the right. "I could have sworn she would've pitched a fit meeting you."

"So why did you bring me down here?"

"Because she needed to meet you. She needed to know that we aren't just fucking and that what we have is so much more."

"And she needed to meet me to know that?"

I nodded. "That's part of it." I took a deep pause. "How about I'm just proud of you?"

"I'll take that. I love you, too." Zach broke into a smile and covered my hand with his.

"Give me a sec." Still following Aunt Pearl, I turned the BMW into a parking lot. "Where the hell are we?"

The parking lot was huge. The restaurant was bigger. Carmichaels name flashed in huge italics over the entrance. I wheeled our car into a spot several rows from the entrance. Zach got out first and I followed. Aunt Pearl stood beside her car, still clutching her oversized purse.

"Come on," she said with a smile. "The rest of the family's already inside."

The rest of the family? Were Drake and the kids here? August and Indie? Why didn't anyone call us? We had all left pretty much around the same time.

Zach noticed August and the girls first as we made our way over to a long table. As staff buzzed around us, I saw my cousin Latrice and a young woman I didn't recognize. There were several unfamiliar people at the table, but I assumed they were family.

Indie wasn't here yet. Drake sat beside his wife, and I went over to them. He stood up and we embraced.

"Why didn't you tell me you got down here?" I pulled out a chair and sat beside him.

He tilted his head towards Aunt Pearl, who stood at the head of the table. She tapped a fork against her water glass, signaling everyone to be quiet.

"Welcome, everyone." She said. Everyone quieted to hear her speak. "I'm so glad to see so many of you here today. This is a day where we are to rejoice in love and family. I'll answer any questions that you may have about the Farm. But for now, let's bow our heads in prayer and thank the lord for all our blessings."

We had just lowered our eyes to pray when a commotion erupted near the entryway. Aunt Pearl stopped mid-sentence and everyone at the table turned to look at the woman who had entered the restaurant.

She was tall…voluptuous. Everything about her screamed sex. She wore a form-fitting two-piece charcoal skirt suit that clung to her round hips and small waist. A huge, sheer black hat sat tilted slightly sideways on her perfectly coiffed head. She was accompanied by three young muscular black men. She moved silently through the room on six-inch black stilettos, long legs encased in sheer black stockings. Her long dark hair flowed over her shoulders to her full bust in a well-styled mane, while her beautiful dark skin and impossibly high cheekbones appeared to have been professionally made up.

One of the men pulled out her chair and she mumbled a cursory, "Thank you," and reached for the menu.

Zach leaned into me. "Real?"

"Drag or trans," I whispered with a smile. The woman looked over at our table.

"Dear Heavenly Father…" Aunt Pearl began again.

I barely heard the rest of her prayer, managing to nod in the right places and say, "Amen" when she was done.

"You sure she's drag and not a real woman?" Zach asked quietly.

"You know any six-foot-two women in stilettos that wear that much makeup?"

"Boys!" August interrupted. "It isn't polite to talk about anyone behind their back." She paused for a moment, then snickered. "But what you're looking at is surgery. Now leave it go."

Zach and I shared a chuckle with August just as a server came to take our orders. She was all eyes and blonde hair pulled back in a tight ponytail. "Can I take your order, or do you need a few minutes?"

"I'll need another minute, but could you answer a question for me?" I didn't understand why I was whispering.

"Sure, sweetie." The server leaned in. "What do you need?"

"Who is that woman over there?"

"That's Lady Onyx," she said with a sideways glance. "She our towns version of a star, even if it's in her head."

# Drake

I followed my brother's gaze toward the woman. Whoever she was, she was tall, sexy…but she wasn't real. All of them fake curves and artificial titties didn't do a damn thing for me. What was real was sitting right next to me. You couldn't beat August. My girl who later became my wife was the best.

The server took our order. I was ready to eat.

Aunt Pearl had asked if we could all meet at Carmichaels for a light dinner and a semi-reunion. I'm not sure if she called Tarek, but I was glad that he and Zach finally made it here.

I knew that my aunt wanted to make this a memorable event. This was going to be something that even though my heart was breaking, I wanted to make it special for my girls. They had never been to the Farm. They wouldn't understand why I was making such a big deal about this, especially since to them it would be some broken-down, old, dusty piece of land that nobody cared about.

They would be wrong. They wouldn't know about the barbecues and celebrations that we had out there. They wouldn't know about the time that I took Tarek out to the chicken coop and had the rooster chase him out because I made him throw sticks at them. They didn't know about the times that Tarek and I lay in bed on lazy summer mornings while grandma made breakfast for us. Bacon, eggs, grits…or rather, hominy. Grandma used to always call grits, hominy.

Granddad would slop the hogs first thing in the morning before going off to work and then we would help him slop them when he came home. Granddad was explicit about what he did to keep the animals alive. And I loved it. Feeding the animals was my favorite part of being on the Farm.

The nights were always warm and from our small bedroom, we could see millions of stars because there were no city lights to block out what grandma would call, "nature's lights."

"So, Drake?"

Aunt Pearl slid herself into the empty seat to my right. There was a glow about her. She looked like the Pearl of my teens…except she had gained a bit of weight and light make-up covered her cinnamon brown features. Her deep brown eyes were round, thoughtful. Her eyes were one of the many things that I loved about her.

"I just wanted to have a quick chat," she began. "I wanted you to know why I sold the house."

"You don't have to go into the why, Aunt Pearl," I said, turning my chair to partially face her. "I understand. We all do."

"Daddy."

I glanced to my left. Autumn looked up at me with her mother's eyes and a smile that captured my heart.

"Baby, Daddy's talking."

"But I just want to go to the baffroom."

"That's bathroom, sweetie. Ask your mom to take you."

August stood up, mouthing, "I got this." She took Autumn by the hand and led her away.

Pearl watched them with a wistful smile, then turned her attention back to me. "So, I wanted to tell you why I sold the Farm."

"We already know. You couldn't afford to keep it up. That's a lot of land." I smiled to myself. "And that was some beautiful land. A lot of good memories are attached to it. But you couldn't do it all alone. We understand that. We didn't come down as much anymore. I can't tell you the last time that we were all down here at once."

"I think that you were about thirteen years old." She settled into the seat, trying to get more comfortable. "My sister had ya'll down for the summer. That was the time we all went to the beach overnight." She smiled again. "Yes, lawd, we had ourselves a good ole time. We packed ya'll kids up in the car and drove to Smith's Grove in South Carolina and had a good time cookin' and such."

I smiled at the memory.

"And at nighttime, your Aunt Merline would sing. Lawd, that girl could carry a tune."

I nodded. I barely remembered Aunt Merline, but her voice was one of the things that I never forgot. She would sing and everyone would get quiet. All you could hear was the crackling of the mini bonfire and her voice. It was almost magical.

"Anyway, I have a check for you, your brother, and your sister. It's not much but you're all family and you each deserve to have some of the proceeds of the sale."

"That's not necessary."

"The heck it isn't," she said with a wave of her hand. "Everyone got a little something. Like I said, it ain't much. I'm picking up the check for this makeshift dinner, so enjoy." She winced as she stood.

"You alright?" I jumped up in case she needed me to help balance her.

"No, honey." She waved her hand again. "It's my back. Nothing you or anybody else can do. I'll be fine."

"Don't drink the Kool-Aid, ya'll." A husky female voice came from somewhere behind me.

We turned our heads to see who was speaking to us. It was the woman who came in a few minutes ago. I hadn't noticed her as she approached the table. "And beware of the smoke."

"What the hell you doin' over here?" Pearl hissed, her demeanor changing so quickly that I had to look at her to confirm the emotion that I was hearing.

"I'm just sayin'." She looked uncaringly from Pearl to me. "Umm, Pearl, you got good genes in your family."

"Mister…"

"It's Miz," she said, raising a painted index finger. "Don't make me have to correct you in front of your family. You know I hate doing that."

"Henry…:

"It's Lady Onyx." She turned to look at me. "And how are you, you fine glass of chocolate milk?"

"You forget that I'm licensed to carry a .45, Henry." Pearl was downright pissed. "You wanna test me?"

Lady Onyx was close enough that I could take in the scent of her perfume. If we had been in a club, aside from her height, I would not be able to detect that she had been a man at one time in her life. She was pretty enough—maybe even beautiful—but Aunt Pearl was clearly agitated by her presence, and I didn't understand why.

Lady Onyx appeared to be unfazed by my aunt's temperament.

"Like I said…" she began. "Don't drink the Kool Aid…huntee. And watch out for the smoke." She turned toward the three men at her table. "Oh, my food has arrived." She looked at my aunt. "I just love their chili cheese fries." Another glance at me. "They're hell on a girl's figure, but I can't help myself."

This chick was purring like a kitten. She was seductive, I could see that clearly. My curiosity peaked as she walked away with the rolling gait of a runway model as she re-joined her friends.

"I can't stand that man." Pearl cut her eyes at the table where Lady Onyx was sitting. "Running around here like he's a real woman just 'cause he had some surgery." She looked directly at me. "He ain't no good. Never was, even before he went through all of that."

"How do you know him…her?" I wasn't sure what to call him.

"I been knowin' him since he was a little boy. But what he did was unnatural. Gettin' feminine pieces put on him like he was some giant jigsaw puzzle."

The waitress returned with a tray that held our drinks. She set them down with precision and then whizzed to another table.

"Well, Aunt Pearl, you have to know that there are some men who were born as men but later found out that they prefer to be female."

"It's not natural, Drake!"

"Okay. Okay. Calm down. I don't want you to have a stroke because of something that you don't have any control over."

"He ain't nuthin' to me. I was talking to my family. He had no right to butt in."

"It's no big deal," I said with a slight chuckle. I heard a child crying from somewhere across the room. "You gotta admit, he does look good as a girl."

"He's still a boy underneath all them plastic parts. Had the nerve to waltz into my church during service. Took a seat right next to all the choir members. Had everybody talking about him."

I raised my hands up in mock surrender. "Okay, Aunt Pearl." I took a deep breath. "The check is a nice gesture but totally unnecessary. Thank you for the meal, though."

"I'll have the checks for you, Indie and Tarek when we meet at the Farm tomorrow."

"What time?"

"Eleven o'clock." Her smile returned slowly to her face. "I planned a day for us."

I gave Aunt Pearl a big smile. She turned to another family member and started talking to them.

"What did I miss?" August pulled out the dull yellow plastic chair and sat down.

Autumn sat next to her sister and dug into the plate of chicken fingers in front of her.

"Nothing much." I shrugged. "Aunt Pearl has some type of day trip planned for us tomorrow."

"What kind of day trip?"

"Couldn't tell you." I stood up. "I guess we'll find out tomorrow. I'm heading to the bathroom." I lowered my voice. "Whatever you do, don't mention Lady Onyx."

"The Lady who?"

"Onyx." I tilted my head towards the table where she was holding court. "Aunt Pearl? Not a fan."

August's mouth formed a silent "O" as I started to the men's room.

My mind kept circling around Aunt Pearl's reaction to Lady Onyx…or Henry. I knew she had homophobic tendencies, but she took Tarek and Zach's relationship well enough. Then again, Tarek was family. She had no reason at all to try to understand Lady Onyx.

# Indigo

2:35 A.M. I was exhausted. My flight got in on time and I was now waiting for my one suitcase to come through the luggage carousel. I was never a patient person but fortunately, there weren't that many people waiting with me. At this point, I wouldn't get to my hotel until sometime around four. That would allow me to get six hours sleep before I would have to make my way over to the Farm…or what was left of it.

Latrice filled me in on the state of the family homestead. If she were correct, there wasn't much left to it. It was going to break my heart to see the house in such disrepair, but there was nothing that I or anyone else could do about it. Pearl did the best she could, but she couldn't have imagined she would not be able to hold on to the land that had flourished so willingly under my grandfather's touch.

According to Latrice, Uncle Shucky was throwing a fish fry on Saturday. I didn't know why Shucky wanted to host a gathering, considering the damage he inflicted on this family. In my mind, he was responsible for Aunt Merline moving to Chicago and away from the family forever. I understood, even though I didn't agree with her choice to leave us. The family didn't abuse her, though she may have felt we didn't protect her enough. We certainly didn't shield her from Shucky's abuse…especially when he was drinking.

But I remember hearing Aunt Pearl telling Aunt Macy there was nothing they could do to intervene between husband and wife. As a young girl, I had no idea what she was talking about. As an adult, I couldn't agree with her less. It *was* her job to intervene. It was our job to protect our own, and we had failed.

The other thing that bothered me was Latrice telling me something weird was going on in Darcy County. Carmichael had been buying up property down there by the neighborhoods, but that was nothing new. Carmichael had been buying up land down there since I was a kid. There was something else going on that she didn't feel comfortable with.

Whatever it was, it was prompting her to move out of Georgia for good.

Finally, the carousel began moving. My suitcase would be out any minute. It held several days' worth of clothes, but everything else—my laptop, my digital recorder, my work and personal cell phones, and a few client files—were in my carry-on. The sooner I could get to the hotel, take a nice hot shower and get a few hours' sleep, the better.

Doing work on a family trip should have been a no-no, but duty has a way of calling when you least expect it. I wanted to make sure that I was still on my game. My mahogany brown suitcase appeared, along with several other pieces of luggage. Rather than waiting for it to reach me, I went to grab it, set it on its wheels and started towards the Enterprise lot to get my rental vehicle.

In a few minutes, I was heading south on I-85 feeling the semi-cool morning breeze blowing through my locs. It was times like this when I felt good. There was simply something about being in the south that stirred something positive deep within me. I came from here. My family came from here. That's what made losing the Farm so painful. It wasn't just the home that Aunt Pearl was selling; it was the memories. I couldn't be mad at her, though. Not one bit. After all, I wasn't willing to step up and take care of the place.

Ten hours after arriving in Georgia, I was standing alone in front of my grandparents' home. The cool breeze on my face reminded me distinctly of fall. I got here ahead of everyone so I could have some alone time with the house. I wanted to breathe in the memories.

The front yard looked barren without the rose bushes that grandmom used to tend. It's funny, I remember this front yard being full of life. And at that moment, I never felt more alone.

I pulled my sweater tighter around me as a late model Jeep Cherokee pulled up in the driveway. I turned, ready to greet my family, but a tall white man with a slim build got out of the four by four. We didn't say anything to one another for a full minute before he spoke.

"You shouldn't be on this land." He took a couple of steps towards me.

Something told me that he was neither friend nor foe; but I took a step back anyway.

"This is my family's land." I said.

"No." He looked me up and down, then then lit a cigarette. "This land belongs to my father."

"Unless your father's name is Otis Robeson, he doesn't own this land. At least not yet."

"Who are you?"

"Does it matter?"

He took a drag of his cigarette, staring at me through deep green eyes, and exhaled a plume of blue smoke.

"My family is coming here so we can say goodbye to this house." I said breaking the silence that fell between us. "Settlement hasn't gone through yet, so technically the property and everything on it still belongs to the Robeson's."

"No need to be hostile, little lady." He took another drag of his cigarette.

I made a mental note on everything about him. He looked to be about six foot four, lean…very intense eyes. He was handsome in a rugged kind of way. His brown hair was thinning at the top and he looked like he spent too much time in the sun without sunscreen.

He also shouldn't be here. This was family time.

"My name is not little lady. You can call me Ms. Robeson."

"What's your first name?"

"My first name is irrelevant." My response was a little harsher than I intended. "You haven't earned the right to call me anything other than Ms. Robeson."

When the man smiled, the wrinkles around his eyes grew more pronounced, but the funny thing was that his smile never touched his eyes. There was something cold about them…something I didn't like nor trust.

"The name's Cal. Cal Carmichael. My father just brought this piece of land."

"That's all fine and well, but right now we still own this land, Mr. Carmichael." I looked over his shoulder to see a black BMW pulling up the driveway. I recognized Tarek's car and was relieved that he and Zach had arrived exactly at this moment. "My family is starting to arrive. This is a private time for us, so if you don't mind…"

"You're kind of feisty." I didn't like his smile. It wasn't the smile of a pleasant man. It was the smile of someone that was plotting…scheming.

"I don't know what that means…but if you can kindly excuse yourself from this property until the sale goes through, it would be appreciated." My gaze bounced back between Tarek, Zach and this stranger named Cal.

"You'll be seeing me again, Ms. Robeson." He took another hit off his cigarette and then flicked the butt away, turning silently and bypassing Tarek and Zach without a word of acknowledgement. They watched him as he got into his Jeep, started the engine, put it into gear and drove off.

"Hey, Indie." Tarek wrapped his muscular arms around me. It felt good…safe.

"How are you, boy?" I kissed him on the cheek. I was never so glad to see him as I was at that moment.

When Tarek let me go, Zach stepped up close. "You okay, Sis?" Concern resonated in his voice, and in his gray-blue eyes.

"Yeah. Now bring it in, silly." I hugged him tightly.

"Who was that guy?" Tarek looked back at the trail of dust the Jeep left in its wake.

"Cal Carmichael."

"Carmichael?" Tarek looked at me, and I could see a flicker of anger in his deep brown eyes. "You mean the Carmichaels that own every damn thing down here?"

I nodded.

"What the fuck??" Tarek was pissed. "You mean Pearl sold the land to them?"

"Apparently." My voice came out sullen.

"That's fucked up!"

"Tee! Calm down." I assumed my role of the big sister. "There's nothing that we can do about it now. It's a done deal."

"Calm down, babe." Zach placed a hand on Tarek's shoulder, running it down his back. "There's nothing that you or anyone else can do now."

"Yeah, but the Carmichaels?" Tarek looked back at the unpaved driveway. "Granddad wouldn't have wanted that."

"We have to abide by Pearl's decision, Tee, you know that."

He shook his head slowly. He didn't want to accept it. I knew how he felt. I understood that Pearl needed to sell the land, but I couldn't understand why she would sell it to someone our grandparents hated.

"Do you want to go inside?" I asked. "Take a last look?"

Tarek nodded, and we started towards the house just as late model Lexus SUV pulled into the driveway. We all turned, watching with smiles as Drake's girls leaped out of the back seat as their parents climbed out of the front. The girls rushed to Zach and Tarek, giving them hugs and kisses. August walked up and embraced me with a loving smile.

"Hey, girl." She took a step back and gave me a once-over. "Girl, you look good. You need to give me your diet plan, cause a sister can use your help."

"You don't need to lose weight, August." I raised my eyebrows. "If your man likes it…"

We both burst into giggles. The thing I loved about my sister-in-law was that she was straight up no-nonsense.

Drake approached and gave me a hug. I could tell he was looking at the house over my shoulder. The loss of this property was hitting him hard, too.

A green Buick pulled up in front of the property. Aunt Pearl, Latrice, a woman I didn't know, and a familiar-looking older woman got out of the car and headed towards us. The older woman moved significantly slower but as she got nearer, my heart leapt.

"Indie!" Pearl wrapped her arms around me and hugged me tight to her large bosom. "God, girl, it's been so long!"

"Hello, Aunt Pearl," I said quickly and then released her so I could hug Latrice.

The older woman took slow deliberate steps, the gait of someone who was recovering from surgery. She was heavier, her silver hair cut short, but I knew it was her. She approached, looking at me with thoughtful eyes. We just stared at one another. My eyes welled with tears.

Drake came over to us with August and the kids in tow.

"Aunt Macy," he said softly.

"Well…don't just stand there." She reached for Drake. "Give your ole' aunt a hug."

And that did it. The dam burst and the tears began to flow…first from me and then from Drake. We hadn't seen Aunt Macy since we were kids and honestly hadn't expected to see her at any family functions on this final trip.

"Now, shush…" She turned to me, reaching out with fingers I could see were bent just a little from arthritis. "Indie."

I hugged her gently, sniffing…trying to get myself together.

Thoughts of a younger Macy filled my mind. Memories of stories shared at night when she came to visit the Farm when we were younger, followed by laughter; how she used to get out in the middle of the yard and dance to Marvin Gaye.

"Little Indie." Her voice came out raspy, her southern accent strong and thick. "Well, not so little no mo'."

"How have you been?" I looked her up and down, wiping away tears.

"Aunt Macy." Drake wiped away his own tears. "I want you to meet my wife, August." He turned to look at her. "August, this is my Aunt Macy."

"Well come 'ere, chile." Macy reached for August, and they embraced.

"It's wonderful to meet you," August said.

"You can call me Aunt Macy, just like Drake."

"Thank you." August stepped aside to allow her daughters to approach Macy with a smile. "I will."

Madison walked up to Macy and smiled up at her while her sister clung to her daddy's leg.

"It's a pleasure to meet you, ma'am. My name is Madison." She hugged Macy as if she had known her all her life.

That's when the tears started to fall from Macy's eyes.

"Aunt Macy, what's wrong?" I asked.

She shook her head, hugging Madison.

"I just missed...so much." Her voice cracked with emotion. "Is that your sister behind you?"

"Yes. That's Autumn." Madison said matter-of-factly. "Momma says she named her that because she was born in the fall."

"Is that so?" Macy looked at Autumn.

Autumn stayed quiet. Drake nudged her towards Aunt Macy.

"You don't have to worry none, chile," she said. "I don't bite."

Autumn took a cautious step towards Macy. Aunt Macy reached into the pocket of her ankle-length dress and pulled out a piece of candy. Autumn took it hesitantly, looking back at her daddy to ask if it was okay.

Drake nodded. "It's okay sweetie." He was smiling broadly now. "What do you say?"

"Thank you," she said shyly, allowing herself to be hugged by Macy.

"Aunt Macy, Tarek and his friend are inside the house."

I was surprised that time hadn't aged her that much. Don't get me wrong, she had lines on her face, but it wasn't what I would have expected from a seventy-seven-year-old woman.

"Tarek has a friend?" Macy looked towards the house.

"For years now." I reached for her arm.

Macy stopped walking before she reached the porch as a crisp autumn breeze caught her from behind. She shook her head slowly.

"So, the house is gonna be torn down, huh?" she said with a wistful sigh.

"I'm afraid so."

Madison ran up to her and grabbed her hand. "I'll walk with you Aunt Macy."

"I think I'd like that, young lady." She smiled sweetly down at Madison as she allowed herself to be led to the front door.

"Macy!" Pearl called from behind her. "You need your cane? You know, to keep your balance?"

She nodded, without looking back at Pearl. "If ya' don't mind."

Pearl rushed back to the car just as Tarek and Zach appeared in the doorway.

"Aunt Macy?" Tarek rushed down the porch steps and gently hugged her.

"Little T." Macy allowed herself to be enveloped by his embrace. She kissed him on the cheek as she released him. "My God son. It sho' is good to see you."

Pearl handed Macy the cane and she started up the steps gingerly. "Let's all go to the house and see what's left."

"Aunt Macy," Tarek began. "Before we go into the house, I want to introduce you to my friend."

Macy paused, looking at Tarek and then at Zach.

"You Lil' Tarek's friend?" she asked Zach.

Zach nodded hesitantly.

"You sure is a handsome thing." She broke into a grin. "Are you Tarek's husband?"

Zach looked at Tarek for a second, and then back at her. "Not yet Ma'am. But I'm working on it."

"Well...if and when you do, welcome to the family." Macy reached out and hugged him. "Now, let's go to the house and see what's left."

She went through the door with Zach on one arm and Tarek on the other. Pearl and the rest of the family followed.

A soft breeze blew, rustling the leaves in the nearby trees.

I remained outside with Latrice and the woman who came with her. She was cute; hair cut close to the scalp and dyed blonde. She had a light brown complexion, with little makeup, and big brown eyes. She was wearing tight blue jeans, a tee shirt, a denim jacket and a pair of kick-ass combat boots.

"Tricee…who's your friend?" I asked.

"I thought ya'll was gonna be ignorant and never ask." She turned to her companion. "This is my friend, Kisha."

"Hi." Kisha gave me a quick smile.

"Good to meet you."

"I heard a lot about you." Kisha said with a pronounced southern accent. "It's finally good to connect."

"I couldn't agree more." I looked around, nostalgia threatening to overtake me once again. "So shall we go into the house?"

Latrice and Kisha nodded and followed me towards the porch.

"There's a lot of history in this house." Pearl spoke up so she could be heard. "Take your time. If there's anything that you want to take, let me know so I can put it aside for you. A lot of this stuff is going to be donated or trashed, so please, feel free."

Drake nodded slowly and wrapped his arm around August's waist. She rubbed his back for a moment, then looked to her left to watch their daughters walking towards the bedrooms.

"Baby," she began. "Why don't you take the girls on a tour and show them the room that you and Tarek slept in? I think that they'd like that."

"Yeah." He raised his voice. "Come on, princesses." He scooped up Autumn. "Daddy's gonna show you where he stayed at when he came down here."

"Then can we go get ice cream?" Madison perked up as she followed him to the second bedroom.

"After lunch." Drake led them away.

I watched Tarek, Zach and Pearl leave the room, leaving August, me, Kisha, and Latrice behind.

"One of the Carmichaels came here," I said to August.

"The Carmichaels?" she responded as we walked through the living room.

"Cal Carmichael. His father brought the Farm." I was suddenly acutely aware of the sagging floor.

"As in the place that we ate at yesterday?"

"You went to a restaurant owned by the Carmichaels?" Latrice asked.

"It was called Carmichael's big as day. Pearl hosted a small impromptu family dinner there."

"Well, we should press pause on telling Drake for a moment. The sale of this place is really hitting him hard."

"It's affecting all of us." I looked around the room.

"Mom tried to hold onto this place." Latrice spoke up. "She really did. She just…couldn't take care of it."

"Oh no, Latrice, we get it, and we understand." I realized that I may have triggered guilt. "I wasn't trying to imply anything. It's just that one of the Carmichaels came to the property before you all came. He gave me a feeling I didn't like."

"You mean like he's trifling?" Latrice asked with just a hint of sarcasm. "Because if that's what you meant, trust me, he is."

"In what way?"

Latrice paused before Kisha prodded her to continue.

"You might as well tell 'em. They gonna find out anyway."

All eyes turned to Latrice as she stood in the decaying living room.

"Maybe we should go outside for a minute." Latrice started towards the front door, her feet kicking up a light cloud of dust.

August followed, giving a backward glance to the bedrooms, where the sounds of her daughters' laughter caused a smile to light on her lips. Drake must have done something in typical Drake style. Of course, he did.

Latrice walked out the front door and into the warmth of the bright sunshine. A welcome cool breeze rustled the leaves again as a flock of birds suddenly took flight.

"Mom sold the land, but it wasn't because she had to," Latrice began. "It wasn't even because she wanted to." She paused. "John Carmichael forced her."

"Forced her?" I wish I could say I was surprised. "In what way?"

"He threatened her." Latrice looked over my shoulder at the door to the house. "Carmichael has been buying up property in the county like crazy. He's already bought enough land to expand his orchard. In fact, Mom is going to have us go on a horse drawn tour of the property."

"Why would she want to go on a tour of his property?"

"She won't tell me, but I think it's just to bring closure to all of this. Once we go on this tour, she will feel like it's all over. This chapter will be closed. We'll move up north and not look back."

August shook her head. "That makes no sense."

"Maybe not." Latrice looked up at the sky and then back to August and me. "But this is how Mom wants to deal with it. With Carmichael buying up all the land, she thinks it will be finished once we leave."

"So, she wants to go on a tour of Carmichael's orchard? The person that's buying our homestead?"

It didn't make any sense. Why would Pearl want to spend time on land belonging to someone who technically stole the land that our parents were raised on? Well, it didn't matter. I wouldn't be going on this tour. I wasn't going to celebrate someone who strong-armed their way into our family losing their home. It didn't matter if we didn't live there anymore. It didn't even matter that we hadn't visited in years. It seemed wrong that our home—and yes, it was still our home—wouldn't be there. It was our heritage. It felt like Pearl was deliberately erasing our memories.

And there were a lot of memories. Too many for me to think about now.

"Well, I'm here for the tour of our homestead." I didn't hide the sadness in my voice. "But then I'll say my goodbyes and head back up to Philly. I got a lot of work to do."

"You ain't goin' on the carriage ride through the orchard?" Latrice asked, surprised.

I shook my head. "No. But I'll do your hair for you before I go." I managed a wistful smile. "Come up to my hotel and I'll tighten you up."

Latrice flashed a huge smile, reminding me why and how much I loved her. I could see why Kisha loved her…assuming she did. I wasn't going to pry. Like with Tarek and Zach, the subject would come up in its own time.

"But you comin' to the fish fry, aren't you?"

I shrugged. "Where's it going to be?"

"Uncle Shucky's house. He brought himself a rancher right outside Darcy County."

"I don't think so." My voice came out low. I didn't want to go, that was the truth. I wanted to put all of this behind me. It was great seeing my family again, seeing Pearl and Macy. But I was ready to head back to my life in Philly. I had work to do, and I couldn't do it while I was distracted with the sale of this property that I will never see again.

I was sad about all of this. Angry? Possibly. I understood what was going on. But maybe Pearl was right: it was time to close the door on this chapter of our lives. It was time to go.

"Good." Latrice turned on her heel and started towards her car. Kisha followed her.

"Well, lawdy, lawdy, lawdy!" I recognized the booming voice before I laid eyes on him. I looked to Latrice first, checking for her reaction to Uncle Shucky walking up from the road.

As I expected, Latrice rolled her eyes and continued towards her Toyota Prius.

"You ain't gonna speak to me?" He came to a standstill.

I shook my head. He hadn't changed a bit. He was decked out in all white: a white running suit with white sneakers and a white Kangol hat.

Uncle Shucky was only an uncle by marriage. He was never my favorite, but I respected his candor. You always knew where you stood with him. Part of me always resented the fact that he abused my Aunt Merline, and after she moved to Chicago, disappearing from our lives, I wrote Shucky off despite his efforts to stay in contact with the family.

Rumor had it he had changed…that time had mellowed him out. I heard through the grapevine that he had even expressed remorse over Aunt Merline leaving him. For me, none of that mattered. Hate would be too strong a word for what I felt for him. I wasn't ready to let him fill the role of my uncle. That wasn't going to happen. At least not today.

"Hey, Shucky," I said as he embraced me.

"Well, lemme look at you." He took a step away from me. "What you doin' now? For work, I mean? I hears that you a lawyer."

"Attorney," I heard myself say, but my mind had gone to back yard barbecues. I could almost hear a younger version of my Aunt Macy hollering for him to get out there and dance while Frankie Beverly and Maze played on the stereo. They were good memories but…

"Well, damn, girl. Good for you." He said through tobacco-stained teeth.

He hadn't changed much at all, just gotten older. Fatter. Gray hair where he had it and thinning where he didn't.

"You gonna be able to make the party at my house?"

I shook my head.

"I don't think so," I said. "I got to get home. I got work to do."

"Work before family?"

"In this instance."

"Well, maybe you can change your plans and stop on through. We won't be havin' too many more of these gatherings. Not with the sale of the homestead."

Anger rose in me so fast that it took me by surprise. But the words I wanted to say stopped short of spilling from my lips. What good would it do? What's done was done. Me layin' out Shucky wasn't going to accomplish anything accept bring up old feelings I should have buried long ago.

"I appreciate you hosting a barbecue, Shucky, but I have to get back to my office." That was a partial truth. I had work to do, but I also had a choice of when I could finish it. I wasn't feeling Shucky right now. He wasn't my blood uncle, so I didn't owe him anything.

"Uncle Shucky!" Drake said behind me.

My brother was coming from the house with his kids right behind him. They watched him as he embraced Shucky.

"Drake!" Shucky laughed while giving him a quick, manly hug. "Damn boy, you grown up as hell." He looked down. "And who are you, little lady?"

"Maddie," she said shyly.

"Well, pleased to meet you, Maddie. My name's Shucky. I'm your daddy's uncle."

Madison took a step back and looked up at Shucky, squinting her eyes until they were almost closed. "You don't look old enough to be my daddy's uncle." Her smile revealed a missing tooth.

He burst into a hearty grin.

"Shucky? I thought that was you." Macy smiled as she made her way down the steps. For a moment, I saw the woman who hosted cookouts, made the best macaroni and cheese in the south, and was now about to hug the man who beat her youngest sister into submission. She held out her arms. "Come here baby."

Their embrace was genuine, with no hint of anger on either side. Is it possible that Shucky had really changed? And if he had, Aunt Macy had apparently accepted that change.

"I understands that you gonna have a fish fry tomorrow?" she asked.

Shucky nodded. "You comin'?" he asked, looking into her eyes.

"If my sister will carry me over there, I would love to."

"Where is Pearl? Is she here?" he asked.

"Back in the house." She pointed with her cane, a smile on her face I swear I hadn't seen since the seventies.

The door banged open, and Tarek exited the house with Zach and Pearl in tow, the three of them in conversation. When Tarek saw Shucky, his demeanor changed. As he descended the front steps, he looked at everything except Shucky.

It was coming. I could feel it. I just didn't know what it was.

# Tarek

Shucky had the nerve to show his face on our land? After all this time? He thinks that time forgot what kind of man he was back then, but I hadn't.

"Tarek? Lil T?" Shucky's lips curled into a wide smile. "Come here, boy. Give your uncle a hug."

"I haven't been Lil T since I was ten." I didn't move. I couldn't. I stared at him, noting how much he had aged since I saw him last. The anger flared up, followed by a fear I tried not to think about. Aunt Merline was somewhere in Chicago, and it was because of him.

"Yeah, but you still be Lil T to me." He took three steps toward me.

Before I could respond, he enveloped me in strong arms. I stood there for a moment allowing him to hug me, and then I pushed him away. By the look on his face, he was as surprised as I was by my reaction.

"You think time can erase what you did to this family?" The anger surged from somewhere deep inside of me, coming to the surface burning hot as emotional lava. "You know how much Aunt Merline meant to all of us? You just tossed her aside like trash!"

Shucky's expression changed in a split second. His eyes went flat, and he folded his arms across his chest as he stepped back away from me.

"Boy…" His voice was low, the voice that he reserved for his enemies.

"I stopped being a boy a long time ago!" The rage boiled over like a pot of water left on the stove for too long. "Talk to me like an adult!" Zach's hand curled around my bicep. I shook him off. "You beat her like she wasn't shit!"

"You were too young to know what was goin' on between your aunt and me. Talk about what you know, not what you think."

"I know you made life hell for her." I took a step towards him. "I know how you treated her."

"Shucky? Tarek?" At the sound of Aunt Macy's voice, we closed our mouths and stared at each other. "You need to find out how to forgive each other."

"There's nothing for him to forgive me for!" I snapped.

"Forgiveness ain't never hurt nobody." Macy shifted her cane from her right hand to her left and took three old lady steps towards Shucky, moving each foot slowly and deliberately. She placed her hand on Shucky's shoulder and said something in his ear.

I didn't want to hear about forgiveness. I wanted to punch Shucky. Not just punch. I wanted to beat him with my bare hands. I wanted him to feel the same amount of pain that he caused us. It didn't matter that Aunt Merline was in Chicago with other family members. I wanted to see her, and I couldn't because of him.

"I'm…I'm sorry," Shucky mumbled.

Zach placed his hand on my shoulder while I looked at him. Something changed in Shucky at that moment. It was as if the arrogance had been sucked right out of him, like I was looking at a version of Shucky that I remembered from my youth. There was a light in his eyes that was there before he started drinking.

"Tarek…Lil T," he began. "I can't make up for what I done. But maybe we can talk for a little bit. Over a beer maybe? Tomorrow?"

I wanted to be mad at him. But I couldn't, not in front of Aunt Macy, who was smiling from ear to ear. I gave him a quick nod.

"I'm gon' head on back to Pearl's," Aunt Macy said, making her way towards a maroon Chrysler 300. "We're having dinner at the house tonight."

"Tonight?" No one had mentioned this to us.

"Yes, tonight." Then she raised her voice, and it came out louder and clearer than I could remember. "Pearl! You comin'?"

"I'm comin'." Pearl followed Macy to the car, watching as she made her way to the passenger side. Macy's body was beginning to fail her, but her spirit remained intact. She still had the same spunk that she had when I was little. I was suddenly overcome with how much I missed the "old" Aunt Macy.

"You ready to head over to the hotel?" Zach said from my left.

He almost startled me. "Oh…yeah. Let's go to the hotel and chill for a bit."

I was still shocked by Uncle Shucky's change of attitude. God knows he had a lot to apologize for, but I never remembered him apologizing to anyone for anything.

I looked at Zach and then back at my brother and the kids. "Let's go."

"Where are you guys stayin' at?" Drake picked up his youngest daughter.

"At the Hampton Inn right off I-85," I said, forcing myself to smile at my niece.

"Well, hit me up on my cell. We can all head over to Pearl's together."

"Sounds like a plan." I looked over at my cousin and her girlfriend as their car pulled slowly up next to our car. "You going?"

"To the dinner?" Latrice smiled broadly. "I wouldn't miss it. Just as soon as can get Indie to come tighten up my braids."

I scanned the property one last time, flooded by a million memories. Most of them were good, and those were the ones I would hold onto. Even though we lived far away, I had a strong connection to this place. I was going to miss this little piece of my history.

The weather-worn mailbox across the road leaned precariously to one side. It was the same mailbox that my grandmother had trotted out to when she went to get the mail. Something else that would die along with the rest of the property. A tidal wave of inconsolable sadness washed over me. My eyes filled with tears, but I wiped them away.

My gaze fell on the wooden electric pole that stood in front of the house like a silent sentinel as the engine purred almost silently in the background. I had seen this pole a thousand times. But this was different. It was completely covered with sheets of paper.

Not paper I realized but flyers. Missing persons flyers. There were dozens of them. Some were new, but others had been faded by weather so that the images were blurred. Worn photos of prom queens and high school football players mixed with pre-teen children whose photos appeared as if they were school pictures. They hung limply from the pole held in place by a single staple.

I looked at the pole one last time before putting the car into gear, the flyers slipping out of my mind.

"See you boys tonight!" Latrice called.

"We'll be there!" Zach said loudly with a huge smile as I eased onto the road.

I didn't give another thought to Shucky as we drove silently up the road to the main highway. I needed a nap.

# PLANTATION

# The Woods

As the sun slipped low in the darkening sky, a crowd of fifty people gathered, speaking in hushed, forbidden tones as a heavy-set, bleached blonde woman made her way to an oversized cauldron of boiling water, big enough to hold two or three human beings. She wore an off-white shift dress that looked more like a uniform than something she would wear for everyday use. She prodded the fire with a poker, bringing it to a roar, and looked over her shoulder with a smile that was almost wistful. Outside of the murmurs of the crowd and the occasional buzz of cicadas, everything was quiet.

She walked with the gait of an elderly woman as she made her way to a lone shed that stood just off center from the clearing where everyone had gathered. The night was warm, almost claustrophobic despite them being outdoors. Three men appeared from a small house that sat on the perimeter of the clearing. Two of the men were white, and they flanked a dark-skinned man who walked hesitantly between them. The dark-skinned man looked malnourished. His eyes darted wildly from side to side; when they fell on the boiling pot of water, he jerked backwards, almost losing his balance. The two white men tightened their grip on his arms as they led him towards the boiling pot of water.

"No!" He tried to turn away from the pot as his fate became clear.

"Let this be a lesson to all ya'll," the woman said in rolling, matronly voice. She adjusted her cat-eyeglasses as her gaze fell on the prisoner. "Anytime you get it in your head to leave this plantation, you'll meet the same fate as Jose."

She looked at the man she called Jose.

Realization of what was about to happen washed over Jose. He struggled and dug his bare feet into the ground as the two men wrapped his wrists in a thick rope.

"No!" Jose pushed back against the two men, but they held him firmly in a wrestler's grip. One of the men walked away, the end of the rope dangling loosely in his hand. He tossed the rope over a low hanging branch in a nearby tree and smiled.

Jose bucked wildly, but his attempts to escape were futile.

"Hold 'em!" she shouted, making her way over to the three men. "Hold 'em!"

She stood silently in front of the men for a moment, then she raised her right hand and slapped Jose across the face, stunning him into silence.

Tears flowed down Jose's face as he looked from her to the tree and then back to her.

"I stay," he said in broken English.

"I already know you don't want to be here," she said in a surprisingly light tone. "I can't keep you here now."

She turned her back on him and started toward the crowd. "String 'em up."

The two men hauled on the rope, pulling Jose off his feet and into the air. He struggled wildly, swinging like a pendulum over the boiling water. A thin layer of steam wafted over Jose's feet. The muscles in his arms bulged; he shouted incomprehensibly in his native language. The crowd looked upwards as Jose struggled relentlessly.

Slowly, the two men lowered him into the boiling water. He let out a blood curdling scream and continued screaming until they hoisted him out again. The skin on his feet and legs had turned bright red.

"Please…please." Tears streamed down Jose's face as they lowered him back into the churning cauldron, causing him to scream again. This time they submerged him into the bubbling water up to his waist.

Just as quickly as the screaming started, it stopped. Jose's head lolled to the side as he fell unconscious.

The crowd took a step back, watching as the men lifted Jose out of the water and then lowered him again, as the skin bubbled and slipped off his body. A few people turned away as Jose's body was submerged fully into the cauldron.

"Let this be a lesson to all of you!" the woman yelled. "You need to appreciate what we do for you! You want to leave…leave. But don't let us catch you, because if we do you…" Her voice trailed off as they all gazed at the example of Jose's unconscious form.

The men lowered his body into the water, waited, and then hoisted him high in the air so the crowd could get a good look at what was left. The odor of cooking flesh filled the air. Someone vomited. For effect, the men lowered him one last time into the boiling water and then pulled his body out and dropped it on the ground as if they were discarding trash.

"Now get back to work." Alone, the woman walked back towards a house that sat off in the distance.

"You heard her," one of the men shouted. "Get back to work!"

# Drake

My girls were curled up on the sofa in front of the television, under a large blanket that I assumed came from one of the bedrooms. I watched them for a second. August was looking beautiful as always. We had rented a two-bedroom condo for the weekend here in Darcy County and right now I was grateful for the down time. My heart was sitting on that couch, and I was smart enough to know it.

I had a few friends who had kids and couldn't have cared less about them. I didn't understand how anyone could have children and not look out for them. I was lucky to have August; lucky in the way that most men should be when they have a good woman.

Most of the guys that I knew were still single…and they were trying to function as though they were twenty-something when they were in their forties. I admit, I was out there for a little while. I chased my fair share of women. But all of that changed when I met August.

We met at a birthday party given by a friend in honor of either his or his wife's birthday. I arrived at the party a little after midnight and was there for a good while before I saw her. She was standing by the front door like she was getting ready to leave. I had never seen a woman as fine as her. She was voluptuous…but there was something more. Our eyes met for a split second and then she looked away while she continued her conversation with my friend's wife. She looked my way again and gave me this smile that just warmed me. It was one of those smiles that turned your stomach inside out and made the tips of your toes vibrate.

Her look wasn't sexual. I couldn't put my finger on it. But I made my way over to her and stood a few feet away as she wrapped up her conversation. My friend's wife looked at her and then at me…smiled and then mouthed something like, "I'll see you later girl," and walked off leaving us in our own space.

"You look like you have something to say," she said with a slight smile.

Her deep brown eyes, partially obscured by wire-framed glasses, were intense.

"You know, I did." I took a couple of steps until I was close enough to smell her perfume. "But now that I'm here, I forgot what I wanted to say."

"That's not the way to get a girl's attention."

"You're right," I said. "In my mind, I had this wonderful line that was meant to sweep you off your feet."

"Really?" Her smile widened just a bit, revealing a hint of Hollywood white teeth. "Well, don't keep me in suspense. What's this killer line that's meant to sweep me off my feet?"

I looked up at the ceiling, smiling more to myself than to her, and then I looked her directly in the eyes…those deep, dark beautiful eyes. "What's your name?"

"That's it?" she asked. "That's your line?"

"It works every time."

She nodded her head, her smile broadening.

"August. My name is August."

"My name is Drake."

"Drake?"

"Yep. But if you don't like it, I can change it to something else."

"No…no. Drake is fine."

She chuckled and I was hooked. Her chuckle was light and girlish…sweet and feminine. I wanted to get to know her.

"Would you like a drink? I mean, I saw that you were leaving but I didn't want to miss my chance."

"No, we can't have that."

I continued to watch them as my youngest nodded off. I would carry her to bed soon, but for now, I wanted to savor this moment. It wasn't often that I could look at the loves of my life in one spot.

August looked up at me from her spot on the couch and smiled, and her smile melted my heart. I would do anything for this woman…and she knew it. And yet, she never abused it.

My iPhone buzzed in my back pocket and without thinking, I answered, never taking my eyes off my family. "Hello."

"Was I right to light into Shucky like that?" It was Tarek.

"That depends," I said, instantly jumping into big brother mode. "Is that how you felt?"

"Yes."

"Then no. You had every right to say what you said."

He sighed on the other end of the phone.

"I'm not feelin' this carriage ride through the orchard. I think it's stupid. Zach and I will probably head out tomorrow morning."

"Well, I think it's stupid too, but you should go. We all should."

"Why?"

"Because it'll be one of the last times we do something together as a family. Do you see yourself coming back down here after this land is sold?"

"No."

"Then go." I spoke clearly, trying to convince him. "I'm not trying to tell you what to do. But I think you should go. No regrets. Remember?"

"Yeah. I remember." I could tell he was reconsidering the carriage ride.

"Besides, it might be nice," I continued. "A final farewell to the homestead."

"Damn man, you make it sound like something to celebrate."

"We should celebrate. It's all about family." I turned and leaned on the counter. "We have bits and pieces of our family left that we can come and visit any time we want. We should want to do it. Besides, the girls will be looking for their uncles."

Tarek chuckled. "So, you're going to play the "Uncle" card, huh? That's underhanded."

"You going on the carriage ride?"

"I suppose."

"Then my job is done."

"Don't you feel a little weird going on a tour of land that's owned by the same man who's buying our farm?"

"Maybe. But it's not about him. It's our goodbye before the Farm's officially sold. I don't have no love for Carmichael, but if I were him and I saw an opportunity to expand my property line, I'd do it too." I looked over my shoulder; the girls were still curled up, but August was watching me. "Look, I'm not going to pretend that I don't feel some type of way about us losing our homestead, but no one's been here to take care of the place. Aunt Pearl…well, she's old. She can't do it no more."

Tarek took a long pause and a deep, audible breath. "We'll go." He said it as if he'd lost a major battle.

"Thank you, Uncle Tarek," I said barely able to suppress a smile. "To hell with you."

I slid my cell phone into my back pocket as August got up from the sofa and came over to my side. "Who was that?" she asked quietly, so as not to wake the girls.

"Tarek. Just wanted to talk about the carriage ride. He also wanted my opinion on how he reacted to Shucky."

"Well, I can't speak to how he reacted about seeing your Uncle Shucky again. But I do want to talk about this carriage ride." She slid her arms around my waist. "Do you think this is the right thing to do, given the circumstances?"

"Are you asking me for my opinion?" I looked down at her admiringly. Even without makeup, she was beautiful.

"Yes."

"It's a carriage ride. I think the girls will love it. And anyway, how long can a carriage ride take?"

She smiled.

"You cool with that?" I asked.

"You like it, I love it." She grinned, kissed me on the cheek and then made her way to the refrigerator.

I looked over at my girls. Maddie had fallen asleep, but Autumn watched the television program intently. I was suddenly aware of my heart beating inside my chest. August came back and sat down beside Autumn, while I gently picked up Maddie. She wrestled for a second, then rested her head on my shoulder and fell immediately back to sleep. I went into the small bedroom next to the kitchenette, laid my sleeping daughter onto one of twin beds she shared with her sister. She could sleep until dinner, which meant waking her within the next hour to get over to Aunt Pearl's.

*Don't drink Kool-Aid and watch for the smoke.*

I paused in the doorway, wondering where that the thought came from. It came to me so quickly that I lost all train of thought. *Don't drink the Kool-Aid and watch the smoke.* Isn't that what the trans woman said to me at the restaurant earlier? *Don't drink the Kool-Aid and watch the smoke.* It didn't make sense to me. And yet, the words wouldn't stop spinning around in my brain.

*Don't drink the Kool-Aid and watch the smoke.*

It had to have a meaning; I just couldn't figure out what it was. The words felt like a warning rather than a statement. I felt like it had something to do with my girls, which was silly. That trans woman didn't know me or August, much less our daughters. But the words were ominous. I just for the life of me couldn't understand why.

# Tarek

When I hung up the phone, Zach had already made himself comfortable on the huge queen-sized bed, sitting with his back propped up against the headboard with two pillows while reviewing a document on his laptop.

No matter what Drake said, I wasn't feeling this ride. And I most definitely wasn't feeling like going to Shucky's for a fish fry. On one hand, my brother was right: it was the last time any of us would see the homestead. All the memories that we shared would be gone forever. There would be no more trips south to visit with relatives, no more backyard barbecues, no more celebrations with the aunts' southern cooking. No more falling asleep to the sweet sound of Aunt Merline's voice. No more dancing to the soul music of the seventies.

I was overly emotional about the whole process and yet, with all of this going on, I couldn't contain what was going on inside of me. I had to talk to Zach…but what we needed to talk about had almost nothing to do with the family. Mostly what I had to say concerned him and me. It felt inappropriate to address this issue now…but it also felt right on time.

I sat down on the edge of the bed, only half listening to his typing.

"Zach?" My voice came out heavier than usual.

"What's up, babe?"

"Do you have a moment?"

"Always." He set his laptop to one side and turned to me. His deep gray-blue eyes looked almost sad, and I didn't understand why.

"Have you ever thought about getting married?" I asked.

"I think about it all the time."

I paused, the whole room going silent.

"Zach…you've been a part of my family for years." All of a sudden, my throat constricted.

"Yeah?" He turned to face me.

"You know I love you," I said. "Quite possibly more than I've loved any man." I paused, my eyes never leaving his. Then, for an instant, I diverted my gaze. I didn't understand why this was so hard. "Will you marry me?"

"I would marry you for the next seventy-five years." Zach leaned in wrapping his arms around me. He sealed his answer with a kiss that brought us to the edge of sex. He kissed me like it was our first date, and I allowed my body to respond, growing…lengthening. And I couldn't give in, couldn't touch him until I said what I needed to say.

I pulled away slowly. "I don't know why it's taken me so long to ask you," I began.

"Does it matter?"

"No." I reached into the nightstand on my side of the bed and pulled out the small black box that held his ring. Opening the box, my eyes fell on the black and silver band with four diamonds.

Zach's smile broadened as I slid the ring on his finger. "Wait…aren't we supposed to wait until we're actually married before we put these on?"

"We could…but why should we? The wedding is just a formality. I couldn't wait a minute longer to give this to you."

"When do you want to do this?"

"When we get back home."

He smiled, showing the dimples in his cheeks. "Then we can make the plans when we get back home. In the meantime," he rolled on top of me, and I placed the ring box on the nightstand. "Hey, where's your ring?"

"In my bag."

"Put it on." Zach kissed me with the same passion as he did before.

"When we're done." I wrapped my arms around his muscular body and the hotel phone rang.

"Fuck." He picked up the phone. "Yeah."

"Hello, handsome. This Zach?"

Latrice's voice came through the phone, light as always.

"It is. Who is this?"

"Come on! Don't play with me. Where Tarek?"

"Underneath me." He started to chuckle, rolling off me regrettably and handing me the phone.

I took it, smiling, as he padded into the tiny bathroom just outside the bedroom.

"Hey Latrice,"

"Tarek, why are you and Zach still at the hotel when you should be here getting lit with the rest of us? You know dinners at eight and we can't be late."

"We'll be there in an hour." I grinned, watching Zach as he brushed his teeth. I looked forward to seeing the girls…Latrice and her girlfriend. We hadn't spoken directly, but gay men could spot another gay, male or female, from a mile away. Most of the time we were right. "We got some great news."

She giggled. "Indie's here. Make it quick."

"We'll tell you when we see you."

"Okay. Hurry up!"

"Duly noted." I said while hanging up the phone.

 I called into the bathroom. "Babe, we gotta get going."

"We going to your cousin's?"

"Yeah."

"We're going to hang out there until your aunt's dinner?"

I nodded.

When he didn't hear me speak, he came out of the bathroom. "So, what's the real reason you don't want to go to your Uncle Shucky's fish fry?"

"What do you mean?"

"You're pissed at your uncle because of your aunt. I get that. But I know you. There's something else going on."

I shook my head.

"Nothing's going on. It's all about how he did my Aunt Merline. Why? Do you want to go to Shucky's?"

"To meet the rest of my in-laws, of course." He pulled out a pair of his favorite jeans and slid into them. "I mean, I already met Latrice and her friend. If you don't want to go, then we won't."

I tried to explain. "Zach, this man almost took down my whole family. He's only related to us by marriage, and he stopped being my uncle the day my aunt left his sorry ass and moved to Chicago."

"I was under the impression that this trip was about healing. If you hold on to the anger you have at your Uncle Shucky, it will remain a part of you for that much longer." He paused for a moment. "I just don't want to see you miss the opportunity to make a wrong right."

I could hear Zach clearly, but his words couldn't touch my heart. Shucky took something from me that I couldn't get back; there was no way to make that wrong right.

"Can we talk about this later?" The anger that had been roiling around inside of me had lessened to a dull ache; the same way that a pounding headache would slowly begin to subside to a pain that I could live with.

"Sure." Zach looked at me and without saying another word, he pulled me towards him and kissed me. He kissed me with the gentleness of a man who understood me. Anger almost always masquerades as hurt. Somehow, he understood that.

"Whatever you want to do, I'll do," he said softly. "For now, let's go see your cousins."

"Thank you," I heard myself say as I pulled him into me. As his hands caressed my biceps, somehow, I felt that things would be right with the world, and yet I carried a secret that I couldn't tell anyone, not even Zach. Everyone keeps secrets from their families and spouse; I was no different. But we would be on our way home tomorrow, back to our life up north. And once we were there, I could put this secret to rest.

Being with my cousins was a riot. We laughed and joked as if no time at all had passed since we last visited. Back then, I had no idea that Latrice was a lesbian. It had never occurred to me; but why would it? She didn't show signs of who she chose to love any more than I did. But then again, it was the seventies, and that era was far less accepting than the one that we are living in now.

As it turned out, Latrice's girlfriend had a terrific sense of humor once she warmed up to us. They told us they had met a year ago and had been inseparable ever since. So inseparable that once Latrice decided she was moving up north, Kisha decided to go with her. I thought that their relationship was cool and, in many ways, it mirrored Zach and me…and yet I wasn't a bit surprised when my cousin whipped out an old-fashioned bong and filled it with marijuana. Zach and I looked at her as if she'd lost her mind, but after a few minutes, Zach decided to give it a try. I stayed on the sidelines, opting to enjoy my glass of wine. In a half hour, we were all mildly buzzed and ready to eat, so we headed to Pearl's.

# PLANTATION

The first thing I noticed was the "For Sale" sign on the front lawn of her split-level home. I suppose I hadn't taken her move seriously…until now. We headed into the already crowded house, where a bunch of family members greeted us with smiles, hugs, and kisses. Most of the people I hadn't seen in thirty years.

I was surprised to see Shucky. Just the sight of him made my blood boil and I turned away to look at Drake and the girls. They were already at the table, and I could see that they had started their meal. A commotion came from the kitchen, pots and pans alongside rattling dishes and silverware.

Aunt Macy entered the dining room with a pitcher of lemonade in one hand and her walking stick in the other. She walked slowly, setting the pitcher in the center of the table, and looked gratefully at Drake as he gave her a sweet smile and pulled out a chair for her. It was moments like this that made me proud of Drake. He was always like this, always looking out for the female members of our family, the aunts and cousins as well as our sister, Indigo.

# Drake

I kissed Aunt Macy gently on the cheek. Her ebony brown skin was as soft as I remembered. She still wore Jergens lotion, which I inhaled deeply as I pushed the seat gently underneath her. From the other side of my aunt, August looked up at me. I knew what she was thinking. I had a family of women which made me acutely aware of how I needed to behave among them. They needed me in ways that women from the family's past had always needed their men to be and were often disappointed. It wasn't enough to be strong. That was a given. I needed to be gentle, loving, and understanding, even when it was hard to be that way.

"You're a good man, D," she whispered lovingly as I sat down beside her.

"Daddy's a good man!" Autumn echoed.

I smiled at her, my heart almost bursting, and then I looked around the table. Tarek had come in with Zach, Latrice, and her girlfriend, Kisha. Aunt Pearl seemed like she tolerated Kisha well enough. Indigo had arrived with them and chuckled as she watched them make small talk.

Aunt Pearl's home was traditional, the walls painted a blue which had faded over time. She still had the Last Supper that had been a permanent fixture in her home ever since I could remember. The dining room was enormous, perhaps the largest room in the house. All the bedrooms were at the back, along with the tiny kitchen and equally small bathroom. Despite the size of the house, it reflected a certain southern charm that was clear in all the homes that ran along Beaumont Road.

Pearl had a huge, fashionable China cabinet that took up half of the wall facing the dining room table. Next to it was a stereo with records stacked in a neat pile. Her taste in music was simple and straightforward: Gospel. Old Gospel. It started with the Five Blind Boys of Alabama and ended with Mississippi Mass Choir.

Latrice had grown up here, and framed pictures hung on the walls…pictures that captured her at every stage of her life. Remarkably, there was one of Latrice and Kisha, although to the naked eye, they looked more like college friends than lovers.

"So, Aunt Pearl…what's with you and the girl we saw at Carmichaels?" I asked, remembering the curvy beauty who walked into the restaurant with her entourage of what I assumed to be gay men. I knew Aunt Pearl was acquainted with the trans woman, but there was something to their relationship that I didn't understand and my curiosity wouldn't rest until I found out what it was.

Pearl bristled and adjusted the scarf she had wrapped around her head.

"That's um…" She coughed purposely and then began again. "That's talk more reserved for grown folks. I'll just say that her real name is Henry and I've known him for most of his life. Now let us bow out heads and thank the Lord for this meal."

A hush fell over the table as Aunt Pearl began to pray. She prayed for a couple of minutes and then lifted her head with a huge smile. "Let's eat." She looked at Tarek. "Tarek, pass me them string beans."

The table was overflowing, the aromas of fried chicken, corn bread, collard greens and macaroni and cheese filling the air. Aunt Pearl had certainly cooked up a storm. I don't know how she found the time to do this and meet us at Carmichaels for a light lunch. And as if on cue, August piped up:

"Aunt Pearl, this food looks amazing. Where did you ever get the time to prepare such a beautiful table?" She scooped a tablespoon full of mashed potatoes and plopped it onto Madison's plate.

"Shoot, there ain't nuthin' to it. Any woman can whip up a great table whether it be for two people or two hundred. My secret is to cook and freeze." Pearl chuckled heartily as she watched everyone load their own plates.

"Aunt Pearl, what's with the ride through Carmichael's Orchard?" Since she wasn't going to address the topic of "Henry," I could at least ask her this.

Aunt Macy looked over at Aunt Pearl with an expression that at first, I couldn't make out. I recognized it as soon as the hush fell over the table.

"You never said that you were takin' these chil'ren on a ride through Carmichaels!" Macy's voice was clear and strong. Gone was the rasp of an old woman, replaced with something else…pure rage.

"Macy, all of us are moving away from here. Do you realize that this is the last big family dinner we'll be having in this house?"

"It don't matter none. Those babies don't have any business carryin' them through that heathen's property."

"What's the issue, Aunt Macy?" August inquired gently. Anyone who knew August would recognize that protective tone in her voice.

Macy took a deep breath, casting a glance at my girls. She smiled slightly and then looked at August. "Chile, everybody knows that Carmichael has been tangled up in shady dealings for years. He brought peoples' land up bit by bit…that's what he's done to your grandfather's house. There's a rumor that he runs with the Klan."

"You mean the KKK?" August impulsively draped a protective arm over Madison's shoulder.

"Yes," Macy continued. "There's rumor that he dapples in witchcraft."

"That's hearsay." Pearl took a mouthful of sweet potato casserole.

"You can say what you want, but I's seen some of his people. They don't look none too kosher." She turned her attention back to August. "Honey, if you want to take your chil'ren to Carmichael's orchard, I can't stop you, but I wouldn't recommends it."

"Well, thanks for the heads-up, Aunt Macy, but I think we'll be all right. Drake will be with me. How long can a carriage ride be?"

Macy shrugged and began eating in silence.

"So, who else is going on the carriage ride?" Latrice cast a long gaze over the table. "Just getting a head count."

"Mommy, can we go?" Madison perked up.

August nodded. "We're going."

Zach looked at Tarek. He replied with a silent nod.

"We're going."

"Indie?"

My sister shook her head. "As much as I'd like to, I have major work to do at my office." Indigo finished the small plate she had made for herself. "But you guys go ahead and enjoy yourselves."

"Well, it looks like we have a full family." Pearl beamed with pride from the head of the table. "That's good. It'll be a good time for all." She turned her attention to Indigo, seated only one person away from her. "Are you sure you can't make it, Indie? It'll be so much fun."

"I wish I could, Aunt Pearl, but I have a ton of work to do once I get back to Philly."

# PLANTATION

She sent a quick smile my way and cast a cautionary glance at Aunt Macy. Indie was a lawyer first, which led to her over-examining every situation. She had been this way most of her adult life. Right now, I got the sense that she was sizing Aunt Macy up for something, but I didn't know what. Whatever it was, it couldn't have been that important. Aunt Macy was up there in years, living in a retirement community. But the way she sounded when she snapped at Aunt Pearl…that was no old woman.

# Indigo

I let my eyes linger on Aunt Macy, but not for too long. Most people don't like being looked at directly. I remembered that from Investigative Training 101. You learned that people, no matter how guilty, will always try to convince you of their innocence and deflect their guilt to someone else. That's the way it worked.

Which is why I was taken aback by Macy's outburst at the table. Maybe it was because she honestly believed that the person responsible for procuring most of the property in Darcy County was into something as nefarious as devil worship. Maybe it was due more to the loss of our homestead, which had to hurt her deeply. We had so many good memories in our grandparents' home. But the house itself was in such bad condition that it was uninhabitable. I had been surprised Drake allowed the girls to run around in there because I wasn't sure how sound the floors were.

The value was not the house. It was the land. It was always about the land. John Carmichael owned most of Darcy County. We all knew this. His family's wealth was nothing short of astounding. From what I had learned reading online publications, including the *Georgia Gazette*, the Carmichaels had exploded overnight in a way that shocked the local politicians.

I did not dive too deeply into the articles that I found. I had more important work to do than to glance through articles that only affected the locals. But I had known John Carmichael for years, and from what I knew of him personally, he was a taker. From the conversations between my grandparents, aunts, and uncles over the years, whenever his name came up, the women were brusque, while the men were outright hostile.

But what's been done is done. There's nothing we or anyone else could do to change that.

Still, Aunt Macy wasn't the type to get angry if it wasn't warranted. She was the jovial one. Even when she lost her husband some twenty years ago, and her home soon after, her spirits were always high. God knows that woman faced enough personal drama to last all our aunts and uncles lifetimes put together. So, I was a little concerned as I watched my aunt quietly eat her meal with a sullen expression on her face. It wasn't like her.

Right now, all I wanted was to go back to my hotel room and soak in a nice hot tub. To be honest, I wasn't keen on any of my family members going on this carriage ride. I understood it was a big thing because it would be the last time that any of us would see our homestead, but it seemed like a slap in the face to go on a carriage ride through an orchard when that land had been procured by someone with questionable intentions.

"So, you really not going on the ride through the orchard?" Kisha asked.

"Yes." I turned to face her. "I have an early flight and a ton of work to tackle once I get back to the office."

"You're not coming, Indie?" Aunt Pearl exclaimed from the end of the table.

I looked up, quickly hiding my annoyance. This conversation was between me and Kisha. I gave Kisha a glance and then turned so Pearl could see my face dead on.

"No," I said with a slight smile. "I'm not. As I was telling Kisha, I have an early flight in the morning and a ton of work to get to once I get to my office."

"Well, you should be there for your family Indie. After all, when are we all going to be gathered again?"

"Probably when Drake and August have the next barbecue at their house." I tried to hide my sarcasm. I didn't want to be rude, but she had no right to try to guilt me into staying when I had my own life.

"I won't get in the way of your work," she said, rising from the table. "I sure wish you would change your mind though."

"I know," I said softly. "Aunt Pearl, I know this is probably the last time that we'll see each other in the south. But if you move up north, we'll see more of each other."

"I surely hope so. And I'm hoping that everything will be okay."

"It will, Momma." Latrice began clearing the table.

"Let me help you." Kisha rose slowly to her feet.

"Are you kids full?" August stood up with her empty plate in hand. "If you are, give me your plates and I'll wash them."

"Ooh, mommy," Madison perked up. "Can I help?"

"We got it, Madison." Latrice carried plates and headed towards the kitchen.

"Aunt Pearl, that was an excellent meal," Drake said. "Thank you."

"Do you want coffee?" Pearl glanced over her shoulder as she walked towards the kitchen. "I can put on a pot."

"No but thank you. I want to get the girls settled for bed and then chill for the rest of the night. If I have a cup, I'll be wired all night long."

Pearl chuckled. "Well, I'm gonna make a little something for myself. If anyone wants a cup, the pot will be on the stove."

"Thank you, Aunt Pearl," Tarek said. "I'll take a cup."

I looked over at Aunt Macy. She was oddly quiet, her eyes closed, as if she had fallen asleep. I waited for a moment and then I stood slowly. I was ready to go but I kept watching Aunt Macy in her chair. It was as if she were totally oblivious to anyone else in the room. Drake's kids were getting up from the table, not being loud, but being kids. Kisha and Latrice were doing the dishes in the other room. August took her family's plates to the kitchen, handed them to Latrice and then headed back to the table just as Aunt Pearl returned to the dining room.

Drake stood. "Aunt Pearl, Aunt Macy…we'll see you tomorrow. Where are we meeting again?"

"In front of Carmichael's," Pearl chirped, "right behind where we had lunch earlier today."

"Okay then." He picked his daughter up with strong arms. "We'll see everyone tomorrow." Autumn wrapped her little arms around Drake's neck and rested her head on his shoulder.

"We'll see everyone tomorrow." August placed her hands on Madison's shoulders and guided her towards the front door. "Good night, everyone."

"See you tomorrow." Latrice stood in the doorway, wiping beads of sweat from her forehead with a sudsy hand.

"It was great meeting all of you." Zach gazed around the table as he stood. "I look forward to the carriage ride."

"It'll be fun," Pearl said with a smile.

Tarek placed a hand on Zach's shoulder. "Everyone sleep well. Aunt Macy, Aunt Pearl. This was a wonderful meal."

"Well, thank you Tarek." Pearl's smile widened.

"Aunt Macy?" He looked at her.

Everyone's eyes turned to Macy, who still hadn't moved from her spot at the table.

"Macy!" Pearl shouted.

Macy's eyes snapped open, and she yawned. "Whoo!" she said. "I musta dozed off."

"Everyone's finished eating and now they're going back to their hotel rooms." Pearl said.

"Yeah. We're just saying goodbye and thank you for helping to prepare such a fine meal." Tarek made his way over to her and kissed her on the cheek.

Sleepy-eyed, she smiled at him and kissed him back. "Thank you, T," she whispered. "Pearl, I'll need you to help me to my room."

"I'll help you, Aunt Macy." Latrice wiped her hands on a dishtowel and helped her up.

I looked around the room and smiled silently to myself as everyone prepared to leave. This was my family…people that I loved.

I had no idea that this would be the last time I would see their smiling faces. No idea.

# Tarek

I hadn't opened my eyes fully before I regretted agreeing that we would go on this carriage ride today. To me, it seemed like a complete waste of time. It didn't matter to Zach because he only wanted to be with me. We had both slept well, and to be honest, all I really wanted to do was make love with him. He looked good with tousled dark hair and matching razor stubble. He rolled out of bed wearing a pair of blue lounge pants, padded to the bathroom and closed the door.

How long the carriage ride took would dictate what time we could get on the road and head home. Indigo was probably packing her clothes and checking her email even as we speak.

Drake and August would be waking up the girls and taking them for breakfast before packing so that they could get on the road early tomorrow morning. This would probably be hardest on Drake, because he wanted his daughters to know where they came from and now there wouldn't even be a landmark to commemorate where we had been. What was left of our home would be demolished, the land going to Carmichael, and that would be that. As much as I detested the idea of the sale of our property to someone so vile, I had no control over Aunt Pearl's decision.

I needed a cup of coffee. I swung my legs over the side of the bed and stretched, hearing my back crack.

"Babe?" I called over the sound of the shower.

"Yeah?"

"You hungry?"

"Yeah. Hotel lobby or Cracker Barrel?"

"Cracker Barrel. Definitely Cracker Barrel." The shower turned off and, in a moment, Zach appeared, a towel wrapped around his waist. He began to dry his hair. He looked amazing.

"Are we still going on the carriage ride?" Zach asked, sitting on the edge of the bed and glancing at the clock on the nightstand.

"Yes." I nodded. "And I appreciate you going on this journey with me and my family."

"Where else would I be?" He leaned over and gave me a peck on the cheek. "I will be your husband soon. I am part of this family."

"Yeah, you are," I said with a smile.

"So, something's been bothering me, and I wanted to talk to you about it."

"Okay."

He paused. "Why are you so angry with your uncle? And before you answer, let me tell you why I'm asking." He gazed at me through gray-blue eyes, and I felt myself simultaneously melting and tensing up. I knew where this was going. I just didn't know if I was ready to deal with it yet.

"I've never seen you respond to anyone as viscerally as you did when you saw him yesterday. What happened? What did he do to you to make you respond that way?"

I thought for a moment. This wasn't the time to deal with this…but at the same time, there was no better time than the present.

"I can't stand my uncle," I began. "He abused my Aunt Merline. You must know that my aunt was probably the kindest woman that walked the face of this earth. Zach, she was the sweetest woman next to my own mother. She would sing when she was happiest…and she had this incredible voice. I always thought that she should cut a demo.

"But my uncle, back then, was a bastard. There's no other way we can describe him. He was a womanizer…used to beat my aunt just because he could. She tried to hide it from us kids, but we saw it anyway, the bruises, the black eyes. We knew it was Shucky. Back then, no one could tell us that he wasn't the cause for the reason why my aunt lost her light."

"Is that all?"

"No." I took a deep breath and shook my head slowly. "But…I really don't want to open that can of worms."

"As long as you're carrying that can, you can't heal."

He was right. I knew that he was right. But I couldn't admit the rest of what Shucky had done. It was too painful. Reluctantly, I agreed with Zach. I had to start the healing process sometime.

"Shucky fucked me when I was a ten. The words fell out of my mouth like a dead stone.

I couldn't bear to see the look of astonishment on Zach's face.

"It happened only once but…" I balled my hands into tight fists. "I don't know why he picked me. He was drunk when it happened. I remember the redness in his eyes…the smell of the liquor on his breath.

It hurt like hell, and I never told anyone. I hated him for it. For years I struggled with this for years, trying to figure out what it was about me that made him think that he could do what he did and get away with it."

Zach moved closer and wrapped his arms around my shoulders. Hot tears slid down my cheeks.

"Why didn't you tell anyone?" His voice was so soft I almost didn't hear him.

I thought about that.

Why doesn't any abuse victim tell on their abuser? I didn't know. I suppose I knew that it wasn't something that you told anyone. Even though I was aware of my sexuality back then, there was nothing enjoyable about what my uncle had done to me. And it was awful. Shucky had always been an obnoxious drunk, at least as far back as I can remember. But the day that he abused me was different. Everything about his demeanor had changed. I knew that he wanted me in a room; alone and defenseless, where no one could protect me. And when it was over, I was left in that room alone to lick my wounds and cry silent tears.

I had kept that secret until today.

"It would be my word against Shucky's," I said. "He was a grown man. Who would believe me if I went up against him? I didn't think anyone would, so I said nothing."

"Baby, I'm so sorry." Zach held me as I cried against him.

I let the tears fall for a few minutes before I sat up. Pride washed over me, and I willed my tears to stop. I wasn't going to allow my aunt's husband to take another thing from me. He had taken too much as it was.

"Are you okay?" Zach gazed at me with uncertainty.

"Yeah." I wiped the tears away with the palms of my hands. "It is what it is, right?"

"It is what you want it to be. But I'll help you get through it. Let's just get something to eat."

I smiled weakly. There wasn't anything that Zach or anyone else could do to make this pain go away. I had learned to live with what was done to me. There was no point in telling anyone what had happened. At the time of the rape, I was too young to know that if I said something, I might have been believed. And like many men who have suffered at the hands of an abuser, I had simply learned to live with the pain that the abuse had caused.

I wasn't going to hold it in any longer, I vowed. One way or another, the agony was going to stop this weekend.

# Drake

"C'mon, girls. Time to get up." I peeked my head into the bedroom that Autumn and Maddie shared.

"We're up, Dad." Maddie said from the closet before magically appearing with an overnight bag in her hand.

"Good morning, Daddy." Autumn pulled an outfit out of the drawer and held it up to herself, decided that she didn't like it and put it back. She looked at me with a look that resonated with exasperation.

"I'll send your Momma in to help you find something," I said with a smile.

August whizzed past me, looking fresh faced and well rested.

"I got this," she said softly. "I have to do their hair. Come on, girls. We got to get dressed so we can get breakfast and do the ride."

I smiled and walked back into the living room. After breakfast, we'll go ride the carriage."

I watched the girls wolf down their pancake breakfast. August looked radiant with a different scarf that tied her hair back. Her makeup was minimal, and she looked stunning. She smiled at me while she sipped her coffee.

"Daddy, are we going to your uncle's house for the party later?" Madison asked me. "Is Aunt Indie going?"

"No, sweetie, and besides that's not until tomorrow" I answered. "Aunt Indie can't come. She has to work. She should be flying home today. But honestly honey I don't know if we're going being that we have to get on the road in the morning. If we go Uncle Shucky's we'll have to stay another night"

"Okay." She reached for her glass of orange juice and took a sip.

"So how do you really feel about going to Uncle Shucky's fish fry?" I asked August as I finished my breakfast of bacon, eggs and toast.

"Honestly, I'd rather get on the road right after the carriage ride." She gave me a wistful smile. "Truth be told, I'd rather start the drive home right after breakfast."

"Are we going to be princesses riding in the carriages, Mommy?" Autumn looked up at the both of us with syrup on her lips.

"Yes, sweetie." August wiped Autumn's mouth with a damp napkin. "You're going to be the most beautiful princess in the whole world. We just have to wait to see what kind of carriage you'll be riding in."

"Oh, goodie!" She clapped her hands together and then began to munch on her last pancake.

"Well, ain't you just the cutest little thang. I said that to one the girls in the back when we was getting your meals." The voice came from just over my left shoulder.

I looked up into the face of a smiling white woman who could have stepped out of the pages of a fifty's magazine with her black cat-eye glasses, chubby cheeks, and a blonde beehive hairdo. She moved closer to the table and bent down to speak to Autumn. "Did you like your breakfast?" she asked.

Autumn looked at the woman, then at me, and nodded hesitantly. I reached out and patted her arm. August had taught our girls not to speak to anyone that they didn't know.

"Well, that's just wonderful. I think that deserves a little something. Are you folks going on the carriage tour of Carmichael's orchard?"

"Yes." I smiled, but something about this woman rubbed me the wrong way. Her smile never reached her eyes.

"Ain't that the bee's knees?" she chuckled. "I have something for you two little darlings. Ya'll waits right there, and I'll be right back with your surprise."

She walked away from our table wearing the white crepe shoes of a person that spent most of the time on their feet. Despite her age, she moved with the agility of someone who had been doing this job for many years. She had taken our earlier and I had really noticed her until now.

"Drake!" August wanted my attention.

"What's up?"

"Your family's all here…even your Aunt Macy. They're coming in now."

I turned in time to see Aunt Macy, Aunt Pearl, Kisha, and Latrice enter through the glass doors across the semi-crowded room.

"Aunt Macy! Aunt Pearl!" I stood up. As they approached the table, the white woman returned with two small boxes in her hand. She smiled through dull red lips and handed a box to each one of my girls. Autumn looked down at the box not knowing if it was okay to open it or not. Madison opened her box at once and pulled out a tiara. Her eyes brightened and her smile widened into a little girl's grin.

"We're both gonna be princesses!" she exclaimed and then turned to her sister. "Open up the box, Autumn! We're both gonna be princesses."

Autumn opened the box and pulled out her matching tiara.

"My name is Ms. Lulu," the woman said, extending her hand to Autumn.

"Go ahead, honey." August looked down at Autumn.

Ms. Lulu placed the tiara on her head, then took a step back and looked at Autumn admiringly. "There, now you look like a fairy princess."

"What do you say, girls?"

"Thank you, Ms. Lulu." Madison was positively beaming.

"You're welcome, sweetheart."

"Thank you," Autumn said shyly.

"Anytime."

"And how are my precious little angels?" Aunt Macy kissed Madison first and then made her way over to Autumn.

"Good morning, family!" Pearl sat down to my right. "Drake, hand me the menu?"

"I'm fine." Maddie looked up at Aunt Macy. "I'm a princess, Aunt Macy…like a real princess."

"And you are a beautiful princess," Aunt Macy said with a smile.

We could hear dishes rattling through the swinging wooden doors that led into the kitchen.

"Well, since I'm here," Ms. Lulu began, "can I take your order? And Ms. Macy! I haven't seen you in a couple of months. Are you well?"

"Yes, I'm fine." Macy glanced at Lulu and then slowly made her way to the head of the table.

"Hey, did Indie change her mind? Is she coming" Latrice asked while sitting down across from us.

"No. She had to fly back home for business," August advised.

"That's a shame." She turned to Kisha. "What do you want? I got you."

"Two eggs, toast, bacon and coffee," Kisha said with a smile.

"You got it," Lulu exclaimed.

Latrice and Kisha turned their attention towards the end of the table where Ms. Lulu was standing…smiling.

"So…Pearl, how long do you think this carriage ride will take?" August pulled Autumn onto her lap and Autumn wrapped her arms around her neck.

"About forty minutes."

"Where you got to be that you got to know how long the ride will take?" Macy asked.

August looked somewhat surprised at the question. "I just wanted to know so I'll know what time to get to bed and get on the road in the morning."

Macy nodded her head as if to say that she understood. She looked tired this morning, but there was something else about her appearance that bothered me. She must not have slept well, or she got dressed hastily. She was wearing a pink collarless dress which did nothing to enhance her shape. She pulled her oversized purse onto her lap and waited for Ms. Lulu to bring her the cup of tea that she had asked for.

"You ain't going to Shucky's tomorrow for his fish fry?" Macy didn't just look tired; she sounded tired.

"Aunt Macy, are you alright?" I finally had to ask.

"Yes, Drake. Why you ask?"

"Because you look tired. Did you get any rest last night?"

"I did," she said, wincing as she stretched her back in her chair. "I put my makeup on too fast, I guess."

"That's not what I see," Kisha whispered.

Latrice cut her a look that silenced her.

"But things should get better after the carriage ride," Macy added.

"What's after the carriage ride?" Latrice asked, brushing her braids away from her face.

"My bed." She chuckled.

"I know that's right Ms. Macy." Kisha grinned.

It was the most that I'd heard Kisha speak since we were introduced yesterday.

"So where are these carriages we'll be riding in?" I directed the question to Macy.

"In the back of this building. They have a place where you can turn in your ticket and then load up."

"I can take you when you and your family are ready," Ms. Lulu said out of the blue. I didn't notice she had returned. "And I brought your girls a slice of my Aunt Emma's red velvet cake."

Before August could object to our girls having sweets so early in the day, Ms. Lulu had put the plates down before Autumn and Madison, who started digging in immediately.

A group of people near us headed towards the back of the restaurant. I assumed they were the first group to head off for the carriage ride.

"Beware of Carmichael's carriage ride."

The voice was so subtle that I almost didn't hear it. I looked across the room at the door. People were coming in and going out of the restaurant acting as if they didn't have a care in the world. I turned to look at August. She was wiping frosting from Autumn's mouth. I looked across the room, taking in the bright yellow walls with glowing red letters outlining Carmichael's name, the people sitting at various tables enjoying the food they had ordered.

"Did you hear that?" I asked.

August looked at me. "Hear what?"

"Something about the carriage ride."

"What about it?"

"I heard a warning about the carriage ride."

"What warning did you hear?" Macy looked directly at me.

"Beware of the carriage ride." I returned her unwavering gaze. "I heard it loud as day. Beware Carmichael's carriage ride."

"Who said that to you?"

I looked around me. Clearly no one had spoken.

"I'm all done," Madison exclaimed proudly, pushing her plate away. "Can I go out to the carriages?"

"Wait for us to walk with you." August didn't even look at her or if she did, I didn't see it. "We'll be finished in a minute."

I knew what I heard. It was a warning not to get on the carriage, but I couldn't figure out where it came from. I looked around. No one appeared to have spoken to me. I shrugged, finished my coffee, and motioned for Ms. Lulu to bring the check. She came over quickly, as if she were waiting for my direction. She placed my check before me with a smile, her doughy arms jiggling by her side.

"Well, it's clear that no one spoke to you, Drake." Macy shifted her ample behind in her seat. "I'm gonna change my ticket and take the next carriage. I'm gonna order me some breakfast."

"Okay. Will we be seeing you after the ride?" I asked.

"Of course, you will. We'll break bread together before you go; whether that's tonight or tomorrow."

"Do you want me to ride with you?" Pearl adjusted her scarf.

Macy looked at her for a moment as if nothing registered, and then she smiled. It was the biggest smile I had ever seen on her face.

"Sure, Pearl." She waved her hand for the server to come to the table. "I could use the company."

"Then we'll meet you at your house I guess," I said, watching as my girls gathered up their belongings.

"Drake?" August touched my arm. "When do you want to get started back home? The girls still have school."

"If they miss a day, it won't hurt them." I looked around once again.

Should we get on this carriage? Something inside was telling me that we shouldn't. The voice telling me not to get on the carriage was light and airy…almost a whisper. But it was loud enough for me to hear, and I know what I heard.

# Indigo

My flight had been delayed by almost two hours…at least that was what I could get out of the information desk. I had no choice but to take refuge at a local Starbucks and drink coffee while I waited. I pulled my carry-on bag close to me and retrieved my cellphone. At least I could read my emails and check in with Lucille to see if anything had changed regarding my workload. I dialed her number as the intercom broadcast flight 1120 for Orlando was boarding at gate sixteen.

"Hello, Ms. Benton?"

"Now you know you don't have to address me by my married name, Ms. Indie." I could feel Lucille's smile over the phone. "How was your trip? Where are you?"

"At ATL International." I crossed my legs and took a quick sip of my coffee. "Anything going on up there?"

"It's quiet," she said. "Nothing's changed. You did receive a message. Someone by the name of LO."

"LO?" I didn't recognize the initials. "What was the message?"

"She was very cryptic. Check on your family. Does that mean anything to you?"

I shook my head. "No. Did she say anything else?"

"Nope. That was it."

Check your family. That didn't make sense.

"Did she leave a number?"

"No. Just the message." She paused. "How was your trip?"

"Okay." I thought for a moment, but those initials didn't mean anything to me. "The trip was good, Lucille. Said goodbye to the old homestead. The house or what's left of it will get demolished and the land will be sold to John Carmichael."

"Save your family."

I looked around me to see who was talking to me while I was on the phone, but no one was close to my window table. I heard the voice just as clear as the day was outside. All I could see were other patrons either typing on laptops or talking on cellphones.

Suddenly I could smell the faint scent of a woman's perfume. I swiveled in my seat and looked around again, not knowing what I expected to see, but I had an impulse to call Drake and Tarek.

"Do you want me to hold on to the message until you get back to the office or should I dispose of it?"

"You can toss it." I gazed out onto the midway. Crowds of people moved back and forth with travel bags and briefcases in hand, yet no one jumped out at me.

"Is there anything else I can do for you?" Lucille asked.

I shook my head, bewildered. "No. I'll see you tomorrow at the office."

"Sounds good. Have a safe flight."

"Thank you." I disconnected the call, looked around once again, and then settled back into my seat. Without thinking, I dialed Tarek's number.

**Tarek**

The carriage looked like something out of a fairy tale…all white with brass accents with four white horses. A short, stout, balding man sat in the driver's seat as he waited for us to get settled. The vehicle rocked on its axles as we boarded and the driver's voice announced the ride's imminent departure from four tiny speakers placed strategically in each of the carriage's four corners.

Just then, my phone rang. I saw my sister's name and answered. "Hey, Indie. What's up?"

"Tarek?" Her voice sounded strained.

"Where are you?"

"At the airport. Is everyone okay?"

"Yeah. We just got on the carriage. Why?"

"I just thought…never mind."

"What's going on?" I watched my niece bounce on the comfortable seat across from me. The carriage had rows of individual padded seats that faced each other. Kisha and Latrice were beside Maddie, and August and Autumn were next them. Drake and Zach sat on my left, and an unfamiliar African American couple sat on my right.

"I just wanted to check on you. I just got this vibe that something was wrong," Indie said with some relief in her voice. "But if you say everything is okay, I'll just wait until we board my flight and head home. Enjoy the ride, little brother."

"Love you, Indie."

"Love you more." She said before she clicked off the line.

"Ladies and gentlemen, welcome to Carmichael's Tour of Darcy County via circa 1800s. On this journey, you can expect to be transported back to 1860 Darcy County. You will see what it looked like prior to modern roadways and bridges.

"We will take a tour of the township, see how they lived, how they made money and what the dress was like back then. You will also take a tour of some of the most beautiful vineyards in Georgia, as well as a first-hand look at the ecosystem in place at that time. We ask that you keep all hands inside of the vehicle.

# PLANTATION

"As we get farther into wine country, we will put the windows up for your comfort. This is towards the end of our summer season, but it's still quite warm and humid. Also, we will be passing over the alligator pit and will pause for approximately ten minutes for you to take pictures and see the alligators that live in the lake. We'll be starting in five minutes. Right now, we ask that you place all electronic devices in the bin to your right. You will get them back at the end of the ride."

"Mommy, can I sit by the window?" Autumn asked August quietly.

August looked down at her and smiled.

"Of course, you can. Do you want to sit on my lap?" Autumn nodded.

A couple of minutes later, the carriage lurched forward and the ride began.

The first thing that hit me was the pungent odor of animals. Clear glass partitions were raised part way up the sides of the coach. Besides the alligators, I didn't know what other animals we expected to see.

The carriage rumbled up a steep incline and then the land leveled off, giving us a view of a cotton field that had been picked over. A gentle breeze caressed my cheek as I watched my nieces look out the sides of the carriage. It looked like we were heading into a small town.

A comforting lull started to take over. Between the rhythmic sound of the horses' hooves hitting the dirt road and the fullness from the food I just ate, sleepiness started to edge its way into my consciousness. Zach's head rested on my left shoulder. Unconsciously, I reached for his hand and held it lightly. The African American woman next to us glanced at me and then looked out the opposite side of the carriage.

We rolled into what looked like the downtown area of a small, midwestern town. There were buildings on either side of us…old-looking buildings. I expected to see a saloon with swinging doors along with guys walking to opposite ends of the town in the anticipation of a shootout.

"People, what you are seeing is downtown Darcy County, 1860. To the right, you will notice the general store with the local apothecary beside it. To the left, you will find our local bank, two-story housing and the stables where a lot of our horses are kept.

"We'll be heading out to what's left of the cotton fields. As you will see, most of the cotton has been picked already, and in a moment, we will be passing through the vineyards."

"Looks like a scene from *Gunsmoke*," August mumbled.

"Mommy, what's *Gunsmoke*?" Autumn looked up with curiosity in her eyes.

"It's an old western television show that mommy used to watch when she was a little girl."

"Me too, sister." The African American woman perked up with a smile. "I used to watch it with my father."

"It was a mainstay in my house." August over at her. "My father didn't give us a choice."

"Your daughter is a very pretty girl," she said.

"Thank you." August's smile widened and she looked down at Autumn. "What do you say to the nice lady, honey?"

"Thank you," Autumn said shyly, and then she looked back at the horses in the stable.

"So, this is what it looked like in the 1800s," Kisha remarked as we rode through the makeshift town. "How long is this ride?"

"Not long," Latrice answered her softly. "Maybe forty minutes?"

"I suppose I can hold out." Kisha settled back in her seat.

"What's your name dear?" the African American woman asked August.

"August," she responded politely. "And that beautiful man sitting closest to the window across from me is my husband, Drake."

"Pleasure to meet you, August." The woman's smile widened and as I looked over at her, I couldn't help but be taken in by her beauty. Her salt and pepper braids had been styled into a cone-shaped bouffant and her makeup was flawlessly applied. She was heavy set, but she carried it well.

"My name's Ida, Ida Monroe. This man to my right is my husband, Wilson."

Wilson Monroe managed to give a smile to everyone in the carriage. He looked slightly older than Ida. I noticed that Ida had a distinctive accent. She sounded Jamaican but I wasn't sure.

"It's a pleasure to meet you, Ida." August nodded at her. "Pleasure to meet you as well, Wilson."

The carriage rolled on past the cotton fields and in a few minutes, we rolled through a small vineyard. For a while, there was nothing to see but trees, but as we came into the next clearing, I was surprised to smell marshland.

"If you look to your right," the driver of the carriage's voice announced, "you will see our infamous alligator pond. If you look at the sandy cove, you will see some of the gators basking in the sun."

"Mommy! Daddy! Look!" Madison yelled as she moved to the opposite side of the carriage.

"Maddie, sit down! I don't want you to fall." Drake's voice carried more authority than needed.

"But I want to see the gators." She moved back to her side of the carriage. "I can't see them from my side."

I nudged Zach, who raised his head at once.

"Hmm?" He suppressed a yawn.

"You're missing the gators."

He turned to his right and squinted. "I don't see anything."

"If you look over at the miniature extension of sand across from the water, you'll see at least two of them sunning themselves." Ida reaching for her husband's hand, carefully intertwining her fingers with his.

She was wrong, but I didn't bother to correct her. There were four good-sized gators lying on the sandy stretch of makeshift beach.

Madison made her way slowly back over to the left side of the coach, pressing herself against the door that allowed access to the carriage. Autumn climbed down from her mother's lap and joined her sister to peer at the pond across from us.

Latrice wrapped her arm around Kisha's shoulders. Ida gave a disapproving glance and then looked away.

We pushed on through a patch of thick brush and appeared into another replica of the town. Here, it looked like people were employed to replicate the citizens of Darcy County from that era. Women in long dresses and full bonnets that protected their heads from the sun, men wearing clothing that looked like they bought it in a secondhand store. A couple of horses were tied to a pole in front of a watering hole. A little Black boy emerged from what appeared to be a general store with a basket of food. The child walked barefoot up the dusty street.

The carriage came to a stop. We waited for it to lurch forward again, but we remained immobile.

August looked to either side of her and then at Drake. "What's going on?"

"I don't know." Drake looked out the side window, then turned his attention to his daughters. "Girls, sit down until we get started again."

"Okay, daddy." Madison perked up.

We heard a loud clunk.

"What was that?" Zach asked, looking around the carriage.

And then the windows on either side of the carriage slid up, sealing us in.

"What's going on?" Panic welled in Ida's voice.

"People, please remain seated. We'll be on our way in just a few minutes." The driver's voice came over the speakers.

I heard the hiss of what sounded like a leak in a pipe. It came from the bottom of the carriage. I looked down, beginning to smell something just as the coach began to fill with a light-colored smoke. But before panic could take root inside of me, I blacked out.

# Drake

My head was pounding, and I lifted my left hand to it. I was lying flat on my back on what felt like a mattress. But the mattress was moving, and it was completely dark around me. I raised my hands and felt wood. I pushed against it, but it didn't move. I was inside a box.

Panic set in. Where were August and my children? Where was my brother and his partner? Where were Latrice and Kisha? And why was I inside of a box that was the length of my body…almost a coffin? I could place my hands against it, but there wasn't enough room to stand. Where was I? And since the box was still moving, where was I going?

I steadied my breathing. I had to keep my wits about me. The scent of freshly cut grass and overturned dirt filled my nostrils.

Where the hell was I?

Maybe I could call someone…if I could get them on my cell phone.

I struggled to reach my back pocket, only to find it empty. I had placed my cell in the basket outside of the coach as they'd requested, and I would get it back at the end of the ride.

Fuck!

Where was August? My baby girl must be losing her mind. I hoped she was with our daughters!

Where the hell was I?

A tear slid down the side of my face. I wiped it as best as I could and closed my eyes to keep the dust from falling into them from the top of the box. Clenching my hands to keep my senses, I realized I would have to wait until they—whoever they were—removed me from this box.

# Tarek

It was hot…stifling hot. My head was pounding. As much as I didn't want to open my eyes, I did it slowly. I tried to wipe my face but couldn't and I realized my hands were chained to the wall. I looked around the dimly lit room. I could sense there were other people here with me, but I couldn't make out who they were.

"Zach! Drake!" I called in a low voice. "Are you there?"

No one answered, but I could hear the murmur of other male voices.

"Hey."

The voice sounded familiar. "Who are you?" I asked quietly.

"Wilson Monroe. Who are you?" the disembodied voice asked me.

"My name's Tarek. Tarek Robeson."

"You were sittin' in the same carriage as me."

"Yes," I responded. "Do you know where my family is?"

"No." Wilson sounded defeated. "I don't know where my wife, is much less your family."

"Where are my nieces?" Whatever happened, I hoped they weren't chained up. "They're only babies! They're gonna want their mother."

"Well, let's think good thoughts about them Tarek." Wilson said from somewhere across the room.

"Think good thoughts?" I was starting to lose my temper. "That's all you got, Wilson?"

"Would you rather think bad thoughts, knowing you can't do anything about it now? Relax. Plan what to do when they unloose your chains."

Wilson was right. But where was Zach? Where were my nieces? Where were my sister-in-law, Latrice and Kisha? Where was my brother?

Sweat beaded on my forehead and trickled down the sides of my face. My shirt clung to my back like a second skin. I couldn't get over how hot it was. I needed air…badly. How the hell did I wind up getting chained to a wall?

I was barefoot, too. And someone had taken my pants. I was standing in my underwear. My head was throbbing, like someone set up shop in my brain and began to jackhammer mercilessly. I pulled on the chains but I couldn't move. My legs buckled, but I couldn't sit down. The muscles in my thighs and calves were screaming. I kept shifting my weight from foot to foot, but it didn't help. The metal cuffs dug into my wrists.

And then the wailing started. It started low and gradually increased in volume. There was something about taking away a man's freedom that elicited terror and a sense of hopelessness at the same time. I had never heard men cry before. The sound was heartbreaking. There must have been at least a half dozen of us in this room…if it was a room. The space felt cavernous.

I never wanted a glass of water so badly.

A door creaked. In the next second, sunlight blinded me as the door slowly opened. We were either in the bed of an eighteen-wheeler or some kind of storage unit.

A tall white man entered. Because the light was behind him, I couldn't make out his face. He was wearing blue jeans and a plaid shirt. He stood in the open doorway not saying a word. I knew that he wanted to add to how we already felt. I wasn't going to give him the satisfaction of instilling fear in me. I wouldn't say anything. As much as I wanted to, I wouldn't allow him to unnerve me. But I had questions…a whole lot of them.

"Where's my wife?" Wilson demanded.

The man didn't respond. Instead, he lit a cigarette and took a deep drag. I couldn't see his face.

"Where's my family?" I heard another voice spoke up.

"Where's my girlfriend?" A man shouted. "Bring her to me!"

"Where are we?" I shouted. "Where are my nieces?"

"Quiet!" the man yelled at the top of his lungs.

Everyone was shocked into silence.

"Now listen here, niggers! Listen good!" He entered and looked each of us over as he walked slowly back and forth in front of us. "Here's the situation," he began. "You belong to me now. You will work on my property. If you try to run, you will be killed."

He walked slowly, pausing in front of each of us before moving to the doorway. I knew that he was trying to intimidate us. Wait! Did he say that we would be working his property?

"You will tend to the fields, pick vegetables and fruit, build additions to various structures on the property. You'll get up at 5:30 every morning and work until the end of the day. You will get an hour for lunch and two fifteen-minute breaks if you're working in the field. You will do whatever needs to get done. Don't get any ideas that you are free. As of today, you're not. It is impossible to get off this compound. To escape, you must get past the various traps including our alligator pond.

"You will be assigned bunks inside this compound, and you will be overseen by managers who will have the aid of the Lords. You will always be watched. There is nothing you can do about this. No matter where you came from…no matter who you were before this; that life is over."

"You won't get away with this." It was Wilson, just to my right.

"I already have," the man said with a smile. "From this day forward, you will refer to me as Massa Cal. Every person you meet on the compound needs to be addressed with the title Massa in front of their name. If you do not adhere to this rule, you will be disciplined by Etta."

"Who's Etta?" I asked hesitantly.

"It's a whip made especially for you men. One strike will leave a lifetime of keloids."

"Where is my wife?" Wilson demanded again.

The man slowly turned his attention in Wilson's direction. "You don't hear too good." The man ran his hand through his dark hair. I could see that it was thinning towards the top. He took another drag off his cigarette and then investigated the darkened corner. "But I'll show you," he said menacingly.

We heard the rattling of chains and then Wilson began to yell. "Get your muthafuckin' hands off me!"

"Since you want to be the first!" the man snapped.

Wilson's form appeared from the darkness, dragged cruelly by a large chain fastened to the metal cuffs. He was nude, except for his boxer shorts. He looked older, like he had aged ten years since he stepped foot in the carriage. The gray in his beard and short cut hair was prominent. I could see Wilson clearly as the man pulled him into the bright light. The rest of us remained in the darkened room that I was convinced was a containment unit.

As he was hauled away, I knew what was coming next. I braced myself for the sounds of what I was sure to be a whipping. I had heard and read about the cruelty of masters and slaves in the 1800s, but now I was going to see it up close and personal.

The crack of the whip striking flesh startled me even as I expected it. Wilson screamed and my heart broke for him. Not only was his wife missing, but he was also a slave.

Hell, we all were.

Slaves.

The idea settled over me like a wet blanket. Slavery? In 2022? It wasn't possible and yet here we were. The crack of the whip echoed and reverberated inside the containment unit. Along with the sound of the whip came the sound of Wilson's screams. They were guttural, painful. I tugged weakly at my chains. I had never felt more helpless.

Wilson screamed again, and suddenly I knew.

We were never getting out of here. We were slaves…forced to work for little or no wages. Our women would be sold. Our children would be auctioned off like cattle. We no longer had any rights. We were now considered to be property instead of people…all because of a carriage ride.

And then the thought hit me…Aunt Pearl and Aunt Macy! They were too old to be productive. They couldn't toil in the fields. What would become of them? I hadn't heard any women's voices in this containment unit, which led me to believe we had been separated. I couldn't imagine what was happening to my little nieces. In many ways I didn't want to.

Zach.

Where was the man that I had pledged my love to? Where was the man that I had asked to marry me the day before? Now that we were captive, what would become of us? Would we be a couple after today? Would I ever see him again?

The whip cracked on, interrupting my thoughts; a grim reminder of where we were and the time we were living in. In the blink of an eye, my home had been taken from me. My family had been taken from me. The love of my life had been taken from me.

I had been reduced to a sense of nothingness that I couldn't wrap my head around. Was this what it was like to be a slave? I had heard of the television mini-series, *Roots*. This was worse. With *Roots,* the channel could be changed, or the television turned off altogether. There was no changing this channel. We were part of the program, whether we liked it or not.

A Mexican man entered the space. He tugged on a chain in the corner of the containment unit and the next thing we knew, we were being pulled out into the open. I took a deep breath of air before my eyes fell on Wilson.

He was bent over what appeared to be a tree stump, his wrists lashed to a set of metal cuffs that had been hammered into the ground. His lacerations were bleeding profusely. His head lolled over the side of the stump. His cries had stopped. I hoped he had passed out.

We were marched past him, a line of men, linked together by the chains that bound our wrists. We had the somber look of the incarcerated. We walked quietly along a path through ankle length grass. The path had been recently cut.

The sun shone on a row of small cabins, the size of a one-room schoolhouse. There were at least ten of them. The cabin closest to the main house appeared to serve as the cookhouse. I would later find out that all the meals for "new masters" were prepared there. The next cabin served as a second cookhouse for the people in chains.

Tears slipped involuntarily from my eyes as I walked past the cabins. Smoke curled from the chimneys, and I could smell burning wood. Had it been a different time, the aroma would have almost been nostalgic. But then I heard the crack of a whip and a scream in the distance. We all knew to be quiet and not say a word.

I couldn't believe this was happening. I closed my eyes as my tears continued to fall. I couldn't believe that we were in a time when it was legal for anyone to own slaves. The man led us into the last cabin. As we entered, we saw six cots. I was shown which bed I would be sleeping in. I sat down on the edge of the cot and the Mexican man tied each of us to the metal posts that served as the frames of the beds, to ensure that none of us would attempt to escape.

Oh, my God. Oh, my God.

# Indigo

Something was wrong. I could feel it in my bones. My flight wouldn't be leaving for another hour. I called Drake's cell phone, and it went to voicemail. They were probably still on the carriage ride. I left a message for him to call me, then dialed Latrice's number. The call went to voice mail. I called Aunt Pearl, Aunt Macy, and Kisha, only for the same thing to happen.

I called Shucky and waited impatiently for him to pick up. He did on the third ring.

"Who this?" His voice sounded rough; like he smoked too many cigarettes and drank too much brown liquor.

"Shucky, this is Indie."

"You comin' to my fish fry tomorrow?"

"No, Shucky." I didn't feel like providing him with a reason, but I could see that I didn't have a choice. "I'm at the airport now. I have work to do."

"What can I do for you?"

"I may be making a big to do about nothing, but I can't reach the family. Can you check on them? Last I heard, they were doing a carriage ride at Carmichaels."

"What are you worried about?"

"Shucky, I can't reach anyone. Not Latrice, Kisha, or Drake. I called Aunt Pearl and Aunt Macy, and I got nothing as well."

"I can take a ride up to Carmichael's if you want me to."

"Do you mind?"

"Naw. I'll go. I got your number. You comin' back here?"

"Only if I must. My flight isn't leaving for another hour. Can you call me the second you reach someone?"

"I can tell that this is important to you. I'll check."

"Thank you Shucky. I'll wait for your call."

The line went dead. I looked around the airport and it hit me again, the scent of a woman's perfume.

"Save your family." The disembodied voice whispered

I stood up and headed towards the desk. I had to change my flight and get a rental to head back to Darcy County.

# Drake

When I woke up to darkness, I panicked. Then I remembered where I was. I had to keep my mind in focus and remember that panicking would not serve any useful purpose. The box wasn't moving anymore, so I assumed that someone would be coming to get me out eventually. I hoped they would get here soon because I had to go to the bathroom.

My mind floated to my girls. It was my job to be their protector. It was my job to protect my wife.

August.

I wanted to wrap my arms around my family and never let go. I couldn't care less if I came back to Darcy County, Georgia ever again.

The lid of the box opened, and I was bathed in bright, warm sunshine. The light was so bright it temporarily blinded me. I raised myself up on my elbows and looked around. Two men stood above me and nothing around me looked familiar.

"Where am I?" I asked.

"Shut the fuck up, nigger!" a male voice yelled.

My mouth snapped shut as someone's hands rudely pulled me to my feet. Normally, I would swing on anyone that put their hands on me. I had to keep that at bay for now. Swinging on someone could get me killed. I stayed quiet as I looked at the man in front of me.

"You have a name, nigger?" He spat a wad of brown colored liquid in front of me.

I wouldn't realize it until later that it was a wad of tobacco. I looked at this dark-haired man from head to toe. He was young, no more than twenty-five.

"Drake," I said quietly,

"Speak up, nigger!" he yelled.

"Drake."

"Drake?" he repeated. "Typical nigger name. Get up there!"

He pointed to a platform where ten other Black men stood all with the same forlorn expression. All of them had their hands lashed behind their backs. My arms were pulled behind me and I felt handcuffs being placed on my wrists. He shoved me towards the group of men. I stumbled up steps to the platform and took my place beside the last man. We were all nude except for our underwear. We were all barefoot. No one said a word. I think we were all thinking about our families as well as how to get out of this scenario. The dark-haired man looked at each one of us while walking back and forth.

"I'll take two, three, five, six and ten," he said to the second man. "I'll pay one thousand for the lot of them."

The second man was bald and overweight. He walked to a pole that had been plunged into the ground, bent over, and rattled the chains. Every man stared forward as the heavy-set man yanked at each one of us cruelly. Five of us were led towards a flatbed truck whose engine was running. We had no idea where we were going. But although I was breathing fresh air and was no longer inside a box, I couldn't help but feel like I was getting farther and farther away from my family.

"How you get here?" one of the men asked me.

"What?" I responded.

"How you get here?" he repeated, sweat glistening off his shoulders and back.

I took a long pause before I answered. "I came down to Georgia with my family. Came to close my homestead. My aunt couldn't afford to keep up the property. We came down to say goodbye to our grandparents' property and then do a last carriage ride – we were in a tour of the vineyard, and we were gassed. I wound up inside a box and when they finally pried the lid off, I was here."

I looked around as the truck rolled through the mostly green countryside. The heat was stifling, and the air reeked of unwashed men and freshly cut grass.

"I was walking along a stretch of road in Atlanta. I was on my way home from work. It must have been around six in the morning. I was abducted."

"Right off the road?" I asked.

He nodded his head.

"I would kill for a Newport," he said while looking far off. "They didn't just snatch me off the street. They snatched me from my family...my wife..." his voice trailed off.

I wanted to say something to him, but words escaped me. Instead, I fell silent. Five of us had been bought for a thousand dollars. We were property. Now I just had to figure out how to get out of here and back to my family. And to start, I had to figure out where I was as well as where I was going.

"My name's Aren," he continued. "You?"

"Drake."

"Pleasure to meet you, Drake. Wish it was under better circumstances."

We couldn't shake hands because of our chains.

"Me too, man." My mind went to August, and my eyes welled with tears. I wanted her. I wanted my girls. Nothing would have given me greater pleasure than to wrap my arms around my daughters and my wife.

"Where are we?" Aren asked in a gruff voice.

"I don't know." I shook my head. "But I don't think we're in Georgia anymore."

"I don't think so, either. But I'm not worried. I don't plan on being here long."

"What are you going to do?"

"I'm breaking away the first chance I get. You wanna come?"

"Sure," I said, relieved that I finally had a comrade. "But we need to figure out where we are first. We won't know that until we get to where we're going."

He nodded, but his eyes never met mine. "If they sold us, then we're probably heading to another plantation," Aren said. "We aren't allowed to talk so when we get to wherever we're going, we need to shut up."

"I figured as much," I mumbled.

"You guys' won't get far." A man with shoulder-length dreadlocks spoke up.

I looked over at him. He was a skinny man with chestnut brown skin.

"This ain't my first time around the block," he began. "I've been going through this now for almost five years."

"Five years!" I exclaimed.

"Yes. There's a whole underground slave circuit going on down here. Plantations are being built and in between those spots are auction blocks. They nabbed me after I went to a bar and got drunk. I passed out in my car and when I woke up, I was in a box.

"I'm originally from Beaumont, Florida. I don't know where I am and have no idea how to get home if I tried."

"Keep 'em confused," Aren muttered more to himself than anyone else.

"Guess we need to find out where we are once we get to where we're going."

The truck made a sharp right. I took note that we turned from a two-lane highway to a dirt road that led past a field of picked cotton. We were lashed to the wooden rails that ran the length of the truck bed, but we still bounced around in the back as we rolled past this unusually large field. There was a lone house in the distance. From where we were, it almost looked inviting…like a cottage nestled in the flatlands of a cotton field that had been picked over. The sky was crystal blue with a few wisps of white clouds in the distance.

Sweat ran down the sides of my face. I became aware of just how hot the sun was as it beat down on my bare shoulders. I looked around me hoping to see a route off this plantation, but I couldn't find any. It appeared as if the entire perimeter had been surrounded by steel fencing. If we were going to escape, it was going to take a tremendous amount of thought and planning.

The tears that had been welling up behind my eyes threatened to fall down my cheeks. I couldn't let that happen. That would show that I was weak. And then, without warning, my thoughts turned to August and my girls.

How was I going to get back to them? Were they okay? Did they need me?

August sat on the dirt floor of the cookhouse, wearing a shift dress. Three women were preparing food over three huge cauldrons. One cauldron held something that smelled like chili. Another held boiling grits, while the last held some kind of soup.

She wrapped her arms around her torso as she tried to calculate how to find her daughters. She had no idea where they were, but they had to be close by. She tried to remember what had happened once they were gassed but her mind was blank.

The cooks were all black and dressed in peasant blouses and floor-length skirts. All had scarves wrapped around their heads and worked quietly, watching the pots to ensure that the food was being prepared properly.

Not only had she lost the girls, but she also had no idea where Kisha and Latrice were. She tried to wrap her mind around the era that she was in. She wasn't sure as she looked around her. She was in a giant one room cabin where the primary function seemed to be to prepare food.

Where was Drake? And speaking of men, where were Tarek and Zach?

"Get up, chile," one of the women said, not turning away from the pot. "I know you new, but they sent you to the cookhouse to prepare meals for the massas. Can you cook?"

August got slowly to her feet. "I only cook for my husband and my daughters."

"You don't got no husband or daughters no more."

"The hell I don't!" August looked towards the doorway. "Where are my girls? Where is my husband?"

"You don't got no husband or children no more." The woman turned to face August; her worn face showing a sense of fatigue reserved for someone that worked tirelessly from sun up to sun down.

"My husband's name is Drake. Drake Robeson." August started towards the entryway to the cookhouse. "I have two girls…Autumn and Madison. Madison is older and…"

"I said you don't got no children and no husband!" The woman sounded irritated.

August got a good look at her. She looked to be about sixty or seventy…older. "They take what's yours as soon as you get on this plantation. I know you don't want to hear none of this, but the sooner you hear it and believe it, the better off you'll be."

"I will never believe that I don't have a husband and kids." August spoke in a tone that came out stronger than she had intended.

"Stay away from that entryway chile," the woman said. "This cookhouse is my responsibility. My name's Tess."

"My name is August." She paused in her tracks.

"Pretty name." Tess wiped her hands on her apron. "They may let you keep it."

"Who are 'they'?" August asked.

"'They' is the people that own this plantation," Tess answered, a tinge of bitterness clear in her voice. "The name of the family is Carmichael. They own all the land around us… including the electric fence that runs the length of the property."

August paused for a moment, looking around the room. A dark-skinned child came in with a tray. Tess turned her back and walked to what August initially thought was an icebox. It was a fully functioning refrigerator. That's when she realized that the building had electricity.

Tess looked down at the child. "Do they want something to drink?" she asked softly.

The child nodded his head.

"Can I ask the boy something?" August asked quickly.

"You lookin' for your chil'ren?" Tess asked.

August nodded.

"I'll ask." Tess looked back down at the child. "Jessie? Have you seen any chil'ren that are new? Maybe they came within the last few days? Two little girls?"

Jessie smiled broadly. "They in the pen with the other kids."

August rushed over to the child and grabbed him by the shoulders. She stooped down in front of him so they were eye to eye. "Where is the pen? Is it far from here?"

Jessie shook his head.

"Can you take me there?"

"Jessie can't take you anymore than he can take me." Tess placed a carafe of orange juice on the tray. "Don't spill none."

Jessie started towards the entryway. August stood up slowly and started to follow. Tess blocked her way.

"Ain't nothin' that chile can do for you. He done tole you everything that you need to know for now."

August pushed her away, watching the child making his way up a flat stone path that led to the main house. "Those are my children," she said, the words slipping from her lips like a dead weight. "Those are my babies."

"And you may never see those kids again!" Tess snapped.

For a moment, all the women in the room stopped.

"Go back to work!" Tess shouted and then she lowered her voice to face August. "Who you came here with?"

August swallowed involuntarily and then took a deep breath. "I came here with my husband and my two daughters."

"I'm so sorry to tell you this," Tess said. "By the time you got here—meaning to this cookhouse—they sent your man either downstream or to the West."

"What do you mean?"

"They divide and conquer. They send the mens away so that they won't be here to support their families. They send them by train in boxes to other plantations. Most of us never see our men again. That's just what they do."

"Drake." August said to herself. She looked into Tess's face who had gone silent for a moment as if she were in intense thought.

"I'm sorry baby," Tess said slowly. "Your man is gone. Plenty of us womens lost our men that way.

"This is insane." August shook her head. "Where the hell are we?"

"You still in Darcy County, but you on a plantation." She continued, "They put you in the cookhouse so you can learn from me. We not just cookin' for the people in the big house, we cooking for all the folks that work on this plantation. Lunch time is coming. We're making them soup and cornbread."

"You said that my husband isn't here," August said. "What about my children?"

"If Jessie says they in the pen, then there's a chance I can get you to 'em."

"You can take me to them? You can take me to my girls?" Her tears began to fall, and Tess almost embraced her, but she knew better.

To convey compassion to another slave was to invite a beating. "I can take you to where I think they may be. Sometimes massa sells the children too. People want smart kids that they can mold into good slaves."

"Good slaves? Slavery was abolished in 1865." August shook her head once again. "Can you take me to my babies?"

"If they still here."

"Where else would they be?"

"Let's just hope that they still there." She turned back to her pot.

August moved to the far side of the room and sat down at an empty table. She would have to wait patiently for Tess to take her to the pen. What would she do if her girls weren't there?

What would she do if, God forbid, the girls had been sold to someone on another plantation or in another state? And what about Drake? Where was he? Could they find their way back to each other and then, together as a family, make it back to Philadelphia?

First things first. She had to find her girls. And if Tess was the means for her to find them then so be it.

# Tarek

I was dreaming I was home. My dog was curled up beside the fireplace and I was in my recliner with an open book lying on my stomach. Teena Marie played softly on the stereo. Zach had dozed off on the sofa. The crackling of the wood in the fireplace was hypnotic. Zach turned his head to me and smiled. And then he stood up and yelled…

"Get up! Get up, nigger!!"

"What?"

"Get the fuck up!" And then he hit me.

I tumbled out of the makeshift bed and woke up.

I was on the dirt floor of the cabin, my left hand still chained to the side of the cot. I carefully raised myself to my feet, shaking my head to wake up fully from my dream. The white man with dark hair scowled at me as if I wasn't even human.

"I'm a man." I muttered to him.

He almost didn't hear me. "The fuck you say, nigger!"

"Stop calling me that."

"Aww." He got up in my face. "You don't like that? You don't like being called 'nigger'?"

He was so close that I could smell his breath. And then he struck me again. This time, he hit me with a closed fist. I didn't expect the punch. I wasn't ready for it, and I crumpled to the floor like a sack of potatoes.

"Get up!" He towered over me.

The ringing in my ears wouldn't stop.

"Get up!" He hauled me to my feet. "You need to get fitted for your work clothes!"

With a rattle of chains, we were hauled out of the cabin. The sun rode high in the sky as they marched us single file past the row of cabins. I wondered where Zach was and if he was okay. What would they have done with him as a white man?

I looked ahead of me to see where they were taking us. All I could see was rows and rows of vegetation standing a foot off the ground. Dragonflies raced across the treetops while bumblebees hummed lazily from flower to flower.

One of the men behind me stumbled and fell, pulling the last fellow in the line down with him. The dark-haired man was on them in a flash, whip in hand.

I closed my eyes as the sound of the whip striking flesh caused me to wince. I couldn't let them see my anger as I rose slowly to my feet. The dark-haired man whipped the man who had fallen mercilessly. With every blow, I could hear the moans of the next to the last man in line. It was the kind of moan that seemed to permeate our souls.

I wanted to yell at the dark-haired man…I wanted him to stop, but I knew that if I said anything, it would only get worse. He wouldn't stop, and he would whip me next. What drove me crazy is how quickly I started to become acclimated to being a slave.

How long was I here, less than a day?

I couldn't accept this. It wasn't just knowing that I was a slave, although that was bad enough. What upset me most was knowing that my family was somewhere on this farm going through the same thing.

Were they beating my little nieces? What were they doing to Kisha, August, and Latrice? Where the hell was my brother? Where were my aunts?

It was hot. I couldn't believe how hot it was. I didn't like the heat and would always go into air-conditioning and cool off if I got too hot. Somehow, I knew that this wasn't an option here.

The whipping finally stopped. For a moment, all that I could hear was quiet sobbing.

"Get up!" The dark-haired man kicked the man he had beaten.

"Puh…please mister."

"Massa! You address me as Massa!" He kicked the man again.

I tried not to be angry but found it hard not to be. I got a good look at the dark-haired man. He was overweight, wore thick framed glasses and looked as if he sun-burned easily. He wore a faded wife-beater tee shirt and ill-fitting jeans.

"You don't have to do that to him," I heard myself shout.

"Yeah? Come 'ere boy!"

It took me a full minute before I realized that he was speaking to me.

"Yes?" I watched the dark-haired man unfurl his whip.

"You niggers don't listen, do you?"

The dark-haired man pulled his arm back and the whip moved like it had a mind of its own. The leather whistled as it sailed through the air. The strap caught me right between the shoulder blades and I fell to my knees. I wanted something to buffer me from the whipping that I was getting for nothing more than saying speaking up for my fellow man. He struck me two more times before he turned his attention to the next man.

I slowly raised myself to my feet when the whip whistled again. The man beside me yelled and reached out to grab it, but the whip was too quick. The dark-haired man lashed at him. And in that moment, I knew the gravity of the situation. We were stuck with a bunch of crazy people who believed they were reliving the old south.

"You will address me with the respect that is due every white man!" the dark-haired man muttered as he back-hand wiped spittle from his mouth.

"Nobody disrespected you," I mumbled.

"Boy, didn't I tell you to address me with respect?"

"I didn't disrespect you!" I raised my voice, the anger overtaking me.

Another man with a whip appeared out of nowhere. Before I could say anything, he unfurled the strap and lashed my bare back. It felt like white lightning across my shoulder blades. I heard screaming and realized that the person screaming was me. I fell to my knees once again as he whipped me. I could feel blood begin to flow from the open wounds. My chains held securely as I rolled as far away as I could. The other men watched without saying a word.

Although they didn't say anything, I knew what was happening. These white men, whoever they were, whipped me with what only could be viewed as joy. I had never been whipped like this before. I fell to the ground once again and didn't get up. I couldn't.

"Stop!" I heard the voice from a distance.

I lay on the ground, my body twitching involuntarily.

"Stop!" The voice had come a little closer.

I dry heaved, then vomited. And then the beating stopped. I don't think they felt sorry for me; they were pausing, waiting for me to finish so they could inflict more pain.

I felt arms around me. I jerked away; the pain too great to stand being touched.

"It's okay." It was Zach. "I got you."

"…Zach?" I barely got his name out.

"I own him!" Zach shouted at the men. "This is my property, and you don't have the right to beat him."

The white men froze, looking at one another. I could tell they didn't recognize Zach.

"You hurt my property!" Zach hissed. "What was the reason?"

"We're sorry, mister," the dark-haired man said. "We didn't know you owned this boy."

"So does that mean you can just beat on anyone if you think they're a slave?" Zach shouted. "Even if the property isn't yours? What's your name? Both of you!"

"I'm Alan," the dark-haired man said in a subdued tone.

The second man didn't say anything.

"Go!" Zach shouted. "Leave me to take care of my property."

The muscles in my back twitched with pain. "Zach…" I croaked as I held onto his forearms.

"Baby, they hurt you." He tried to pull me toward him.

It hurt. I jumped, pulling away. "Shit." And then I let him gently pull me close and I wrapped my arms around his waist.

# Indigo

Keeping my attention on the road, I sped towards the only place that I could remember my family being. I wanted to hear back from Shucky before I got there, and when my cellphone rang, I hoped it was him. "Hello?"

"It's Shucky. Where you at?"

"I'm heading towards Carmichael's Restaurant."

"I'll meet you there along with my crew."

"You have a crew?"

"I know some folks who will show out if I need 'em to. How long before you get to the diner?"

"I'm about half an hour out."

"Okay. I'll meet you there."

"The ride is less than an hour," I said. "A whole family doesn't just vanish into thin air. Something is wrong. I can feel it."

"Is that what you're going by? A feeling?"

"That and the fact that no one has seen them since they got into the carriages."

"How you know this?" Shucky asked.

"You're gonna think I'm crazy but…well, I got a weird feeling. That coupled with the fact that I can't reach none of the folks that went on that ride."

"None of 'em?

"Not a one." The asphalt rolled out ahead of me like an endless stretch of black licorice. "I've been trying to reach everyone, and no one's answering their phones."

"You gonna feel foolish when you get here, and everyone is in their hotel rooms."

"But I'll know where they are, won't I?"

"I ain't gonna tolerate gettin' disrespected, little girl."

"Who's disrespecting you? I'm simply trying to find my family." Shucky fell silent.

"Shucky…you still there?" I said after a minute of silence.

"Yeah, I'm still here. We'll see you in a few." The line went dead.

When I got to Carmichael's, I pulled up to a crowded parking lot. I had to park a distance away from the front door. I sprinted across the lot and entered the building. Dishes clattered, waiters buzzed about, but when I looked around, my family did not magically appear.

But in the corner sat someone who looked vaguely familiar. I walked towards her. She sat with her legs crossed, reaching into her purse and retrieving a compact. She began to re-apply her makeup just as I approached her table. She looked up at me with green eyes, her hair spilling over her left shoulder.

"Why hello," she said with a smile. "I saw you yesterday."

"You remember me?"

"You were with your family yesterday." Her perfectly painted red smile broadened. "I'm Lady Onyx."

"Do I call you Lady or Onyx."

"I'm Lady Onyx. Lady O for short. And you are…"

"My name's Indigo."

She nodded. "Pretty name."

"So is yours," I found myself saying.

The woman was beautiful; long shapely legs stretched below a short black and white pencil skirt that was part of a two-piece suit. She wore six-inch stilettos, and I couldn't help but notice that her nails had been recently done in a vibrant red with one middle nail painted gold. A wide-brimmed hat sat slightly off center on her head.

Lady Onyx took a sip of coffee. "You're here because your family may be missing."

"How did you know?" I sat down next to her.

"I tried to warn you not to go on the carriage ride," she said. "You're here. That tells me that you didn't go with your family."

"You're right. What else do you know?"

Lady Onyx bit into a scone, took another sip of coffee and then carefully blotted her lips before re-applying her lipstick. "Your family's in trouble." Her tone was nonchalant.

"How do you know?"

"Because anyone who goes on those carriage rides don't come back the way they went in."

"What do you mean?" I asked.

Her eating that scone reminded me that I hadn't eaten anything since I checked out of my hotel. I'd had coffee at the airport, but nothing else.

"I mean, I know that your family went on the carriage ride…and you haven't heard from them since. Am I right?"

I nodded my head slowly.

"The only way you can get your peoples back is to go on the carriage ride yourself and get them out."

"Why can't they come out by themselves?"

"They can't."

"Why?"

"They can't."

"But why?" I repeated.

Onyx leaned back in her seat, looking like she was deep in thought. I wondered for a moment why her entourage wasn't present. She took a deep breath, placed her napkin beside her water glass and looked me straight in the eye. For the first time, I noticed that her eyes were green almost completely obscured by long dark lashes.

"Honey, where you from?" She asked.

"Philadelphia."

"Most people that go on those carriage rides don't come back. Especially if they look like you and me." She leaned into me which caused me to lean in as well.

"You mean women?" I asked.

"I mean black." She shook her head, looked down to her right and then back into my eyes. There was a sincerity that grabbed onto me and held my attention.

"Then why do you patronize a place like this if this is what they're doing to 'our' people?" I asked, trying not to get angry with her.

"Look, go on the ride. If you come out on the other side, I'll tell you everything you want to know."

"Why can't you tell me now?"

"Because you won't understand it if I tell you everything I know."

"Try me."

"I can't."

"Why?"

"Just trust me when I tell you that you wouldn't understand. I could tell you stuff that'll blow your mind. But I'm not going to."

"Why, Onyx?"

"It's Lady Onyx," she corrected. "Trust me when I tell you that you're better off not knowing than knowing."

"Damn! Ain't you a sweet, dark glass 'a chocolate milk."

The male voice took me by surprise. I didn't think Shucky would get here so quickly. It didn't surprise me that he'd hit on Onyx. Shucky always struck me as a man who would chase after any female.

Onyx looked up at him, then went back to eating her scone as if he weren't there.

"What am I better off not knowing?" I reached across the table and grabbed her wrist. "Please. Tell me what I need to know, and I'll go on the stupid carriage ride."

When she didn't respond, I pulled out my cell phone and dialed Drake's number again. The call went straight to voicemail.

"My name's Shucky." He took Onyx's hand from mine.

Lady Onyx pulled her hand away. I couldn't blame her. There was something about my uncle that made my skin crawl. It was the way he looked at people. I knew a lot about his past escapades. He was a sexist and womanizer. I knew it and so did any woman who met him.

"My name is Lady Onyx." She gave him a disparaging look.

"The pleasure is all mine." Shucky was trying to be suave.

"Yes, it is," she said. "So, what can I do for you?"

"I'm trying to get to my family." He looked back at me. "My niece can tell you more about what's happenin'. I got my army wit' me."

"She did." Onyx took a small sip of coffee and then looked back at me. "You have an army?"

A group of ten men walked into the restaurant and headed towards our table. They looked like they would associate with Shucky. They all appeared to be in the same age range, seventy or so, all trying to hold onto their youth as it slipped away from them.

"This is your crew?" Onyx finally addressed Shucky directly.

"Yeah," he said proudly. "And whatever we got to do to get my family outta there, we will."

"So, all of you are going on the carriage ride."

"Naw, five will go, five will stay behind in case we all don't make it out."

"Okay."

"Damn, you is fine." Shucky's eyes roamed over Onyx's legs.

"Shucky!" I raised my voice. "Focus! We got things to do."

"You right, Indie. Let's go for this carriage ride."

# Drake

We were in the forest, chopping down trees. I had never used a chainsaw in my life, and yet, here I was in the woods cutting down trees to build another cabin. I had been whipped for no other reason than being black and speaking out of turn to a white man.

My back hurt. Once again, my mind turned towards my little girls. How were they coping? Were they with August or were they all alone?

I had to get to them, which meant that I had to get to Aren. If he was leaving this hell hole, I would go with him. I still didn't know where we were, but I was hoping it was close enough to the original plantation that I could find them and escape to back to our real lives.

I wasn't a lumberjack, but I was surprising myself with the ease in which I was able to maneuver the chainsaw. I looked around me for a quick second to see where the overseers were.

"Keep cuttin', nigger!" The voice came seemingly out of nowhere.

I kept the chainsaw going. I couldn't risk being beaten again. The wounds on my back were open and the sweat running into it inflamed it more.

I noticed some differences in this new age of slavery. They gave us tools that could be used as weapons. Maybe that's why the overseers were hidden, so we couldn't get an estimate on just how many of them there were. No matter their numbers, I had to get back to August and my daughters. But how could I protect my family from something like this?

I was no Nat Turner or Frederick Douglass. I wasn't Sojourner Truth or Harriet Tubman, either. And yet they managed to get through this shameful time of our nation.

The muscles in my shoulders, forearms and biceps began to ache due to the exertion behind the chainsaw. My back was screaming.

And then I heard it.

It was a sound that I wasn't familiar with at first. But I had heard *about* it. The men in the forest were doing a call-and-answer routine to get through the day. It started with two guys, then four, then eight. Their voices came to me clearly over the roar of the chainsaw; without thinking, I heard myself join in.

In that moment, I made up my mind that not only was I going to survive this, but I was also going to get to my wife and my daughters, no matter what it took. But the elements were against me. When we stepped out of the shade of the forest, the sun beat down mercilessly on our backs and shoulders. I was thirsty and there were no sources of water to be had. Was I foolish to think that they would send a boy or girl with water and a dipper to quench our thirst?

I finished making a deep cut in the base of a tree and stepped back, calling out to two men who had wrapped a rope around the upper part of the tree to pull it down. Wiping the sweat away from my eyes with the back of my work-gloved hand, I looked down at the clothes they forced us to wear. The shirt and pants were cheap and nondescript from Wal-Mart or Target, dark handyman pants and a plaid shirt too heavy for the hot weather. My construction boots didn't fit properly and rubbed at my heels.

There was another group of men nearby clearing out foliage for what I assumed to be the next area where cabins were to be built. I could also hear other groups of workers, although I couldn't gauge how far they were from us.

Another tree splintered and fell to the ground, and an oversized golf cart with extra thick wheels appeared beside me, with a white man riding inside.

"Get workin', nigger!" he shouted at me.

"Okay." I hoisted the chainsaw from the ground.

"Okay what?

A full minute passed before I realized what he was demanding. He wanted me to call him 'massa.'

I couldn't bring myself to say it…but if I didn't, I would get a whipping. I didn't have the strength to go through that again, and it would only delay my escape.

"Okay…massa."

The smugness on the man's face told me everything that I needed to know. They were denigrating me. To them, I was no more than the many Black people that had come before me… just another nigger. I wasn't human. I was like livestock worthy of taking care of if only to get the creature to work for them the next day. They were going to try and break me, and I couldn't let that happen. I had to remain strong to get back to my family. That was the only thing that mattered.

Aren had been whipped for merely speaking out of turn. He had the audacity to yell at one of the overseers because he had been whipping a smaller man who looked terrified. Aren spoke up, which cost him several lashes across his back. They whipped him until he bled…and then whipped him some more. I hadn't seen him since. A part of me didn't want to.

The cookhouse was full of the aromas of food. August smelled bacon, biscuits, collard greens, pork chops, cornbread, rice and some kind of gravy. She looked down at her shift dress staring at it so long and hard that she didn't hear Tess speaking to her.

"August?"

"Yes?" She looked up at Tess's round dark face.

"You ready to go see if your kids are still here?"

"Yes."

"Follow me." Tess said quietly, and then she turned to face the other girls. "Keep stirring that soup and take it into the house to start their dinner in five minutes. Fifteen minutes after that, take in the main meal. I'll be right back." She turned to August. "Let's go. We gotta make this quick."

August followed her out of the cookhouse and down a narrow dirt path outlined by tall grass growing on either side. It was hard to walk in the slippers that they gave her to wear instead of her chukka boots.

The path led around the big house and to the back. She saw another row of crude cabins. August hoped that her children weren't there, but at the same time, she would have preferred instead of being inside of a pen.

They entered one of the cabins, where they found three Black pre-teens.

"Hey." Tess addressed the children with a voice of authority. "I'm looking for two girls." She turned to August. "What are their names again?"

"Autumn and Madison."

"Yeah." One of the children perked up. "They inside. They being trained to serve in the big house."

"Oh, hell no!" August left the cabin just as quickly as they had entered and headed towards the main house.

"Wait, chile!" Tess yelled from behind her.

August whirled on her. "My babies are in there being trained to wait on white people?" She shook her head. "No! I'm getting my girls!"

"Wait!" Tess raised her voice. "Let me go first! There's a way you gotta do this. You just can't go marching in the big house."

"Listen, Tess, no matter what, I'm getting my children. If they're in that house, I'm getting them."

"If you march in there, you will never see those kids ever again! Do you understand me? You will never see your girls again!"

August paused. Tess was right. Getting out of this scenario was going to take planning. She was this close to getting her babies. Once she got them, she needed to find Drake.

"Go ahead." She exhaled in exasperation. "I'll follow your lead. Take me to my babies."

Tess walked through the tall grass heading towards the screened in back door. They entered the house to hear a commotion going on. Two women were in the kitchen standing as if they didn't know what to do.

"What's going on?" Tess demanded.

The women couldn't have been any older than fifteen. They looked frightened. One of them pointed towards the dining room. Tess marched past them with August following on her heels. They found a group of people seated around a huge Victorian dining room table. Madison was standing in front of her little sister, who was in tears.

August raced past Tess. "Babies!"

"Mommy!" Both girls ran to their mother's arms. Her eyes filled with tears; Madison spoke up. "I tried to protect Autumn...but they wouldn't let me..."

"It's okay, baby." August embraced her daughters and gave the blonde woman seated at the head of the table a hard look. "Mommy's here."

"Don't leave us again, Mommy." Madison's tears began to fall.

"Where's Daddy?" Autumn choked through her sobs.

"I don't know, baby."

The blonde woman at the table stood. "Who is this nigger bitch?"

"Please, Missus Carmichael," Tess began, maneuvering herself so that she was between August, her children and the woman at the table. "These is her children."

"None of you nigras have any children," the woman sneered.

"Oh, my God." August pulled her daughters closer. "You're Ms. Lulu! You waited on us yesterday!"

The blonde removed her cat-eyeglasses and placed them beside her plate. The room went quiet.

"Where is my husband? Where's my family?"

"Girl, you don't have no husband," Lulu took two steps towards August who recoiled.

"I don't know what you have going on, but you need to get the police here right now!"

"Who do you think you talkin' to, chile?" She looked down at the two girls. "I'm gonna let you keep your cubs with you, for now. They wouldn't have made good servers no how."

She reached for Madison, who clung to her mother tighter.

"Don't!" August warned.

"Tess, take this nigra out to the cookhouse. We need supper for the rest of the staff." She turned towards August. "I have something special planned for you."

"You can do anything you want with me. Just don't touch my girls!"

"Chile, you don't have no power here. You don't tell me what to do, I tell you!"

"Come on, girl." Tess said in a low voice, dragging August and her daughters toward the back door.

August walked out of the house holding both her girls protectively. "How can you live like this?" she asked angrily. "What is wrong with you people?"

Tess kept walking back to the cookhouse in silence.

"Answer me!"

Tess whirled around. "I don't have to pay rent! I don't have to pay for insurance!" she shouted. "I don't have to pay for my food or the clothes on my back!"

The girls whimpered, then grew silent.

"For once in my life, all my bills are paid. And all I have to do is cook! For me, it's worth it!"

"Your freedom is never worth it!" August yelled back. "What am I supposed to teach my daughters?"

"That they're taken care of."

"By who? Some white man that doesn't give a damn about them?"

"Hush your mouth! Wait until we get to the cookhouse…then you can say what you want!"

August wrapped her arms around her daughters again and followed Tess back to the cookhouse.

"Mommy, I'm hungry." Madison's tears dried when they entered the cookhouse, and she smelled food.

Tess gestured toward the food. "Go fix your girls something to eat and then I'll tell you everything I know."

# Indigo

The carriage bounced as we rounded corner after corner, eventually coming to cotton fields that had been picked over. In the distance, I could see some field hands crouched down low as if they were weeding a garden. I wasn't crazy about having to turn over my cell phone, but I did it anyway to keep the peace.

We rode slowly past a makeshift replica of a town being built in the early 1800s. I would have been mildly intrigued had it not been for the circumstances. Shucky and two of his men sat across from me and I was hemmed in by the remaining three men who rode with us.

The driver guided us past rows and rows of vegetables ready to be picked. There were more people bent over in those fields.

"You scared?"

The voice was deep, rough. I looked at the man seated to my right. He was handsome in a rugged sort of way, dark-skinned with a close beard, full lips, broad nose, and deep dark brown that appeared as if he was always in thought.

"No." I looked out the side of the carriage as it rolled along the unpaved road. "I just want to find my family."

"And you think you won't?"

"I think I'll find them when I find them."

He chuckled to himself and then yawned. "Sorry about that."

"No worries." I looked at his face for a moment, then back outside the carriage.

We rode past either a small lake or large pond.

"Goddamn! You see that, Levi?" The man to my left perked up, speaking across me. "Damn gator snatched something!"

"I didn't see it and I don't want to see it." Levi responded.

"Goddamn!" The man stared intently out the right side of the carriage as the driver guided the horses onto a narrow path that cut through dense foliage.

"You want to want to watch our mouth, Teddy." Levi stared straight ahead. "There's a lady sittin' right next to you."

"You right, Levi, you right." Teddy ran a nervous chubby hand over his scraggly beard.

Levi glanced over at him, then at me. I could tell that he was looking me over. I wasn't sure if he liked what he saw and right now, I didn't care.

I caught a whiff of smoke, but I couldn't figure out where it was coming from since the sky was a pristine blue.

"You smell that?" Teddy said.

"Yeah." Levi's voice was barely audible.

"Hey, Levi?" Shucky called from across the carriage.

"Yeah?"

"Did you know that all this shit was back here?"

For a moment, all we could hear was the clop of the horse's hooves striking the dirt road beneath us.

"No," Levi grumbled, "but I heard rumors."

"What kind of rumors?" I asked hesitantly.

"They have crops back here…lots of crops. The kind that need to be harvested and not enough hands to gather them."

I nodded my head as the carriage come to a slow halt. The glass on either side of the carriage began to slide upwards.

"What the hell?" Shucky sat upright just as smoke started to fill up the interior.

Panicking, I reached over Levi to try to open the door. It was locked.

Levi wrapped his arms protectively around me as all of us began to cough. I turned to him, burying my face into his shirt and taking measured breaths. Teddy rolled onto his side, kicking at the door with his feet, but it wouldn't budge. The other two men started banging on the roof. I remember hitting the glass door before feeling what felt like extreme fatigue overtake me.

I came to in Levi's arms. We were both on the ground. I jumped away from him instantly and looked around me. All the men were looking around them with bewildered expressions. We were in the middle of a town that looked more like a set from *Rifle Man* than any place in 2022.

"What the fuck?" Shucky looked up the dirt road towards the end of town. A group of young white men were headed towards us. I took a step back, feeling slightly disoriented.

"Be prepared to run." Levi whispered to me.

"Why?"

"These folks don't have our best interests at heart."

I understood, but I wasn't sure where he expected us to run. We had no idea where we were, much less what direction to run in. We watched as the men slowly approached. The man in the lead was heavy-set, with dark hair and thick framed glasses. He frowned when he looked at me.

"What are you niggers doing out in the middle of town?" His voice was loud and authoritative.

"Who are you calling 'niggers', you fat, thick glasses-wearing motherfucka?" Shucky snapped.

"Oh, so you don't know how to behave!" The dark-haired man looked off to his right.

Two men armed with twelve-gauge shotguns cocked their weapons while the first unfurled a whip from his belt. I couldn't believe what was happening. Were these men really going to try to arrest us? What kind of offense could they charge us with?

"Shit." Levi instinctively pushed me behind him.

"We can do this the easy or hard. It's up to you." The dark-haired man sneered. "And you…" He turned his attention to Shucky. "You got a problem with authority. But I'm gonna show you."

"Show me what?" Shucky growled.

"Who's boss, coon!"

"You tryin' to take me out of my character, snowflake?"

"The girl comes with us!" the dark-haired man ordered.

"That's not gonna happen!" Levi stayed in front of me, and I was grateful for his presence. I was fine until the first gun went off.

Teddy flew backwards, a hole blown in his chest the size of a volleyball. I screamed, covering my face with my hands. Someone grabbed Levi by the arm while another man grabbed me.

"Get off me!" I screamed.

"Bitch!" He backhanded me across the mouth stunning me into an abrupt silence. Blood trickled from my lip. He slapped a pair of handcuffs on my wrists as if he'd done this a million times before and proceeded to drag me toward a row of cabins that ran the length of the big house and into the back woods.

He pulled me through thigh-high grass past the big house and into the first cabin. A million thoughts flooded my mind, the first one being that he was going to rape me. I was preparing myself to fight back when I saw other women in the room.

"Indie!" I heard my sister-in-law's voice.

"Aunt Indie!" Madison yelled; and then I felt small arms wrapping around my waist.

August looked more like a slave than my brother's stylish wife. She threw her arms around me. I would've hugged her back if I could.

"August…how…what?" I couldn't find the words to ask all the questions I had.

"I don't know!" She held me tightly. "Are you okay?"

I looked around me. The man was gone.

I shook my head and then the tears began to flow. Based on what August was wearing and the way those men had treated us, I had to conclude that we were the victims of people who wanted to bring back the era of the slave. My sister-in-law looked ridiculous in this runaway slave get-up. I looked at my nieces.

"Girls, are you okay?"

"Yes." Madison nodded.

"I wanna go home," Autumn said in a low voice.

I wiped the tears from my face. "August, where are we? And where is everyone else? Kisha and Latrice? Aunt Macy and Pearl?"

"I don't know." August shook her head. "Macy and Pearl were supposed to be in the carriage after ours. I haven't seen anyone since we left."

"Well, where's Drake?"

"I wish I knew."

And then it hit me…we were caught in the mind of someone that wants to live in the era of slavery. The question was, what did we do now?

It was well after midnight. The cot I was lying on was the most uncomfortable thing that God had created. I knew that I had turned in my regular cell phone but not the phone that I only used for work. More than once during the day I tried to call my office and speak with Lucille, but I couldn't get a signal. I had to get her to contact the FBI and send someone to free me and my family.

After we had served everyone their last meal of the day, I noticed just how many women there were on this farm. I didn't know how it was, but I counted at least fifteen in the cookhouse alone, most of them black.

The odor of animals hung in the air like a thick mist on a spring morning, but at least the roosters had stopped crowing, and the cows were silent.

Autumn and Madison shared a cot while August slept next to them on the floor. The cabin door was open to allow fresh air to flow to the back of the room, but steel bars stood securely locked to prevent any of us from escaping. I needed the downtime to take everything in.

The white men who took me were between the ages ranged from 24 - 39. They were armed with double-barreled shotguns and Glocks. They could have killed us in the blink of an eye, but they didn't, which meant they had a reason to keep us alive.

I thought slavery had been abolished, but I guess I was wrong. At least I had found my nieces and my sister-in-law. But where was the rest of my family? And what about Shucky and his friends?

I heard a mixture of sobs and snoring. I couldn't understand why the people who had appointed themselves as our masters insisted on dressing us in traditional slave garb. Why were we in a cookhouse and not a kitchen? None of it made any sense. How did they expect to get away with this? Or rather, how long had they been getting away with it?

Tess seemed to be the person in charge. If anyone had information, it would be her. And then the thought hit me…how long had she been here? And why was she so comfortable with this life?

I hid my phone behind the cot, not wanting to take the chance that it would be discovered. I needed information and I didn't want to wait until morning to get it.

The room was lit only by four or five large candles. I crept over to where Tess was sleeping and tapped her sleeping form so I wouldn't startle her. She awakened instantly.

"Girl, what you want?" She stifled a yawn.

"Tess…sorry to wake you. I have a couple of questions for you if you don't mind."

She rolled over on her back and propped herself up on her elbows.

"What you want to know?"

"How long have you been here?"

"Two years I think."

"Two years?" I was incredulous.

"Shh. Chile, lower your voice!"

"Sorry." I paused for a moment. "What kind of place is this?"

Tess took a deep breath and exhaled slowly. Even by the light of the candles her eyes were thoughtful, but they reflected a sadness that I recognized. It was the same look that I saw in the faces of the mothers of defendants whose cases stood no chance. Too many young Black men were becoming victims of a system that seemed more intent on killing them than rehabilitating them.

"This is a plantation." She spoke as if it pained her to acknowledge that truth. "It's owned by some corporation who stands for a 'surgence of the old south. I think they call themselves the Confederation of the New South.'"

"Is this the only one?"

She shook her head. "No. There's a string of 'em that run from Florida to the Midwest. We just one of many. August's man…"

"Her husband." I interrupted. "My brother."

"I'm sorry."

"Why are you sorry? You didn't do anything."

"That's not why I'm sorry." She paused, "Your brother…August's husband. He's gone. What's your brother's name?"

"Drake."

She nodded her head. "They sent him out west or they sent him to the plantations in Florida."

"Why?"

"It's what they do," she said. "They separate us and then send the men to different plantations. They don't keep them here. It makes the women and children easier to control."

I sat in silence on the floor, not believing what Tess was telling me. How could my brother be gone? And how would we get him back? Someone must know where he is. And why didn't she mention Tarek?

# Drake

I lay on my back, staring up at the ceiling of the darkened space that I shared with at least ten other men. It felt like a twisted version of the summer camp that Tarek and I used to go to from time to time as kids. At a time when I should have been resting because of the hard work well done, my mind was racing a mile a minute trying to think of ways to escape what I'd come to understand as the deadly circumstances of our situation.

I was on what could only be described as a slave plantation. I heard whispered rumors that I wasn't in the state of Georgia anymore. Maybe I was in Florida, maybe Alabama. I wasn't sure. All I knew was that I had to get back to my girls.

I knew that Aren planned to escape but I hadn't spoken to him since his whipping. His bunk wasn't far from mine, but a nurse had come in, dressed his back, and gave him something to make him sleep.

Whoever owned this plantation had gone to great lengths to keep us comfortable, even if we had been abused. We were viewed as valuable property and therefore they did not feel the need to mistreat us unless it came to discipline.

While I worked to cut down trees, girls had come out with carts of water to help us get through the day. The work was backbreaking but, in some ways, our modern-day slavery was easier than how my ancestors had it. For starters, we had better tools to work with. We had three square meals a day and thirty minutes for a lunch break.

One old man told me this was not the only plantation in the area. Whispered conversation during lunch and after dark revealed that there were dozens of them and each one held slaves. I heard horror stories of people snatched off the street. Others had been found in soup kitchens and shelters for the homeless. No one was allowed to leave once they entered the plantation.

I kept thinking of my little girls and how hard it must be for them to adjust to their new circumstances. I didn't know if they were with August or not.

I wanted to crawl over to Aren, but I would have to wait. We were all chained with a chamber pot situated between the beds in case we had to pee in the middle of the night. If we had to do anything else, we were on our own.

I wiggled my hand to see if I could free it just a little. It didn't give at all.

The door to our confines opened and someone enter quietly. I didn't say a word as they crept into our darkened room. Whoever it was tiptoed right past my bed and approached Aren. Soft words were exchanged, and I could make out that one of the voices was female. I listened intently and realized that the nurse had come to change the dressings on his back.

All the women wore garb that appeared more suited to the eighteen-hundreds…long skirts, peasant blouses and head wraps. The men wore flimsy work pants, plaid shirts, and work boots. There was no contact with the outside world: no radio, no television, no phones. In many ways, we were alone and painfully isolated. There would have been no way of knowing that other plantations existed if we hadn't heard the overseers talking among themselves.

Still, outside of being chained to my bed, it was oddly peaceful. Except for the sound of crickets, it was quiet. There was no odor on the men that slept in these quarters. At the end of our workday, we were allowed to wash up, eat, and then rest. We just weren't allowed to roam free on the plantation.

I wiggled the hand that was cuffed to the bed. Surprisingly, this time it gave a little. If I could free myself, maybe I could find out some valuable information and flee this plantation, whether Aren was able to go or not. I closed my eyes, resting for a moment, and listened to the barely audible exchange between Aren and the woman. I felt myself dozing off when the door burst open, and three men entered the cabin and headed for Aren's bed. The woman was still there. She looked like she wanted to run but there was no place to go.

I remembered the first man, the one with dark hair, beer belly and thick-framed glasses. Within three strides and without saying a word, he was on her.

"I, I'm sorry, massa!" she exclaimed.

Her using that word caused my stomach to turn over. The dark-haired man punched her in the face, and she flew across the room, crumpling to the floor like a lifeless ragdoll.

"Bitch, you don't ever do anything without my say so!" He sneered down at her. "You don't tend to no one's wounds unless I tell you!"

"I'm sorry! I'm so, so sorry!" Her words came in gulps; I could feel the fear coming off her.

He reached down, hauling her to her feet, and smacked her again, this time with his open palm. The sound reverberated throughout the room. All we could hear were her sobs. Aren didn't say a word.

"Get to your quarters!" the man barked.

The woman scurried out of the room like a frightened mouse, and I was once again faced with my own helplessness.

"Listen up, niggers!" he shouted. "I will not tolerate any back talk, mutterings under your breath, cussin' or talk of any kind! You speak when you're spoken to!"

I heard the jingling of keys, a rattle of chains and then a groan. Two of the men hauled Aren to his feet. My heart sank. What were they going to do to him?

"When we loosen your shackles, you'll be going right outside this building! Meet me at the pot by the clearing."

Pot? Now what was he going to do with Aren and a pot?

August was sleeping soundly when she was seized by two pairs of strong hands, awakening her abruptly. She began to struggle, which woke the girls. They began to scream. Tess raced over and wrapped her arms protectively around them. Everyone in the cookhouse had awakened and was now lying in their beds, eyes opened…frozen in fear.

"Indie! Indie!" August screamed. "Look after my girls!"

"Mommy!" Madison yelled at the top of her lungs.

Autumn burst into tears as the men hauled her mother out of the cabin into the Georgia night.

"It's gonna be all right." Tess cuddled both girls, not allowing them to follow their mother outside. "Just stay with me!"

The men tossed August to the ground. Before she could get up, one of them seized her again, turned her around and grabbed the neck of her shift dress. In one swift motion, he jerked it down, ripping the fabric and exposing her bra. Without saying a word, he reached for her bra strap and yanked it down exposing her chest. August screamed hysterically, trying to cover her breasts.

Someone slapped metal cuffs on her wrists and pulled her across what looked like a tree stump. August didn't know what they were going to do to her, but she knew it wasn't going to be pleasant. The first thing that came to mind was rape, but when they bent her over the stump and hooked her cuffed wrists to the base, she found herself having difficulty breathing.

She didn't know when the first lash was going to come, but when it hit her bare back, she stopped breathing. The second lash felt like white lightning. August tried to wrench away out of range, but her wrists were firmly fastened. The third lash made her body buck wildly. She took a deep breath as her tears began to flow.

Lulu lashed August several more times before tossing the whip away. She looked down at August's bleeding back and smiled.

August's vision had doubled and then trebled because of her tears. As two men exited the cookhouse with Autumn and Madison, Lulu walked slowly back to the wrap around porch of the big house. The girls screamed, while Tess and Indigo followed them in tears, begging the men to let the girls stay. August screamed once again, knowing it would not affect the men who had been told to take her daughters away from her.

She had no way of knowing that her little girls were being removed from the plantation...permanently.

# Tarek

I woke up to the sound of screaming and bright morning sunlight streaming through a break in the light-colored curtains. Sitting up in bed, I took in my surroundings. I was in a bedroom, lying on a bed with a sheet and comforter engulfing my body. I could hear the lazy hum of the central air conditioning. Zach had been dozing in the heavy armchair seated next to the bed because he jumped up at the same time I did. He wrapped his arms lightly around me and then let go, painfully aware of the wounds on my back.

I looked at Zach. He was dressed differently than he had been when we'd left the hotel just the day before. It might as well have been years. He was wearing an off-white cotton shirt with the sleeves rolled up to his elbows, dark blue acid-washed jeans and workman's boots.

"Calm down," he said gently. "I got you. You're safe."

"Where am I?"

"In the main house. But don't worry. You're safe," he repeated. "As long as you're with me, no one will hurt you."

"How did you know to tell them I was your property?"

"White skin carries a lot of weight here in the New South."

"New South?"

"That's where we are." He looked directly at me. "We're on a plantation owned by Gordon Collings. He's a friend of the Carmichael's. He owns most of this…"

Zach's voice trailed off.

"Most of what?" I asked.

"He owns at least five acres of this plantation. They produce cotton, potatoes, peanuts, peaches, apples, oranges, tobacco, watermelon, and cantaloupes." He leaned into me lowering his voice. "We have to get out of here."

"Do you know where the girls are?"

"I'm going to check on them now that I know you're awake. For now, just rest and save your strength. You're going to need it."

"What happened to us in the carriage?"

"They gassed us. But they don't gas everyone…only the ones they think they can use."

"Where's the rest of my family?"

"August and Indie are in the cookhouse. Kisha and Latrice are on laundry duty."

"What about my brother? Have you seen him?"

Zach paused, then took a deep breath almost as if the news he was going to give me would shatter my spirit. "Drake isn't on this plantation. We think he is either in Florida or Alabama."

"What?"

"They separate the men from their families. It makes it easier to control people that way."

We fell silent as we listened to the bustling of household activity in the house.

"If I can corral the family, I think I can get us off this plantation. I just have to be careful," He whispered to me. "They think I'm a wealthy white from outside and that I want to be part of the power structure in this place. They think that I want to be part of the New South."

"Is this what white people have become? They want to stay in power so bad that they're willing to reinstitute a whole new racist society inside the society that already repress people of color?"

"Looks that way." He paused. "But it doesn't matter what they've become. They can think what they want. I'll get us out of here."

"One more thing, babe." I whispered to him.

"What is it?"

"Have you seen Aunt Pearl or Aunt Macy?"

He shook his head.

"No. I'm sorry babe."

"Excuse me, Massa Zachary."

We both looked up to see a small Black child standing in the doorway. How long had she been there? What did she hear?

"What is it?" Zach asked gently.

"Missus Lulu wants to see you, sir."

"Okay. Tell her that I will be down in a moment. Thank you."

"Yes, sir. She's in the library."

He turned his attention back to me and I was struck with just how easily everyone had accepted their designated roles in this backward hierarchy. Zach especially. He had suddenly become aware of his whiteness as well as the power that his white skin carried. I knew he was protecting me and that we had to take certain precautions when we talked to one another. But I didn't like that he was now in a class above me…and that he had accepted it so easily.

He got up off the bed and walked out of the room. I wondered who Ms. Lulu was, and what she wanted with him

Then my thoughts turned to Drake, and I forgot all about Ms. Lulu. Zach said he wasn't even on this plantation anymore. If that was the case, how many plantations were there, and where was Drake being held?

The lacerations on my back ached dully. One of the girls in the field had given me a salve made with herbs that took care of some of the pain. I thought of what it must have been like for people directly involved in the Civil Rights movement and I was grateful that there wasn't someone like Bull Connor or George Wallace around. But just because they didn't have those types of figures didn't mean that they didn't share their sentiments. If Ms. Lulu wanted to see Zach—was it that same Lulu who had waited on us yesterday? There had to be for a good reason.

I wondered briefly what had happened to Ida and Wilson. I hadn't seen them since the carriage ride, either. I moved and my back screamed. I settled into my pillows and pulled the comforter up around my shoulders and gingerly turned onto my left side.

I couldn't shake the thought that this was going to end badly.

Zach took the steps two at a time but instead of going to the library, he raced out of the house. He had to find out what had happened to the rest of the family so that he could plan a means of escape.

Bees buzzed drunkenly, landing on flowers and then flying off. There was no one around…no one to ask. Zach turned left and headed down the path through the waist high grass. Someone in the cookhouse would know what was going on.

# Indigo

I was crushed. August sat unresponsive on the floor in a corner of the cookhouse. She hadn't said a word since her girls were taken. I couldn't blame her. She had been whipped mercilessly and then they took her children. She had no idea where Drake was. In her mind, she probably felt like she'd lost everything. Tess tended to her wounds as best she could, but she had to start preparing breakfast for the morning crew.

The cookhouse was filled with the smells of frying ham and bacon, and I could see a huge pot of oatmeal or grits boiling over an open flame on the cast iron stove. Tess navigated the cookhouse more like a head chef than a slave.

In many ways, the cookhouse served as more than just as a place to prepare food for the master and the slaves; it also served as a place where many of the women would go to seek solace after they'd endured mental or physical abuse. A woman sat in the far corner of the cookhouse; her knees pulled up to her chest. She rocked while humming. I found the sound to be oddly soothing, almost like a balm to my soul. I tried to sit close to August, but she pulled away. I didn't know which was worse, her pain or her grief.

I tried not to think about what was happening to my nieces. Where were they? Were they safe? Were they in pain? There was simply no way of knowing.

A disheveled woman trudged forlornly into the cookhouse. She approached Tess slowly. "The people in the big house want biscuits with their breakfast."

I recognized the look of someone that had recently arrived here and was still shell-shocked "August, I'm gonna talk to that woman right over there," I said, pointing. "Call if you need me."

The only thing I got from August was a low moan. I stood, smoothing my hands absently over my skirt. "Ida!"

She looked at me.

"Who are you?" she asked.

"I'm sorry. My name is Indigo. My family took a carriage ride and got stuck here…on this plantation."

"Who is your family?"

"That's my sister-in-law right behind me."

Recognition resonated in her eyes. "August…and her girls. I remember her children.

What's going on with her?" Ida looked at August once again.

"She was beaten," I said. "She lost her kids…lost her man…my brother."

"I'm sorry." She stepped into me. "How did you get here?"

"The carriage. I came here with my uncle Shucky and some of his friends."

She looked to her right and then back at me. The bitterness in her expression told me all that I needed to know. A tear slipped from one of her eyes and she backhand wiped it away. She sniffed and stifled a sob. "Looks like everybody lost something."

"Except for the white folks that have us on lockdown," I said bitterly.

"I haven't seen my husband since we got here."

Tess pulled a tray of biscuits from the oven and handed them to Ida. "Take those up to the big house," she said with no emotion.

Instead of turning to head back to the big house, she waited for a moment, her jaw tightening. It gave me a chance to look carefully at her face. She was tired, worn down by fear and loss.

Zach burst through the door, gasping for breath. I couldn't have been happier to see him. I rushed to him and threw my arms around his neck.

He embraced me, which caused some of the women to give disapproving or fearful glances.

"How did you get here?" he asked, trying to catch his breath. "Have you seen the girls?"

"They took the girls!" I told him. "August hasn't been right since. Have you seen Tarek?"

"Yes." He nodded. "He's safe."

I was so happy that I could have kissed him, but I restrained myself.

"He's upstairs in the big house." He continued.

"How about Kisha and Latrice?"

He lowered his voice. "They're in the laundry room."

"Aunt Pearl and Macy?"

"No idea." He slowly relinquished me.

"Indigo," Tess called out. "Maybe you want to go to the laundry room and call your friends to breakfast."

"Tess, this is Zach." I hoped introducing them would ease the tension in the room. "He's a good friend of the family."

"Pleasure." Tess nodded at him before turning her attention to me. "Maybe your friend would like to run to the laundry room and tell 'em that it's time to go to the lunchroom for breakfast."

I looked back at August, then at Zach. "Go," I said softly, knowing Tess was listening. "I'll stay here with August. Shucky and some of his crew are here, too. I just don't know where they are."

"Then it'll take me longer to get us out of this place."

"We at least have to find Shucky and Levi."

"Who is Levi?"

"One of Shucky's men."

He nodded and gave August one last longing look before turning to leave the cabin.

"Zach?" I called.

"Yeah?"

"Be careful."

"I will. And I'll try to find out where they sent the girls." He disappeared through the doorway.

Dishes rattled as the first batch of plates came back from breakfast being served in the big house.

"You know you ought to be careful trusting them crackers," Tess said tersely, her voice hushed.

"He's okay." I sat down beside August and put my arms around her. This time she leaned her head against my shoulder.

One of the women sitting in the corner began singing softly to herself. I recognized it as an old Aretha Franklin tune. I began to stroke August's hair while joining my voice with hers, silently hoping we wouldn't be on this plantation much longer.

# Drake

The scent of burning flesh hung heavily in the air. We stared incredulously at the remains of Aren's body. They had dipped him in boiling oil or water until his skin slid off, then the muscle tissue cooked, followed by his internal organs. All that remained was a skeleton and some residual tissue and cartilage. Aren had been killed for no other reason than having the audacity to speak sternly to his master.

He had been a strong man. He could've done a lot of work for them with the muscle mass that he carried but they thought of him as disposable.

We went to breakfast with heavy hearts. No one said a word and we ate our oatmeal in silence.

Our detail today was to pick snap beans, cauliflower, cabbage and collard greens. The sun rode high in the sky and there was a slight breeze that sailed through the open doorway of the cabin that served as our eating quarters. Rumor had it that more slaves were coming in today. That didn't concern me. What concerned me was getting off this plantation and back to my girls. Silently, as we finished our breakfast, I began to plot my escape.

I couldn't stay at a place that boiled men alive for no reason at all. I could plot my escape while we were out working in the fields digging up the vegetables that we were assigned to pick. I could take a bathroom break and pray they didn't see me as I escaped through a bathroom window and into the woods behind the outhouse. I remember the outhouse they constructed for the workers having three evenly spaced toilets separated by metal partitions. The last toilet sat beneath a small window that faced the woods. That would be my line of escape.

Thoughts of returning to my family overruled any fear that I may have felt in my core. It didn't occur to me to think what they would do to me if I were caught. If they boiled the skin off a slave for talking out of turn, what would they do to a runaway?

I purposely hadn't attempted to make friends since Aren. I was trying to fly under the radar. Not knowing anyone would make it easier for me, and I wouldn't put anyone else at risk. I was determined to get back to August if I had to walk to find her.

All morning, I worked cutting cabbage and throwing them into a cart like an over-sized child's wagon being pulled by an ATV. I couldn't understand why they had us out in the fields doing all this back-breaking work when there were machines that could do the work twice as fast and more efficiently than we ever could.

Maybe it was all about one race thinking they are better than another, believing it is their right to take away the freedom of others for their own personal gain. I assumed they felt as if it was their right to denigrate and reduce men to playing the roles of animals. We were no longer considered human.

I thought about our women. How many Black women had been raped or beaten? I thought about my own wife and daughters...but I couldn't allow my mind to go to the depravity that might befall them.

I found out through the grapevine that I was in Alabama...one state away from my family. There were many back roads I could take to get to them, but there were the dense woods that I would have to go through. I had no idea what might lie in wait for me in there. I couldn't think about that either.

Just two days ago, I was a father with a loving family. I had a home that I was proud of, and a good job. In just twenty-four hours, I had been reduced to being a thing that existed solely for the enrichment of another race of people for no other reason than because I was Black. The thought of this was almost enough to break my spirit; if I didn't have a family, I might've succumbed to those thoughts.

As I cut cabbage, I kept them in mind. I traced the lines of August's face, remembering the color of her deep brown eyes, the softness of her lips, the curve of her jawline, the warmth of her smile...

My heart broke all over again.

How was I going to get from Alabama to Georgia on foot? Well, I thought, how did Harriet Tubman get a multitude of slaves from the heart of the deep south to the north? I would walk if I had to.

The sun was unrelenting, beating down on my back and shoulders as I worked. Sweat rolled down my face, neck and back.

I could see the big house from here. It looked like they were having some type of event. Cars and limousines were lined up in the front and the people getting out were dressed like they were attending an upscale gala.

Women in their finest ensembles headed into the house one by one. I recognized one of the attendees as the transgender woman I had seen in the restaurant. Lady Onyx, I think she called herself. She was wearing a striped outfit with a short pencil skirt and a matching hat.

Another woman walked behind her, wearing a black bodysuit and extremely high heels. She was dark-skinned with short natural hair and reminded me of a much younger version of my Aunt Macy.

I looked down at the cabbage that I was cutting. By the time I looked up again, the women had disappeared into the house. The homeowner emerged wearing a wine-colored evening gown. I had to stop for just a moment at the sight of her because it had never occurred to me that the owner of this plantation was Black. But there she was, standing on the huge wrap-around porch greeting her guests. She didn't act like a slave at all; she had to be the head of the house.

It looked like they were having a dinner party. That meant that the plantation's women would be working overtime to make sure that the food was kept flowing. Would they even notice if I simply took off?

"I hear that you thinking of leaving."

A male voice sounded right next to me. I looked around. There were a few rows of us working the fields but the nearest man of Latin descent was bent over cutting cabbage, and he was not even facing me.

"Take me with you." He said in a hushed tone.

English was not his primary language; his accent was so thick that I could barely understand him. His face remained turned to the ground as he continued working.

"I'm not planning on leaving here," I lied.

"I knew Mr. Aren." He spoke without looking at me. "I cannot stay here but I'm from Ecuador. Not sure where to go."

I didn't say anything to him. I didn't know what to say. How did he know what I was secretly planning?

"I can help you." He tossed two bushels into the wagon that was slowly creeping up the row behind us.

"I told you…I'm not leaving this plantation."

"I seen you when you come in."

"So?"

"You don't want to be here anymore than I do." He never broke the rhythm of cutting cabbage.

I paused, glanced over at him, and then continued to cut. "What's your name?"

"Miguel."

"Okay, Miguel. My name is Drake."

"Where you from, Mr. Drake?"

"Philadelphia. I started off on a carriage ride with my family at Carmichael's restaurant. I wound up here."

"You have family?"

"A wife and two little girls."

"I have a little boy. He's with my wife back home. We have family in Box, New York."

"You mean the Bronx in New York." I cut and bound.

"They have a fleet of ATVs. They use them to…" He paused. "They hunt us."

"What?"

"I seen 'em. It's runaways they hunt. And if they catch you, you wind up like Mr. Aren."

"Shit."

"But there's a time when you can break away from here and they won't know."

"What are you talking about, Miguel?"

"Every six months, they have big party…like what they doin' right now. It must be big 'cause so many people from other plantations come."

"And?"

"That's when we leave."

I kept cutting and binding.

"Are you still leavin'?" Miguel asked. "And can I come?"

"Don't you need to know where I'm going?"

"Are you leaving this place?"

"Yeah." I nodded.

"I'm coming with you." He said matter-of-factly.

I took all this in. Miguel could slow me down or, depending on what he knew about this area, he could help me get back to my girls sooner. I looked him over once more. He was short, with dark skin and a wiry build. I don't know how long he'd been on the plantation, but he obviously knew more about the "goings on" than I did.

"Do you know where they keep the keys to the ATV?" I asked.

"Yes. In the main hallway of the big house. I have a friend on the inside that will grab a set for us when we ready to leave."

"They're not going to turn you in?"

"No." He shook his head and tossed a couple of bushels into the wagon.

A gentle breeze cooled my forehead, and I wiped the sweat away. "You speak good English," I said.

"My mother taught me. She thought I would need it."

"She's right about that."

He nodded.

"So, this party that you're talking about…is that's what's going on in the main house today?"

"Yeah."

"Okay." The wheels in my mind began to turn. One way or another, I was going to see my family again.

August sat on the floor of the cookhouse, watching everyone else move about preparing the afternoon meal. After her tears stopped falling, she managed to hold her head up. She recognized her sister-in-law, but that was about it. She couldn't bring herself to serve the people in the big house. How could she? They were the same people that took away her babies.

Indie was looking for her children though. She knew that she shouldn't place all her hopes in her sister-in-law, but that's all she had. She would wait silently in the cookhouse until she heard some positive news as to where her children had been sent, and then she would go get them. She didn't know how; she just knew that she would.

She listened to what was going on in the cookhouse, hearing everything. She listened as Tess barked out orders to present lunch to people in the big house. The same people that stole her precious babies. She listened as the woman in the corner murmured the lyrics to a gospel hymn that she remembered from her childhood.

"Amazing Grace, how sweet the sound, that saved a wretch like me."

The women in the cookhouse stirred briefly when Zach had appeared with Latrice and Kisha in tow. How he had managed to get them out of the laundry was a miracle. They were ecstatic to see her and Indie. There were hugs and tears that vaguely registered an emotion in her heart, but it couldn't resonate too deeply. All that mattered was her daughters and Drake.

Where did they send him? Was he at a nearby plantation? Were they whipping him the same way that they whipped her?

Zach ducked out of the cookhouse as quickly as he appeared, mentioning something about going back to the main house to check on Tarek. That was good. That meant more of the family was coming together. She heard a faint but distinctive buzzing noise and initially dismissed it; it was a sound that didn't belong with the familiar noises of the cookhouse.

# Indigo

I couldn't believe my ears when I heard the buzz of my work phone. I quickly reached into the inside pocket of my skirt to shut it off. I didn't want anyone else to know that I had any kind of communication device. That buzz meant my assistant was trying to get hold of me—and a signal could be reached in the confines of this place after all.

I watched out of the corner of my eye as Kisha and Latrice settled around August, but she didn't need comforting. She made that perfectly clear.

What she needed was her children.

Ida came in once or twice before settling in a chair next to the woman who continued to sing softly to herself. She sang "Amazing Grace" and "Nearer My God to Thee." When she finished singing, she hummed.

I felt bad for Ida. She appeared isolated and alone, her eyes vacant. I couldn't blame her. She'd lost her husband, too.

My mind turned towards Levi and Shucky as I wandered slowly outside. Where were they? Were they alright? I hadn't seen them since Teddy was shot and I'd been dragged away.

The air outside felt good, but I needed to get to a place where I could have some privacy.

"Indie…where are you going?"

I turned around and swore silently to myself. Latrice had followed me out of the cookhouse.

"Hey, Latrice." I didn't want her to know that I had a phone.

"Where you headed off to?" She asked.

"I needed to get out of there minute. I needed some air."

Latrice nodded in agreement. "Glad that Zach came to get me and Kisha out of that laundry room. They like to break our backs washing sheet set after sheet set simply 'cause they want to have some company over."

"Be glad you don't have to work in the cookhouse."

"It's hot up in that piece!" Kisha appeared, brushing off the front of her skirt. The top of her blouse was damp with sweat, sticking to her body.

"You got that right." Latrice leaned up against the back of the building. She reached into the inner pocket of her skirt and pulled out a dwindling pack of cigarettes, lit one and took a deep drag.

"Where'd you get those cigarettes from?" I asked.

"I never go anywhere without cigarettes." Latrice flipped her braids over her shoulders and took another puff.

"Let me get one." Kisha extended her hand.

Latrice handed her the pack. She shook one loose, lit it and took a deep, satisfying drag.

"I've been wanting one of these forever," Kisha exclaimed, "Why didn't you offer me one earlier?"

"This is the first time that we've been alone outside of our sleeping arrangements. Now be quiet and help yourself."

We sat in silence for a moment while they smoked, listening to the distant sounds of farm equipment and livestock.

"How did we get here?" Latrice asked more to herself than any of us. "And has anyone seen the girls?"

"Where is Drake, for that matter?" I added.

"I heard that they ship the men off immediately." Kisha exhaled a plume of smoke.

"Ship them to where?" Latrice asked.

"Other plantations, I guess." Kisha looked across the rows of bush snap beans and cabbage.

"You think there are more places like this?" Latrice was flabbergasted.

"All across the south. They're calling it the 'New South.' Rumor has it that they have plantations just like this in Florida, South Carolina, Mississippi, Alabama, Louisiana, and parts of Texas."

"That's crazy."

"What are you bitches doing out here?" The voice was deep, white, and male.

We turned to run but the only place that we could make it to would be the cookhouse. The fear in Latrice's eyes told spoke volumes.

But where fear took root in Latrice's, anger took form in me. I recognized Cal Carmichael, John Carmichael's son. He stood tall and lanky, the ever-present threatening whip hanging on his hip like a vicious snake ready to strike.

"Sorry sir," Latrice said meekly.

I was surprised at her tone. She had acquiesced so easily. In fact, everyone seemed to adjust easily to being relegated to second class citizenship. But I understood it. That whip was enough to elicit fear and respect even if it wasn't earned. Kisha looked at him disapprovingly.

"What the fuck's wrong with you?" He snapped at her.

She didn't say a word.

"Bitch! I'm talking to you!" he barked, reaching for his whip.

I shook my head while mouthing the words, "No, Kisha…don't."

"No…sir." She glared at him, and I could tell by the way she said 'sir' that she was forcing herself to be obedient.

"No sir, what?" he said, stepping close to her. She took a step back and he closed the distance between them, his fingertips dancing lightly on the handle of the whip. "You know, you need to learn how to mind your master." He relinquished the whip and placed his hand on her shoulder. She pulled away.

Latrice, sensing that something bad was going to happen, quickly stepped between them. Cal slapped her hard across the face with the back of his hand. Anger leapt into Kisha's dark brown eyes.

"You got something you want to say, bitch?" Cal snapped.

"You know, you wouldn't be doing this if…"

"If what?" He cut her off, grabbing her by one arm and marching her towards one of the cabins. Latrice burst into tears as Kisha struggled against from him. He punched her in the face with a closed fist. She shook her head as if she saw stars, and blood began to trickle from her upper lip.

What happened next couldn't have been foreseen. Kisha hauled off and punched Cal dead in the face, his head snapping backward on his neck. He was stunned for a moment before he seized her with both hands, lifting her completely off the ground. She managed to wriggle free and clawed at him, sinking her nails deep into his left cheek.

"Please don't!" Latrice yelled as Cal pulled a screaming Kisha towards a cabin that stood on the edge of the field of collard greens.

"No!" I grabbed Latrice. "Let them go!"

Kisha's screams echoed across the field, reverberating against the cookhouse until it was silenced by the slamming of the cabin door. I put my arms around Latrice as she sobbed uncontrollably. I fought back my own tears. I couldn't be weak. Now was not the time. I had to hold it together because I knew what was coming next.

I waited impatiently in the cookhouse, absently helping to make the stew for lunch. Latrice didn't say anything as she baked the rolls that would be served with the stew. We were both concerned about Kisha. It had been over a half hour since Cal Carmichael had taken her to one of the cabins on the outskirts of the rows of collard greens.

The window was closing on when I could call my assistant since she generally left the office at four, but I couldn't run the risk that someone would see me using my cell phone.

August sat at a table shelling peas. All was quiet in the room except for the rattling of pots, pans, and dishes. Everyone was waiting for Kisha. Everyone knew what was happening. By now, everyone knew that when the Cal Carmichael came calling, you went. There was no choice.

I looked around at the other women and realized that we all wore the same mask of despair and concern. Whether we knew each other or not, when the head of the household assaulted one of us, he assaulted all of us.

One of the girls said she had seen a man that fit Wilson Monroe's description picking apples on another part of the compound. There was another rumor floating around that something was brewing with the men assigned to pick sweet potatoes, pumpkins and peanuts.

This was the biggest fear of any slaveowner. They didn't want the men to congregate for any reason other than at breakfast, lunch, and dinner in the makeshift cafeteria.

Shucky had to be involved with this. I knew my uncle. He was a schemer. There was no way that he would settle for being a slave. It didn't matter how many times they beat him—if they had the opportunity to beat him at all. I had to assume that Shucky and his crew were still on the plantation and not shipped off somewhere else like cattle. Cal Carmichael wasn't stupid enough to keep them all together. He had to have shipped off some of them.

Word spread that the lords of the house were going to an event at another location, possibly another plantation. We only knew this because they cancelled the dinner menu; we only had to cook for the field staff and the help.

Ida came barging into the cookhouse with the unmistakable look of anger on her face. We stopped what we were doing waiting for her to speak.

"Why didn't ya'll tell me you saw my husband?" She scanned the room, her eyes pausing on every woman in the cookhouse. She stopped when she came to Tess. "Where is he?"

"Rumor has it that he's picking pumpkins on the other side of the plantation."

Ida turned to walk out of the cookhouse.

"You can't go there!" Tess shouted. "You better off going right before they call all the field hands for supper."

"I'm going to him right now and then we're leaving this godforsaken place." she hissed while walking back out the way she came in.

"Ida, wait!" I called. I couldn't let another one of us become a victim of their cruelty. I followed her outside. "Please don't go."

"I have to find my husband, Indigo." She turned to me with tears in her eyes.

"I know, but there's a place and time for everything," I said as quickly as I could. "If they find you in a place where you shouldn't be, they'll whip you for sure! You know that!"

Ida paused. I could tell that she was listening to me.

"You won't be doing Wilson any good if you're maimed trying to get to him! And there's a good chance of that happening if you're found in a place that you shouldn't be. Wait until a little later. Please." I could tell she was thinking. "They already got August. She's gonna have keloids on her back for the rest of her life. I don't want that for you!"

Ida looked down and fresh tears began to flow hitting the dirt in droplets.

"I have to get to him." She began to sob. "He needs me." Her shoulders began to shudder and then her sobs became wails.

I threw my arms around her shoulders, and she sobbed uncontrollably as if she were releasing all her frustrations in one tearful exchange. I held her, stroking her back, hoping that I was able to relieve some of her pain.

But I knew better.

Nothing short of handing her husband to her on a silver platter would console her. So, we stood in the cookhouse yard, both of us now in tears.

# Tarek

I lay on my stomach as one of the girls dressed my back. Whatever salve she used really helped with the pain. She told me that the likelihood of me having keloids from the whipping would be slim to none because they had treated me right after it had been done.

Zach entered the room, which was decorated like a bedroom in a country B and B while I waited for her to finish. She told me to remain on my stomach while the salve worked its way into the lacerations on my back. When she left, he settled onto the bed by my side.

"Are you in pain?" he asked softly.

I nodded, mumbling into my pillow, "It'll pass."

He leaned into me. "We're getting off this plantation tonight."

"We are? You figured out a way to do it?"

"Yes. I found your sister, Kisha, Latrice, and August."

"My nieces?"

"Not yet." He shook his head slowly. "But I'm still looking."

"We can't leave without them."

"I know," he whispered. "I'm working on it."

"How do the people of the house feel about you working to free some of their slaves?"

"They can't say anything if they don't know that we're leaving."

"Okay." I reached for his hand.

He held it for a moment before releasing it.

"I'll take care of it." He said quickly and in hushed tones.

"Can you find Drake?"

"I think I know where he is. But let me manage it."

"Have you seen Aunt Pearl or Aunt Macy?"

He shook his head. "No."

My heart sank. My aunts weren't young. They couldn't survive in this environment.

"Is this your buck, D'Angelis?" a female voice asked sternly from behind us.

Zach turned his head. Ms. Lulu was standing in the doorway in a full-length, light blue gown. How long had she been there? How much had she heard?

"Yes." He nodded his head. "And so are the two I pulled from the laundry."

"Weren't you sitting with them folks just a day or two ago in the restaurant?"

"No," Zach lied.

"I see." She came in and looked at Zach for what felt like a full minute, and then she extended her right hand, her fingers curled into a semi fist. Her smile was ice-cold as she pointed her extended arm at Zach's face, and slowly began to raise her arm.

Zach grasped his throat as he began to slowly lift off the bed. I turned my head as far as I could without rolling onto my back. Zach rose higher and higher, gasping for breath, first six inches, then twelve, then two feet.

"Now...who are you?" Lulu sneered.

She twisted her empty fist. Zach tried to scream but began choking instead.

I turned onto my side. "Stop," I croaked. "Please...don't hurt him."

"Who are you?" She ignored my pleas and twisted her hand once again. "You best answer me, boy! I can really hurt you if you don't!"

"Let me..." Zach began before he started coughing again. "I can't..."

"Tell me!"

"I'm his...owner."

"You lie!"

"Wha...what are you?" Zach managed to ask before he started choking again.

"I can snap your neck like a twig." Lulu opened her extended palm and Zach fell to the floor. "I have a gathering to get to. If you're still here when I get back, we're going to continue our little chat."

She turned her back, not acknowledging me in the least bit. Her attention—and her power—had been laser-focused on Zach. I remembered Aunt Macy's talk of witchcraft.

Zach lay on the floor like a broken doll, still gasping for air. He took a few deep breaths and then looked up at me. "We leave tonight."

# The Escape

# PLANTATION

# Drake

Clouds rolled in that afternoon and with the clouds came rain. We couldn't work, so they chained us indoors. That gave me time to think. Now that I knew Miguel wanted to come with me, I was in a quandary as to when we should make our move.

From what I understood, he was only interested in getting off this plantation. They received a load of new slaves earlier that afternoon. A few men were led into our quarters, chained to their cots, and left until morning. No one said a word, but I believed that we were all thinking the same thing…how to escape.

I thought of those ATVs and how Miguel and I could get to them and get away before they knew we were gone. That was key...splitting before the powers that be knew some of their property had gone missing.

We would have to take the back roads to Georgia, and duck anything that looked remotely like law enforcement. I hoped the ride wouldn't be long. If we weren't chained, I would've been tempted to leave tonight, but we would have to take our chance in the morning as soon as they came to get us for breakfast. They were weakest when we were going into the fields after breakfast, and again when we came out of the fields to dinner. Miguel told me this and ordinarily, I would've dismissed the idea but then I saw it for myself I believed him.

The other issue that sat in my mind, like the creaking door that slowly swung open to have you face whatever horror that lay within, was what would we do if we got caught?

Aren had been boiled to death. The odor of his burnt flesh still haunted my sinuses. If Miguel and I were caught, it would be like a Fourth of July celebration for the people that owned this place. They would make examples out of us. Our deaths would be gruesome.

I couldn't allow my mind to go down that rabbit hole. If it continued down that path, it might never come back.

But would I sacrifice Miguel to get back to my family? I hoped I would never have to face that question. The mission was simple…get to Georgia without being killed.

I lay on my cot and listened to what could only be described as "quiet commotion" going on around me. The newer slaves were talking amongst themselves. This group of guys wasn't "having" being slaves and planned to do something about it. They talked about some women and children that they planned on taking with them when they left.

But there was an even bigger reason for leaving though this hasn't been confirmed. There were rumors of an uprising. I didn't know what that meant but I wasn't going to hang around to find out.

A drop of water hit me squarely on the forehead. I opened my eyes and stared directly into the darkness of the ceiling, trying to drown out the chatter. I couldn't see anything.

The loneliness was unbearable. I had never wanted to hold my wife in my arms more than I did at that moment. Not knowing what was going on with my girls was more than my soul could take. Still, I had to give this new crop of field hands credit. They were looking out for the women and children that had come with them instead of taking off leaving them to fend for themselves. That was admirable.

The lights in our quarters suddenly flicked into life. Instantly, all the chatter ceased. Four big, burly men stormed in. They marched down the center row of the cabin, whips and guns in hand. We had no idea what they were planning to do.

"Niggers! Heads up! No fuckin' noise while the tour is going on!" one of them barked. "If you say a word, you will be whipped!"

The voice was familiar. I tilted my head up, but I couldn't see who was talking. The room was so quiet that you could have heard a pin drop.

"Good," he said. "Tell them they can begin the tour."

My first thought was that they were going to whip someone for sport. If they did, I hoped that they would skip over me. I wanted to be in good shape when it came time to leave. I was going to be on my best behavior.

"Nice. Very nice," a woman's voice said softly.

The tour had started. One by one, women adorned in their finest gowns and men in black tuxedos streamed into our quarters, looking us over as if we were meat in a butcher's counter as opposed to the men we were.

"I like this one." A woman wearing a fluorescent pink backless gown exclaimed. "Are we sacrificing any of them tonight?"

"Yes," one of the heavy-set men answered, and my testicles withdrew into my body.

They continued making their rounds. They were going to sacrifice one of us. Most likely it would be by boiling us to death.

"And here are my main field hands." The woman sounded like she was just beyond my line of sight.

I laid my head back as much as I could, considering the flatness of my pillow, but raised it again as the voices came to the foot of my bed. I lay perfectly still hoping they wouldn't pick me for anything. I wanted to remain unnoticed. Pass me by and don't look in my direction, I prayed.

Another drop of water hit me on the forehead. With the lights on, I could see there was a watermark spreading on the ceiling above my bed. And at that moment, the idea hit me. I just hoped that it would work.

"Excuse me." I addressed the people standing at the foot of my bed.

They turned to look at me. I noticed a Black woman in a maroon gown. Her eyes were huge, almost as if I had startled her. Then I realized she wasn't frightened; she was enraged. I was taking a gamble by doing what I was about to do.

"Boy, I could whip you where you lay!" she hissed through clenched teeth.

"All due respect, ma'am," I said in a gentle tone, "but I can see that you have a hole in your roof. I can fix it for you."

"What do you mean?" She had sharp, angular features with medium brown skin. Her beehive hairdo was so tall that it was clear the dark hair atop her head wasn't hers.

I looked upwards in time for another drop of water to land squarely on my cheek. Her eyes followed mine resting on the stain on the ceiling. One of the burly men started to uncoil his leather whip.

"In my past life, I worked with my hands…ma'am." I spoke slowly and carefully, so she wouldn't think I was being arrogant. "I could patch that hole up in no time if I had the assistance of one of the other field hands."

"Who did you have in mind, buck?"

I couldn't believe she was Black. A Black woman enslaving other Black people. That made no sense. But then again, nothing about this altered universe we were living in made sense.

"I was thinking Miguel could help me. He used to be a carpenter before...well before all of this."

"Are trying to sass me, nigger?"

I had to play it cool.

"No, ma'am." I shook my head. "I thought maybe this would be a way to make you happy."

That should do it. If she thought that I was about keeping myself in her good graces, maybe she wouldn't grill me. She thought for a moment as a slow murmur started among her other guests.

"I say let him do it." A woman's voice spoke up from the back of the crowd. The voice sounded familiar. "Let him do it in the morning before breakfast," she said. "He can't do anything now. It's pouring raining outside."

The woman in the maroon gown paused then turned towards the burly men who had accompanied her into our quarters.

"Get them up an hour early to patch the roof." She lifted her hand as if for emphasis. "Check the other cabins and see if their roofs need fixing, too. Might as well make these niggers work for their keep. In the meantime, let's continue with the tour. I have a wine shed that I want to show you. Come. Come." She clapped her hands, and the crowd began to move towards the doorway at the end of the passage that separated rows of beds.

I lay quietly and at peace...probably more at peace than any time since I've been here. As they turned off the lights, I smiled to myself. I would be on my way to see my girls soon.

Two of the men came into our sleeping quarters and roused me and Miguel out of our cots. Miguel had no idea why they were waking us up so early. I hadn't had a chance to tell him. It was still dark, but the sky had started to turn that beautiful robin's egg blue before the sun rose.

They herded us to a cabin I had not been in before. I looked around quickly to see if this was where they kept the keys to the ATVs.

Miguel rubbed his eyes, suppressing a yawn. I watched the other men carefully. Instead of using flashlights to guide us, they used kerosene lamps, and they were dressed like they had stepped out of the 1800s.

What scared me was that most of the people around us seemed to genuinely believe that we were living in that period. What didn't make sense to me was the odd combination of old and the new. Like our cabin. The walls of our cabin were cement gray and the room we slept in was cylindrical in shape. It felt more like a summer camp setting rather than slave quarters from a previous century. We slept on cots, while I'd heard that slaves normally slept on pallets created from hay and or corn husks. There was none of that in our quarters.

When we worked in the fields, they used ATVs to gather the produce that we picked. Horse drawn carriages weren't used unless it was for effect. My best guess was that they wanted to live in the 1800s, but only when it was convenient for them.

Things were slowly coming into focus. I was starting to understand what was going on. As they marched us into the shed where they held all the equipment we needed to do the work around the plantation, Miguel followed my lead and didn't say a word as we selected the materials that we would need to patch the roof. The men watched carefully as we carried the materials back to our slave quarters.

"And when you mules are done with that, there's more cabins that need patching." one of the men barked.

We marched through the knee-high grass like we were marching off to war. Birds had started to chirp, and I could smell food in the air. A thin wisp of smoke rose from the cookhouse chimney. A fine mist was falling, remnants of the downpour we had the night before. Maybe we wouldn't be able to work out in the fields which meant we wouldn't be able to leave.

The smell of earth intermingled with the scent of marshlands assaulted my nose. Because the morning was so quiet, I was aware of all the sounds around me. Over the birds, I could hear wailing. At first, I wasn't sure what I was hearing but the sound carried over the sounds of the woods coming to life. The voices were young, but I couldn't make out whether they were male or female.

Miguel looked over at me in confusion as the cries grew louder. The cries were coming from children outside a fenced yard just to the right of the big house. Two Black women with head wraps and floor-length skirts were leading the children into the yard. All of them were crying and most of them appeared to be Black. They looked terrified and my heart went out to them instantly.

"Stop that cryin'!" One of the women shouted. "I'll whip you good if you don't stop!"

I counted heads. It looked like there were nine children. For me, that was nine too many. I was a father first, and I could see my daughters' faces on each of those kids trapped in the makeshift pen.

"I said shut the fuck up or so help me I will whip your little asses good!" The woman's shouts made the children cry even more.

"They're scared!" I shouted before I realized what I was doing. A blow across my back brought me to my knees.

"What's going on over there ain't none of your concern!" one of the men hollered at me.

"Daddy?" one of the children yelled. "Daddy! Come get us! Please come get us!"

"Baby girl?" I struggled to my feet. It was my girls. My precious babies! Now where was August? And how did my daughters get here? Were they okay and had anyone harmed them?

"Daddy!" Madison screamed.

"Daddy!" Autumn ran to the fence. "Daddy, come get us!"

"Where's Mommy?" Madison was hysterical.

"I'm coming!"

Another hard blow to my shoulders caused me to stumble. I caught myself and kept running towards my babies. I was so happy to see my girls that I didn't see or notice Miguel running alongside me. I felt another blow across my back.

"Daaaddeeeee!" my girls screamed.

"Miguel, stay back!" I yelled, pushing forward. Nothing was going to stop me from getting to Autumn and Maddie.

I felt another blow; the strap tore through the fabric of my shirt and into my back. I couldn't falter. I had survived being locked in a box, transported to another state, watching someone being boiled to death, watching a friend get whipped for doing no more than asking a question. I had survived all of that and my babies were finally in front of me. Nothing could stop me.

I reached the fence considerably ahead of the overseers and fell to my knees, grasping my daughters' fingers through the makeshift fence. I had never seen Maddie this hysterical.

"I'm here now baby," I said through the fence. Could I get in the yard before the overseers caught up to me?

"Daddy, where's Mommy?" Maddie cried. "Where are we? I want to go home."

"I know, baby, I know." I tried to console her, but it was difficult, knowing that I was going to be torn away from them and whipped at any moment.

Strong arms wrapped themselves around me and a male torso pressed itself against my back.

"These are your kids, Mr. Drake?" Miguel asked, a few inches from my right ear.

I nodded. "Yes." My vision blurred with tears as I clung my girls' fingers through the chain link fence.

Maddie and Autumn held tightly to me on the opposite side, still crying. A woman came up from behind Maddie and tried to lift her up and she started screaming.

"I have you, Mr. Drake," Miguel said.

The whip whistled through the air and struck flesh. Miguel moaned but held me tightly, using his body as a shield between the whip and me.

"Let her go!" I yelled. "She's my daughter! These are my girls!"

"Let him go, wetback!" one of the overseers shouted. The whip struck and Miguel moaned again, loudly this time.

"Please!" I begged. "Please let my girls go."

Maddie began to kick at the woman, screaming even louder.

"Let the boy see his cubs," one of the overseers said in a barely audible voice.

Miguel's body was trembling. He had defended me, taking the lash of the whip for me and my girls. If I had thought I would have to make a choice between saving myself or Miguel, I now had to include him. Leaving him behind was not an option. He had taken a beating for me. He had proved to me that he was my ride-or-die.

He straightened up and extended his hand to me. It was at this gesture that Autumn's tears ceased. She slowly released her grip on the fence as the woman lowered Maddie to the ground, then whirled on her.

"How can we get to our daddy?' she demanded, sounding like August. "I want to see my daddy!"

The woman smacked her.

"Don't you sass me, little girl!" she hissed. "I'm doing you a favor! Don't you forget that!"

"Don't you put your hands on my child!" I yelled.

Rough hands hauled me to my feet and then shoved me towards the right side of the cabin. My girls ran alongside as they pushed me towards the entry into the pen. That short walk seemed to take forever. One of the overseers pushed me and I almost fell but it didn't matter. My babies were here with me, and I was going to fight like hell to keep them by my side until we found August.

The woman opened the gate to the yard at my approach and my daughters raced into my arms. There were tears…lots of them, and not just from the girls. They were with me, and they were safe. No one was going to hurt them…ever.

If I had to take a beating every day until we found our freedom, I would do it. No one was going to hurt my girls. If they did, I would have one more thing to do …and that was to kill whoever dared to put their hands on my children.

# Indigo

Early the next morning, Kisha limped into the doorway of the cookhouse. She entered without saying a word. Latrice raced to her side first and started crying, wrapping her arms around her girlfriend. But the damage had been done.

Kisha was battered and bruised. Cal must have beaten her mercilessly. Her clothes were torn; her blouse ripped right down the front. I didn't know how bad it was, but I knew it was beyond the time for us to leave this place no matter the cost. I listened to Latrice whispering to Kisha. We all did. It was so quiet in the cookhouse that you could've heard the slightest whisper.

We all held our breath collectively until Kisha came back. We had expected her to be returned to us the day before. That would have made it better. But Cal Carmichael kept her out all night long. We don't know where they slept, but I knew for certain that he couldn't have slept with her. She would have killed him in his sleep if she'd had the chance. Kisha was strong, but at the end of the day she was still a woman. No matter how hard she fought, she was no match for Carmichael's strength.

"Clean her up," Tess said without turning away from the pot of grits that she had been stirring. "Take her down to the stream, then to the cabin so she can rest. I'll get some sheets and towels for her."

"No! No! Don't leave me!" Kisha threw her arm around Latrice and held on.

"I won't leave you," Latrice whispered to her. "I promise."

"Do not let the massa know you are hurting because of something he did to you." the woman in the corner said to no one in particular.

Tess walked over to a small refrigerator that sat in the corner by the humming woman. "You talk crazy talk, Lean," she muttered while retrieving half a stick of butter from the refrigerator, returning to the stove, and absently pushing it into the grits.

"You say that now, Tess, but I knows what I'm saying," the woman said. "You can't let him know, lest he do it again. They like that you know.  They find your weakness and then they keep hitting you on your wounded spot. For us womens, it's going to be silence even as they lay claim to your body."

"Look," Tess whirled on her, "you stays quiet most days unless you decide to sing! Why don't you stick to that and keep your mouth shut?"

I mouthed the word, "damn."

The woman got up slowly from her spot on the floor, smoothing her skirt and giving a Tess a stern look. "I don't say nuthin' to you when you boss these womens like they work for you!"

Tess ceased stirring the grits and the other women stopped working to watch.

"Lean…"

"Don't you "Lean" me. I never say nuthin' when you tell these womens, 'go here, go there.' Most times I just shut up and keep on singin' cause that's all I got. This chile here was just raped and used like the toilet paper they use in the bathroom. How you gonna justify that? Just have her cleaned up in the lake like nuthin' just happened to her?"

"What do you expect me to do?" Tess snapped hotly. "Every day I got to cook breakfast lunch and dinner for this whole compound! No one's gonna step up and run this kitchen but me! That's my job! That and to somehow hold you wenches together!"

"Then comfort this chile!" She took a step towards Kisha, who had turned her face into Latrice's chest so that no one could see she was sobbing uncontrollably. "You can't just say 'business as usual', send this chile down to the riverside to be washed clean and hope that everything will be okay."

"I know this is going to sound silly, but is there a doctor on this plantation?" I asked.

"No." Tess responded without looking at me. "Closest we got is a midwife in the last cabin to the right of the big house. She just delivered a baby so she should still be there. Her name's Doreen."

"I can go get her." I started towards the entryway.

"Take her to Doreen," Tess said with no emotion. "If the massa comes around here, I'll tell him where she is and that he shouldn't bother her. Chile needs rest after what she's been through."

"Then you shoulda' said that." Lean walked towards me. "I'll come with you."

I looked hard at the woman they called Lean. Something about her was familiar to me. Very familiar. I was almost certain…her hair was grayer and longer. But she looked at my face and didn't recognize me.

Latrice stood slowly; her arms still wrapped protectively around Kisha. I took hold of them both and together, we made our way to the cookhouse door. I didn't know how I knew this woman, but I was determined to find out.

"Tess, can you watch over August, please? I'm just going down to the midwife with Kisha. I'll be back."

"Go." It was said in the same tone that she would use to correct a child. "I'll watch her."

I walked with the others out into the cloudy day. I didn't feel like I was any closer to leaving than when I got here. Deep in my pocket I still had my work cell phone which I planned on using on my way back from the midwife. I held tight to my cousin and her broken girlfriend, praying that she would heal and become her old self soon.

But I knew better. I had tried rape cases before, and it was always the same. The victims always changed; their personalities permanently altered because of the attack.

The plantation seemed unusually quiet. I assumed this was due to the weather. The rain created a fine mist that hovered over the ground like a low hanging cloud. Thunder rolled in the distance as we walked through wet, knee-high brush. The hems of our dresses were black with damp before we reached the midwife's cabin. Latrice murmured to Kisha; I could barely hear what they said. I felt bad for them both.

I looked over at Lean and it occurred to me who she was…or at least who I thought she was.

But that would have to wait; we had arrived at the cabin. The door was wide open as we entered, and I understood why. The humidity was stifling. You would think that the mist and all the rain the night before would have made the air more breathable. Instead, the humidity was cloistering and the visibility over the fields of the plantation were temporarily obscured.

A heavy-set woman rushed towards us. She had a round, somber face…the kind that I associated with a midwife. She instinctively held out her arms to Kisha, flicking her fingers so that they extended and curled towards her.

"Here, chile. Come."

Latrice released her friend reluctantly and Kisha moved unsteadily towards the midwife.

"Can Latrice go with her?" I asked tentatively.

"Yes." She nodded. "I need to get this girl into bed and evaluate her for her injuries."

"What's your name?"

"Doreen." she said in a raspy voice.

"Thank you," I said, stepping towards her. "My friend was raped and beaten."

"I know. That's what massa does. It don't pay to be a pretty girl on this plantation."

I turned away from her slowly watching as Lean went outside. I followed.

"So, you think you know me?" she asked without giving me a glance.

"How did you know?"

"It was the way you looked at me." She pushed her disheveled hair away from her face, looking at me directly. "So, who do you think I am?"

"You remind me of my Aunt Merline. Is that who you are?"

She nodded her head.

"How long have you been here?" I couldn't believe it was her! I hadn't seen Aunt Merline in years, at least two family reunions ago...the equivalent of twenty years.

"About three and a half years." She looked across the field. "Who are you?"

"I'm your niece. I'm Otis Robeson's grand."

"Indigo," she said slowly. "You have two brothers, right? Drake and Tracey?"

"Tarek," I said, and then on impulse, I embraced her, and she hugged me back.

"How did you get here?" Merline asked, relinquishing me. "I mean, here of all places. Are your brothers here?"

"Yes. Tarek is upstairs somewhere in the big house with Zach, and I have no idea where Drake is. Rumor has it that he was sent to another plantation."

"Probably the one in either Alabama or Florida." She paused. "Who's Zach?"

"My brother's boyfriend."

"I see."

I regretted revealing what Tarek's sexual orientation was and I tried to change the subject.

"How did you wind up here?" I was curious. It seemed like most of the women lived willingly on the plantation; it was almost like they liked wearing slave-garb and waiting on the occupants of the "big house" hand and foot. Women like Tess seemed to revel in the fact that they could make "massa" happy.

Merline paused, looked across the rows of vegetation and spoke in a slow, measured tone. "I could tell you lies but I'm not going to do that." She took another deep breath. "You remember what it was like for me when I lived with your Uncle Shuckland?"

"Shucky," I corrected absently.

"Shucky," she said with no emotion, and then said nothing else for a few minutes. "You got a cigarette?" she asked, breaking her silence.

"I don't smoke."

She didn't say a word, staring across the field at a grove of what I believed were fig trees. "I've been out here for a minute now," she said. "I have no regrets."

"Aunt Merline, nothing is worth your freedom."

"You don't remember what it was like for me, living with Shuckland." The bitterness was slowly starting to show. "It was the beatings that I couldn't take anymore, chile." She shook her head as if that could dispel the memory. "He was an awful man, Indigo."

I inhaled the scent of grass and wet earth.

"He wouldn't stop cheating and lying. When you kids weren't around, he drank liquor like water. And when he drank, he became violent and then wouldn't remember what he did the next day." A lone tear trailed down her cheek.

"I guess it's safe to say that you don't miss him at all." I kept thinking about the 'Shucky' that came with me on this journey.

"Hell, no, I don't miss that bastard!" she said hotly. "Let some other woman deal with him. I know I won't."

"But Aunt Merline, you're a prisoner here. You can't leave. Don't you miss your freedom?"

"Chile, I am free. I don't have a mortgage or rent. I get fed. I'm taken care of when I'm sick. And all I got to do is cook."

"That doesn't seem to be like a fair trade."

"It is to me." She turned back towards the midwife's cabin.

"So, you *want* to stay here?" I asked.

"Yes, I want to stay here. What choice do I have?"

"We all have choices, Aunt Merline. It's what we do with those choices and right now, you're throwing away something that so many Black people died for. We died for freedom. We're supposed to move forward, not backwards."

Merline took another deep breath, but before she could speak, I blurted out, "Shucky's on this plantation."

She looked at me as if I had slapped her. "Where is he?"

"Somewhere. I don't know."

"Well, he can burn in hell if I never see him again!"

"What about your family? We've missed you. We thought you abandoned us."

"My soul was long gone, girl, even when my body was present." There was deep sadness in her voice. "I'll be fine right where I am. And if you see Shuckland, you can let him know that."

Without another word, she started back towards the midwife's cabin.

I thought of the questions I hadn't asked: how did she get here? Was she hoodwinked into a fake carriage ride, too, or were there other ways?

Instead of following Merline, I made my way behind the cabins. I wanted to make sure that I had enough privacy to make a call.

A blackbird crowed, flying over the cabin and into the trees beside it. My heart slammed in my chest as I clutched the phone and held it firmly between my breasts. I listened for the sounds of anyone approaching, prepared to shove the phone into the inner pocket of my skirt to prevent myself from being discovered.

I looked around. The day was still dreary…misty…and the humidity was building. I didn't know if rain was coming or going.

I dialed my office number, waiting anxiously as the phone went through a series of clicks before I received the automated message that the number I was attempting to contact could not be reached at this time. I swore silently and tried to remember where I was when my call went through. I simply wasn't sure.

A strong hand clamped itself securely over my mouth while my captor's equally strong arm wrapped itself around me. I tried to scream but it was stifled. Visions of being whipped filled my head. I started to struggle.

"Shh!" a man's voice whispered in my ear. "Indigo…Indigo, is it?"

I wrenched myself out of his grip prepared to bolt off into the woods; then realized that the man who had grabbed me was Levi. I suppressed the urge to run to him, but I still didn't trust him.

He held his index fingers to his puckered lips.

"How did you find me?" I whispered.

"I saw you from across the way." He pointed to a spot in the field that I couldn't make out. His eyes must be like an eagle to see me from that distance. "Shucky and them is coming. I'm glad I found you. Did you find any of your people?"

I nodded. "August is in the cookhouse." I stepped closer. "Levi, they took her kids. We don't know where they are."

He shook his head.

"She hasn't been right since. And Drake being missing makes it worse."

"Drake is your brother, right?"

I nodded my head. "We found two of the other girls that were in the carriage with us. Kisha and Latrice. They're in the midwife's cabin because…" I paused. "The owner raped Kisha. She and Latrice are devastated."

"Shit," he murmured. "I want you to get to the last cabin on the left. It's empty. You need to stay there until I come get you."

"Levi, what's happening?"

"There's something not right going on here," he said softly. "And I don't want you to get caught up in it."

I nodded my head as I absently reached out to touch him. The hardness of his body was comforting. He must have misinterpreted for my touch because instantly I felt him pulling me into him. His hug was more comfortable than I thought it would be. I stayed in his embrace for a minute or two before backing away from him. He was looking at me intently.

"What do you mean about something not right going on here?" I asked, averting my eyes from his.

"You wouldn't believe me if I told you." His face appeared somber.

I knew something was wrong but was almost afraid to find out what. "Try me."

Levi didn't say anything at first. He just stood there, looking at me. I couldn't read him at all; his expression didn't betray his thoughts.

"Indigo, I saw some things around here that don't make sense." He paused. "They kill people by dippin' them in boiling oil. I personally saw them do it. I don't know why they kill folk like that, but they do.

"I saw men being beaten, women being raped, kids being abused. All in the name of whiteness."

We stood in silence, listening to the birds in the trees that surrounded us.

I found myself nodding in agreement. "Whiteness huh?"

"Yeah."

And then suddenly, he pulled me into his body and held me tight.

"Shh," he whispered in my ear. "Don't say nothin'."

I closed my eyes and waited for whatever the danger was to pass. I listened to the noises around me…and then I heard an ATV pulling an empty wagon along one of the rows of vegetation. The wagon rattled and bounced behind the vehicle as it rolled past us, the white driver seemingly oblivious to our presence.

When I let go of Levi and pulled away from him, he looked at me strangely. "You need to go to the last cabin on the left. I'm gonna round everyone up and then we're gonna bounce up outta here."

"Okay." I looked after the sound of the ATV as it faded into the background but didn't move.

"I don't know if it's all of 'em…" Levi began. "But some of 'em have some type of power that I can't even describe."

"Try," I said dryly.

"They can do things that normal human beings can't do. Yesterday they had a party…a formal of some kind and they sacrificed someone. I think it was to keep their powers. And then Shucky said he seen something that couldn't be right."

"What was it?"

"He said he seen your Aunt Macy…I think that's the aunt he said."

"Well, that's a good thing." My heart leapt. They had found our aunts.

"He said what he saw couldn't have been her because she was young, like he remembered her from the backyard barbecues he used to throw when you all were much younger."

"So, are you saying that he saw my aunt, but it really wasn't her? It was a younger version of her?"

"Sounds crazy, right?"

"That's more than crazy. That's insane."

"I wasn't the one that saw her," he said. "You talk to your uncle about what he thinks he saw. But for now, you need to gets to that empty cabin and wait on us to come and scoop you up."

I couldn't take in what he said. "So, are you telling me we're in a den of witches that enslaved us?" I asked disbelievingly.

"Maybe. But girl, you gotta go! And stay put while I corral the others."

I headed towards the last cabin without looking back, retrieving my work phone from my pocket. Other than Levi, no one was around. When I got to the cabin, I raced to the side facing the dense woods and rapidly dialed my office but received the same message. I swore and rushed to the front of the cabin, ducking inside to wait.

Levi believed we were in a den of witches. I didn't believe in that. It wasn't possible. But I did believe that we were in the midst of people who wanted to return to a time when slavery was legal. They wanted us to dress the way they did back then; they had us cook their food in a cookhouse as opposed to a kitchen; they had men out in the fields when they could easily have machines pick their produce. And then there were the beatings and the rapes. I could only imagine what Cal Carmichael did to Kisha. And it must have been even worse for her, being an avowed lesbian. Kisha. My heart ached for her.

I tried my office again and received the same message as before…my call could not be completed as dialed, please hang up and try your call again later.

Disappointment washed over me. I tried to calm myself, inhaling the mixture of trees, earth, and marsh. It was extremely cool inside the cabin. I ran my hands over my arms as I crossed the empty room. It looked recently built; there was no furniture. I took in the scent of fresh cut pine boards and made my way to a corner of the cabin.

I couldn't believe how bad I felt. My sister-in-law was incapacitated, we had no idea where my nieces were, we couldn't find my brother, Kisha had been brutally raped, and now Levi thought we were in a den of witches.

It was all too much for my mind to process. What did he mean by "witches?" What had he seen that made him think they had any type of supernatural powers? And assuming they did have some type of power…how much harder would that make it for us to escape? How could we combat someone or something with powers not of this world?

He had to have been mistaken.

I looked around the room again, my eyes coming to rest on a lone door. Curiosity got the better of me and I walked over and opened it to find a closet filled with paint cans, brushes, and a drop cloth.

Outside, the rain began to fall again. Another ATV rolled up a row of vegetation and I froze. My heart beat steadily inside my chest. For some reason or another, I wanted Levi beside me, but I didn't know where he had gone. The ATV slowed to a halt right outside the cabin door. I looked around one last time and dashed into the closet, closing the door behind me.

Work boots thudded against the hard, wooden floor and then I heard voices. They muttered something I could barely hear. Cold sweat trickled down the small of my back and I tried not to breath in case they could hear me.

Footsteps stopped in the middle of the room, and a male voice said softly, "We have to sacrifice someone today."

"Yeah…but who?"

"How about that bitch in the cookhouse, the one that don't do diddly?"

"You mean the one that lost her cubs?"

"Yeah. It's either her or the other one, the one who just stays in the cookhouse singing."

"Lean. Yeah. I like her. She's been with us for a bit. She's one of the good ones."

"So, we ain't dippin' her in oil?"

"No. Not Lean. That other bitch seems like the most likely candidate."

I freaked out silently. They were planning to kill August! I had to get her out of here. It didn't matter that Levi told me to stay put. I moved, bumping into one of the paint cans. It didn't fall, but just in case they heard me, I crawled under the drop cloth.

The voices went silent and then the door opened. My bladder nearly gave way as I crouched low under the drop cloth, breathing shallowly and praying not to be found. Eventually they closed the door, mumbling something I couldn't hear. I didn't move or breathe until their footsteps faded and the cabin door shut behind them.

They were going to kill August! I had to get us out of here. I reached under my dress, found my phone, and frantically dialed my office, waiting for the familiar message that my call couldn't be completed as dialed.

Instead, the phone rang.

# Drake

"Daddy?"

My oldest daughter was looking down at me with a look of concern. I sat up quickly.

"You, okay?" I asked.

"Yes." Madison hugged me and I hugged her back fiercely.

We were in a cabin surrounded by other children with their mothers. I was the only father. Other kids started to awaken on their small cots. As I held my daughter in my arms, my youngest still slept soundly in the cot beside us. My mind turned naturally towards my wife. Was she alright? What had happened to her while we were in this godforsaken land?

"Daddy, I want to go home," Madison whispered into my chest.

"I know, baby girl," I whispered back. "I know."

"Where's Mommy?" she asked in a barely audible tone.

"I don't know, baby. But Daddy will find out, and when I do, I'll make sure we all get home."

"Children!" The female voice came from out of nowhere. "Children, make a single line by the door and get ready to head to the cafeteria for breakfast."

I looked down at my daughter and then at Autumn, who was now awake and sitting on the edge of the cot. The woman stood in the entryway to the sleeping quarters. She clapped her hands twice to get the children's attention, and then she pointed towards the line that was beginning to form. Autumn looked at me as if to ask what she should do.

"Girls, follow the other kids out so you can get your breakfast."

"But daddy…" Madison began.

"I will come get you after you've had breakfast." They didn't want to leave my side. I couldn't blame them; I didn't want them to leave but they needed to eat.

Where was Miguel? I hadn't seen him since he had intervened on my whipping. I had been hit, but he took most of the blows as he hugged my back tightly while they beat him. I needed to find him, but I was afraid of letting the girls out of my sight. I waved my hand in the air hoping that would get the woman's attention.

She turned and began to make her way over to me. She stood before me, smiling an inauthentic smile. I waited until she said that I could speak.

"What do you want?" she asked.

She was an attractive, rail-thin woman with red hair elegantly styled in an updo. Her dress was long, cinched at the waist, her blouse cut low, nearly exposing her cleavage. I was careful to avoid making eye contact with her and even more certain that I didn't look at her bosom.

"Ma'am," I began, measuring my words carefully. "I'd like to stay with my daughters if that is okay with you."

She looked at me as if I were speaking Greek. "We don't do that here, nigger, you know that." She watched the line of children disappear through the open doorway. "You need to get ready and get out there and pick those figs. They ain't gonna pick themselves."

"All due respect, ma'am." I started to panic. "I need to keep my children near me. I also would like to check up on a friend of mine. He took a beating for me, ma'am…or rather, he took a beating with me."

She looked at me for a long time…or at least it felt like a long time and then she called to one of the men who had come with her into our quarters. "Take him to the Recovery Room," she said with a twinge of bitterness in her voice.

Strong hands grabbed me by the arm and hauled me out of the room and into a steady drizzle with rapidly darkening skies.

"You think that you gonna get outta workin' the fields today nigger?" he asked.

I shook my head. He was gaslighting me. I was going to have to ignore him, so I just kept walking. Put one foot in front of the other and keep walking. A sharp blow to the center of my back caused me to lose my footing and fall to the ground. I leapt to my feet; my hands balled into fists. I couldn't let him goad me into fighting or I might never see my girls again.

"You got somethin' you wanna to say, boy?" He took a deliberate step, as if to intimidate me.

I didn't move, but I uncurled my fists. The anger was visible on my face and I didn't want him to see my hands.

A scream came from the direction of the midwife's cabin. I didn't want to know what was going on there. I couldn't understand how one race of people could want to inflict so much pain and despair on another race of people. I looked away from the man who glared at me through crystal blue eyes. His auburn-colored beard was full and thick stopping at the top of his chest. He was a stocky, broad shouldered, with larger than average biceps. It would be a hell of a fight if it came down to it, but make no mistake, I would whoop his ass if he came at me.

He took another menacing step towards me, but I didn't move. I didn't know if he was going to swing on me or not. He had already hit me once.

"So, you one of them bucks that need to be broken." He placed his fingers on his chin as if to evaluate what he was going to do to me.

In that moment, I knew what my ancestors had gone through. They lived under an umbrella of hopelessness in which white people were their lords and masters, capable of inflicting pain and misery at the drop of a hat. Men were separated from their families and sold to other plantations. That I had my kids back was nothing short of a miracle.

"Boy, I'm gonna break you. Not because I want to, but because I have to." He took a step back. "And I don't want you getting any ideas in your head about leavin'. There are things in the woods that you don't want to meet. Bad things, boy."

"May I check on my friend?" I asked hesitantly, ignoring what he said.

"Go." He pointed towards a cabin at the far eastern part of the plantation. "Last cabin on the left. The midwife's cabin."

The drizzle that enshrouded the plantation slowly turned into a steady rain.

Another shrill scream caught my attention as I slowly made my way towards the cabin. I looked across the plantation and saw one of the overseer's whipping a woman. I made a beeline to the midwife's cabin. I couldn't allow myself to get involved. The lives of my daughters and Miguel depended on me.

"How can I help you?" I heard the woman's voice before I saw her. She stood slowly, wincing as she placed her hands on her lower back.

"I'm looking for Miguel," I said, as if I were trying to figure out if she was friend or foe.

She nodded and raised her hand indicating that I should follow her. She pointed to a bed at the end of the room that sat directly underneath a window. Miguel lay on his stomach. He must have heard his name because he turned his head towards me, simultaneously releasing a low groan. His back was a crisscross of lacerations although they were no longer bleeding.

"Mr. Drake." He extended a hand to me. "You still here."

"Yeah, man." I looked over my shoulder.

The midwife had gone to another section of the room, presumably to care for another patient.

"I couldn't leave you." I leaned into him.

He gave me a weak smile. His jet-black hair was disheveled. He reached out to me, and our hands clasped in friendship.

"Thank you," he said softly. "There's a transport van at the end of a parking field. I can get the keys to it." He winced. "We cannot go through the woods. There are things in the woods."

"But there's a road that leads out of here?"

"The same road you came in on." He swallowed and then pointed towards a pitcher of water that sat on a small wooden table beside his bed.

I reached over, poured a small glass of water, and handed it to him. He accepted the glass and took a couple of sips gratefully.

"What's in the woods, Miguel?" I wasn't sure I wanted to know the answer, but I had to know what danger I would be placing my daughters in when we make a break for it.

Miguel paused for a moment, took a deep breath, and spoke slowly. "If we go…into the woods." He took another raspy breath. "The things out there will kill us. We won't be seen again."

# Tarek

"Come on." Zach put his arm around my waist as we made our way down a narrow set of steps that ran from the rear of the second floor to the first-floor kitchen.

My back was screaming, blood still trickling through my shirt. More than anything, I wanted to crawl back into that bed and cover myself with the down comforter. But I also couldn't overlook the fact that Lulu had lifted Zach's two hundred ten-pound body without laying a finger on him. I had looked at the soles of his feet to confirm I was seeing what I was seeing. He had levitated in front of her, suspended at least two feet off the ground.

"Where are we going?" I winced in pain.

"To the cookhouse to get the girls. Then we're headed into the woods."

"What's in the woods?"

"Our way out of here."

"Going somewhere, boys?"

We both froze. It was Lulu's voice.

Zach looked behind us just as we hit the bottom of the stairwell. The blood and sweat on my back turned to ice.

"You know…" And then she froze.

We stared at her in bewilderment. She stood approximately five steps from the bottom, and she was frozen. She had stopped moving…almost like she was in a movie and we had pressed the pause button.

Zach looked at me and then we both turned our attention back to Ms. Lulu as she stood in a state of suspended animation. A shadow moved at the top of the steps. A look of sheer panic passed over Zach's face as Lady Onyx stepped around the frozen Ms. Lulu.

"Hello, boys," she said, and cast a judgmental glance at Ms. Lulu. "That should keep you for a while."

"Onyx…what's going on?" Zach asked.

"You remembered my name…how sweet." She gave Lulu a disparaging glance. "You boys are safe…for now."

As always, Lady Onyx looked stunning, this time in a tight red pencil skirt suit with matching hat and bright red stilettos. Her long, impossibly straight hair was draped over her right shoulder.

"I can help you if you let me," she said through ruby red lips.

She descended the few steps to the floor. My attention bounced from Lulu to her and then to Zach.

"I tried to warn you before all of this occurred. I'm so sorry, boys." She looked back at Lulu. "I wish I could've stopped what Lulu had been planning from the beginning. She targeted your family."

"What?" I couldn't believe what she was saying. "Why?"

"Because she thought you would make good slaves. Don't you know? You're in the middle of the New South. You're also in the middle of our coven."

"Coven?" Zach's grip on my waist tightened, causing me to wince. "As in witches? That's a thing?"

"As real as I'm standing in front of you." She bent down and ran her fingers lightly over my forehead. "That should take care of your pain."

I looked down at the wooden floor and then back into her eyes, realizing that she wore deep green contact lenses. I also realized that the pain in my back had evaporated like smoke. I pushed myself up slowly, prepared for the pain to overtake me but miraculously, there wasn't any.

Zach looked amazed. "What did you do?"

"I cast a spell of healing. He should be fine." Lady Onyx looked over her shoulder at the immobilized Lulu. "We should get going. She's the strongest witch here. I don't know how long my spell will hold her."

Her stilettos clicked on the wooden planks as she passed us. I inhaled deeply, taking in the scent of her perfume. She paused in the doorway, looking at the steady drizzle of rain.

"Guess I'm gonna have to shake my shell," she mumbled.

She raised her hands over her head while murmuring something I couldn't hear. What followed next was something that neither Zach nor I was prepared for. A wave of static electricity, much like that of an old-fashioned television when it went off the air, started at her feet and swirled in clouds of yellow, red and blue, wrapping around her until she was fully enveloped. When the cloud dissipated, what was left was a thin, Black, teenaged boy dressed in blue distressed jeans, construction worker boots and a black tee shirt.

Zach and I were speechless.

"Yeah, I know." He spoke in a voice too soft for a man "I know…it's not glam. But I ain't ruining a pair of pumps in this weather. Come on. Let's go."

He darted out into the mist, and we followed behind him. The scent of wet trees, grass and vegetation filled my nostrils as we sprinted through the mud. We didn't see or hear any ATVs that would normally be in the area.

As we got closer to the cookhouse, I could smell frying ham. My stomach did a slow roll as I tried to remember the last time I had eaten.

"Can you explain what's going on?" I asked while trying to catch my breath.

The boy turned to face me "My name's Henry. You're in the middle of the Southern Middlesex Coven. You are in what's called the 'New South' and in the New South, they enslave people that look like you and me to work the fields, prepare the meals and to make the lives of these good ole white folks comfortable. Got it?"

"So, you're part of a coven…of witches?" Zach asked. "Like Samantha from *Bewitched*, witches?"

Henry turned his attention to Zach with an expression of disbelief and a tilt of the head that suggested sarcasm. "Yes. Now keep it moving." He hurried towards the cookhouse. "I could be stripped of all my powers if Lulu knew I helped you."

"You said she's the strongest witch here." Zach said. "Won't she figure it out?"

"Only if she catches me."

When we stumbled through the doorway to the cookhouse, we startled Tess. I raced over to August who was sitting on the floor, and hugged her fiercely…but she pushed me away.

"August, it's me." I hoped that she would recognize me.

"I need my children and my man," she said firmly, turning her head away from me.

"Where are my nieces?" I stood slowly turning my attention to Tess. "Where's my brother?"

"We don't know where your brother is," Tess said with no enthusiasm, turning back towards the stove where she was frying bacon. "Your nieces were shipped off to another plantation. Don't know which one."

"What?"

"Henry, tell them what they do here," Tess said.

"They separate the mens from their families first," Henry responded.

We turned toward the source of the words. Indigo stood in the doorway with my Aunt Merline. I rushed towards Indigo and embraced her, holding her tightly.

"What the hell are you doing here. Indie?" Her body shuddered with emotion. "I thought you went back to Philly."

"I almost did." She released me slowly, wiping away the remnants of tears. "But I got this feeling while I was in the airport that something was wrong, so I came back."

"That was me," Henry said with a slight smile. "Glad to see that my spell worked."

"What?" Indie looked at him incredulously.

"Did you smell my perfume?"

"Your perfume?"

"Lady Onyx's perfume."

"This is Lady Onyx," I said to Indie. "Out of drag."

"It's not drag." Henry gave me a hard look. "What you're seeing in front of you is who I was…who I used to be. Who I really am is Lady Onyx. What I'm in now is drag."

"Where are my babies?" August asked, rocking back and forth on the floor.

"I don't know where they are." Henry knelt close to August. "But I can help you find them."

She instantly stopped rocking. "You can?"

Henry nodded, smiling at August. "I need a strand of your hair," he said. "Anything with your DNA on it. This should be easy since I cast a spell of protection on your babies since the day we met."

"But I don't remember meeting you." August's voice was barely above a whisper.

"You met me as Lady Onyx." He reached for her head, but she pulled away quickly.

"Sweetie, if you want me to help, I'm gonna need a strand of your hair."

"Why?" She was apprehensive; everyone could see it.

"August," I began, "let him help you. If he can get the kids back, you let him do what he needs to do, otherwise, you'll be rocking on the floor for a long time. And I know you want to hug and kiss Maddie and Autumn again."

My sister-in-law looked at me, recognizing my face for the first time. I took a deep breath, and the aroma of frying ham and bacon made my stomach growl again. I turned my attention to Zach as he slowly approached the table that held a stack of oatmeal cakes, bacon, eggs, fresh-squeezed orange juice imported from Florida, and several plates of thinly sliced ham. Tess stopped, waiting for Zach to do whatever she thought her master would do. The hatred was clear.

Zach stepped away from the table quickly turning his attention to Henry and August. Henry had plucked a strand of August's hair and had placed the strand between his closed palms. He whispered some barely audible words almost as if he were praying, and then his hands parted and for a second, the room went silent except for the sound of frying food.

"Your girls?"

She nodded her head. "Yes. Yes. Maddie and Autumn."

"They're at a plantation in Alabama or Florida…but I see that they're safe."

"How do you know?" August's voice quivered.

"I see someone…possibly a man, watching over them."

"Who's the man?"

"Does it matter? What's important is that they're safe." He looked over his shoulder at the empty doorway. "Whoever's leaving needs to come with me now!"

"August, we need to go." I said quickly.

She shook her head, adamant. "I hear what you're saying," she said, looking directly at Henry with the determination I was familiar with. "But I'm not leaving this place without my children." She turned her gaze to me and Zach. "You guys get out of here. Get out and send someone for us!"

Several of the young teens looked at Zach and me, then back at Tess, who nodded silently with a tight lip. They picked up the trays of food and marched out of the cookhouse.

"I can't leave you here," I protested.

"And I can't leave this place without my babies or my husband." She paused. "Tarek…Zach, get out of here. Send help. Some of us want to go." She looked over her shoulder at Tess, who had started chopping onions. "Others will want to stay."

"We don't have time for this," Henry said, exasperated. "We need to get going right now!"

"Then go!" August ordered.

My sister knelt beside her. "Are you sure?"

A tear slipped from August's right eye; a tear that she wiped away as quickly as it had begun to fall. "I've got to stay here Indie. I must wait here for my babies. If they make it back here, I have to be here waiting for them."

Indie nodded, tears starting to form in her own eyes. She stood up slowly looking at Zach and me. "Let's go." Her voice was stern and without emotion.

Zach, Henry, Indie, and I turned to leave. Indie turned back, giving August a last longing look before we disappeared into the steady rain.

# Drake

Miguel told me a tale of creatures in the Alabama woods that made my head spin. According to him, there were things that could only be described as part man/part creature living just on the outskirts of this plantation. He said that they were deformities of whatever cruelty that the owners inflicted on their captives.

He also said that he had access to the shed where they kept the keys to the ATVs. How he gained access, I had no idea, and this wasn't the time to ask questions. Right now, the only thing that mattered was getting my daughters out of this godforsaken place.

As I made way to the makeshift cafeteria where all the "help" ate, I couldn't help but think about what Miguel had told me. He spun me a tale that was so wild, so unrealistic, that I had to pause and shake my head just to get my thoughts together. He said we were in the middle of a coven of witches, that they were the reason for the cars I saw pulling up to this plantation, with the people getting out in their evening gowns and tuxedos. He told me that they needed to make sacrifices once a month, boiling the person being sacrificed in a specially prepared oil.

My girls were not going to see or experience that.

Our plan was simple: we were going to meet at the shed in an hour. After grabbing two sets of keys, we would make a break for it. Since we wouldn't be pulling a wagon, I could only take one of my daughters. I would have to rely on Miguel to carry my other child.

"Hey, nigger!" The voice came virtually out of nowhere.

I turned my head to see a white man in jeans, boots, and a loose-fitting cotton shirt. He was holding a long-barreled rifle in his hand, and I could see that his finger was on the trigger. I froze, becoming acutely aware of my blackness. For a brief second, I wondered if this was what slaves felt like over a century ago. I had to think quickly.

"Sir," I began, "I was headed to the eating room to have breakfast and see my little ones."

"Boy, you ain't got no children here!" He pointed the rifle at me.

"I don't think we need to talk like we're from the eighteen-hundreds," I said, my mind going a hundred miles an hour. "We can talk like civilized people from the current era."

"You ain't got no children here." I heard the distinctive click as he leveled the rifle at my chest.

"Sir, my children arrived last night. Not their mother…just the kids. I'd like to be with them because they're afraid, sir. They don't know where they are or what to do. I need to comfort them."

He paused, never letting his gaze falter. I didn't dare move. I had no idea if he was going to shoot me or not.

"You can't go unsupervised. March!" He gestured with the gun toward the cafeteria.

I had no idea what he had planned. I had to do something. I couldn't trust this man to do right by me or my daughters. I raised my hands high in the air above my head and turned towards the eating room. I took one hesitant step, and then another. I could hear the man's pants against the un-mowed grass. I had to do something, but I couldn't think of a single thing. What would he do to us once I gathered up my girls? I wasn't going to wait around to find out. I crumpled to the damp earth clutching my abdomen as if I were in pain.

"Get the fuck up, nigger!" The man shouted at me.

I waited. One, two, three…

When he poked me with the barrel, I grabbed the rifle as if my life depended on it. And then I summoned up all the strength I had and kicked him in the ribs. He grunted in pain as he teetered to his right side. The adrenaline coursed through my system as I jumped up, planting my feet squarely on the grass. I swung at him, hitting him hard on the side of the head. He went down like a sack of potatoes.

I grabbed his rifle and raced towards the eating room. "Maddie! Autumn! Come here!" I scanned the tables. One of the men at the back of the cavernous room started towards me until I pointed the rifle at him. I had no idea if there was more than one round in the chamber and I had no extra bullets to refill it should I need to.

"Daddy!" Autumn clung to my leg, involuntary tears running down her face.

"It's okay, baby," I said in a low voice, scanning the room for anyone else that could be viewed as a threat. The woman who had ushered the children into the room stood frozen, looking at me in horror. I pointed the rifle at her, pushing my girls gently behind me as we made our way to the entrance.

One of the other little girls started screaming. Another joined in, then another.

"Come on babies, we gotta go." I pushed them out the door, not sure of where we were going. And then I knew.

"Daddy, where are we going?" Madison's eyes were wide with fear.

"Run across the field." I risked a glance behind me. No one was pursuing us, at least not yet. "We're going into the woods."

We made it across the field intact, but in the distance, I could hear the revving of engines. They were coming for us. My youngest had her arms locked around my neck. Her heart beat like a bass drum inside of her tiny chest. Maddie held onto my waist breathing heavily. She needed to rest, but we had to keep moving. If we could get to the wooden fence that surrounded the entire plantation, we could get off this land and into the woods and hopefully find shelter.

"We gotta move, baby," I said to Maddie.

"Daddy..." she began.

"Keep moving, sweetie." I glanced over my shoulder. The engines were getting louder. They reminded me briefly of the go-carts I had raced with friends when I was a child.

The fence was only a few hundred yards away. If I could just reach the split in the fencing and get the girls to the other side of the dense growth with a straight swath of land running through it, we would be safe. I started to pray as my daughter grew heavier and heavier. Normally she felt as light as a sack of pillows...only now the pillows were starting to feel like they were filled with rocks.

A voice reached me from a good distance away. "Don't let that nigger get to the fence! If they get out, we'll never find them!"

I pushed on, the high grass like greedy fingers pulling at my clothing. I had to get my girls off this plantation. They might end up as slaves for the rest of their lives if I didn't. And then there was August. I couldn't think about her right now. I had to save the girls first.

My chest caught as the fence got closer and closer.

So did the engines of the ATVs.

With one major thrust, I threw Autumn over the fence like a rag doll. She screamed as she sailed through the air and came down hard on the dirt road leading to the woods.

I turned to Madison. "Come on, baby! We got to move!"

"Daddy, I can't!" She started to sob.

We didn't have time for this. I grabbed her by the waist, lifted her into the air and tossed her over the fence after her sister, then propelled myself over the rail and landed on my right side with a sickening thud.

"Daddy…" Madison rushed to me, followed closely by Autumn.

I stood up quickly. We were on a dirt road approximately the width of an automobile. I looked at the woods and for the first time, I noticed just how dense they were. The dirt road appeared to be swallowed up by the forest. I knew that the girls wouldn't want to venture into the woods, but we didn't have a choice.

"Babies," I started, looking over my shoulder. The ATVs were getting closer; we were out of time. "Maddie, I know you don't want to do this, but I'm gonna need you to be a big girl today. I know I hurt you and I swear I didn't mean it. But right now, we gotta move. Can you do that for me?"

Madison looked up at me, nodding her head slowly.

I grabbed her arm, clutching Autumn to my chest. She kept a death grip around my neck as I looked above at the darkening skies. I tried to judge how far away the ATVs were. They were close. We had no choice. We had to enter the woods.

The first thing I noticed when we went into the trees was that the temperature seemed to have dropped by ten degrees. I felt as if the woods were swallowing us whole. My heart pounded in my chest as I looked from side to side. The woods were dense and could hide so many things…things that I didn't want to know about.

But we couldn't outrun an ATV, that much was for certain. Without thinking further, I ventured into the dense brush, pulling Madison after me. I couldn't let anything happen to my girls. My youngest was whimpering softly into my shoulder while my oldest sobbed aloud.

"Shh!" I looked down at Madison. "I need you to be quiet until the bad men pass us by, okay?"

The area was thick with vegetation. All I could smell was leaves and dirt. I held tightly to my girls as we stepped off the road and into the dense woods. I squatted down low to the ground trying to make myself as small as possible. Madison buried her face in my shirt. My arms were screaming from holding Autumn, but I couldn't risk putting her down.

I waited impatiently for them to pass. I wasn't sure what I would do once they did. If they passed us, then they would be ahead of us. If we went in that direction, we would run into them. At the same time, we couldn't go back the way we came. That would simply take us back to the plantation. And then August's face flashed before me. I had never wanted her more than I did in that moment. I had my girls, but where was the love of my life?

An ATV came to a slow halt about three feet from where we were crouched. My arms trembled. What would they do to us if we were caught? I had no doubt they would kill me. But what would happen to my girls?

Heavy footsteps crunched on gravel just behind us. The sound sent shivers up my spine. The warning that Miguel had given me about what could be lurking in the woods rang in my head, making it spin. I didn't know what was going to happen, but I was going to protect my girls at all costs.

"Mr. Drake." The voice was just above a whisper. If I had tilted my head in the wrong direction, I wouldn't have heard it at all. "Mr. Drake. Are you there?"

I recognized the voice at once and climbed out of the ditch, Autumn still in my arms. I had never been so glad to see another person in my life.

"Let's go, Mr. Drake. There's no time." Miguel pointed towards a white van which took up most of the roadway.

"Girls, get in the van." I looked back towards the plantation where I could hear several ATVs in the distance. I looked behind me at the woods and then climbed into the van. Miguel climbed into the driver's seat, wincing in pain, put the vehicle in drive and took off.

"Put your seatbelts on," I barked as the van bounced from side to side.

"Daddy, are we going to be okay?" Madison's voice quivered. Both girls were in tears.

"Yes," I said without looking at her. "We're gonna be fine." I turned to Miguel, who was laser focused on the road ahead of us. "How did you know where we were?"

"I made myself...get up from the bed when I heard the commotion. I knew you...were getting your children." He glanced into the back seat. "These your girls?"

"Yes." I glanced back at my girls, momentarily admiring the fact that Maddie had wrapped her arms protectively around her younger sister.

"Maddie...Autumn...this is Mr. Miguel. He is going to help us."

"Thank you." Maddie wiped tears away with her hands.

"So where are we going?" I asked.

"Away from here." Miguel replied and pressed his foot on the accelerator.

# Indigo

By the time we reached a clearing to the south of the main house, it felt like we had run a marathon. Thank God we were able to stop so that we could catch our breath. My heart ached for August, as well as the plight of my nieces.

"So, what now?" Zach bent over, taking deep gulps of air.

"There's a shed behind the main house that holds all of our carriages." Henry answered.

"And horses? Or are these motor propelled vehicles?" Tarek asked.

"Horse-drawn," Henry said. "So yes, there are horses pulling the carriages."

"Can you cast a spell on us to get us back to the restaurant?" I looked back toward the main house.

"Unfortunately, I can't." Henry shook his head. "I can only cast a spell of protection for the children. I can't do anything with the adults. I can pause other witches, but not for long periods of time. Most of my powers are put toward transforming myself into Lady Onyx." He looked directly at me. "I can reach out no matter where you are and warn you, like what I did with you."

"Like when I was at the airport?" I asked, more to myself than Henry.

He nodded. "Exactly."

"So that's why I smelled your perfume. That's when I got the urge to come back."

"That was just me telling you to come save your family," he said with a smile. "And it worked!" He looked over his shoulder and then back at the three of us. "The carriage house is about a mile across the plantation. The best way to get off this place is to hop in one of the carriages and go! How long do you think it will take ya'll?"

"Where will the carriage take us?" I asked with caution in my voice.

"Off the plantation. I know that this road will lead you to another clearing and from that it will take you to a main road. Just stay in the carriage with your windows rolled up when you get into the woods."

"Not liking the sound of that," Tarek said.

"Look, ya'll don't have much time. Get across that field and get to the carriage house." He looked at Zach. "You'll need to look like one of the drivers. I can cast a cloaking spell to give you a uniform that looks like you are supposed to be driving the carriage…"

"Hello, Henry." The voice made my blood run cold.

Lulu approached us slowly, with a smile that only belied what she was getting ready to do to us. "First things, first."

She raised her hand, aiming it at Henry. I wanted to run but felt powerless to do so. Henry opened his mouth to protest but nothing came out. We looked at him as an invisible force closed his lips. Lulu smiled without humor. Henry rubbed at his mouth but there was nothing he could do.

"So, you want to leave us?" Ms. Lulu approached us slowly. Her eyes had gone from an older person's blue to slate gray.

I moved closer to my brother, not knowing what to expect next. Henry waved his hands and smiled at Ms. Lulu.

"You think your cloaking spell can save them?" Lulu extended her right hand and curled her fingers into a semi closed fist. "I don't need to see them to find them. Or did you forget?"

Suddenly, Henry's mouth popped open, and he began to giggle. His giggles turned into a steady laugh. "Just because you're the most powerful witch on this plantation don't mean that the others are without power." His laughter turned into a smirk. "I have more power than you think." He mumbled a few short words and then colorful smoke appeared at his feet and swirled upwards like a miniature tornado. When the cloud dissipated, Lady Onyx stood before us, perfectly made up, with long red hair draping over her left shoulder and descending into a fall of loose curls. She faced Lulu down, wearing tight jeans, open-toed wedge shoes and a hot pink crop top.

Lulu took a step back and looked her up and down as if she were admiring her. "Pretty. But that's all you are."

"Or so you think." Onyx's smile crept over her lips. "Run!" she shouted.

We bolted towards the carriage house. My arms pumped as we raced across a field of knee-high grass. I could see Zach and Tarek out of the corner of my eye. They were barely keeping up with me.

Voices shouted behind me; one of them I was certain was Lady Onyx. Tarek stumbled and I paused, watching as Zach stopped and helped him to his feet. The three of us started running again. My breath came in gasps as we drew closer to the carriage house. Tarek stumbled again and then fell flat. Zach reached down, trying to pull him up with both arms. I rushed to them and grasped Tarek's left forearm while Zach took his right.

"Tarek, get up!" I screamed.

I couldn't see Lady Onyx or Ms. Lulu but I could hear them. Their voices were muffled. And as we pulled Tarek to his feet, it hit me. Lady Onyx had done something so that we were cloaked in a state of invisibility. As we broke into a final sprint towards the carriage house, I could see that the three of us looked as if we were a hologram.

Zach stepped into a hole, twisting his ankle violently to the right. Tarek wrapped his arm around Zach's waist and pulled him up, and the three of us broke into a wild run again. The gray and brown carriage house was just a few yards away...and then the structure vanished.

I stopped, rubbing my eyes as if they were playing tricks on me and then rushed to Tarek's side. I gave a final glance to what should have been the carriage house, blinking as if that action would bring the building back. It was useless. If it had been there before, it wasn't there now. All I could see was a field of rapidly drying corn stalks.

So where could we go now? And how long could Lady Onyx hold off Ms. Lulu?

# Tarek

I could feel something wet and slippery on my back so I knew the wounds had opened and were bleeding again. I looked over at my sister and followed her unbelieving gaze to the open field and stopped dead in my tracks.

"We can't stop!" Zach gasped, tugging at my right arm.

We were between the woods and the main house. Men burst out of the front door. They looked around until their eyes fell on us, and then they bounded off the porch and started towards us.

We looked around but there was nowhere to run. And then a movement to my left, just beyond the cookhouse, caught my eye. Someone was calling my sister's name.

"Tarek! Zach!" my sister yelled. "It's Uncle Shucky! Come on!"

We started towards them, me on wobbly legs. Zach motioned for Indigo to run ahead of us. He wasn't leaving my side.

Indie reached Uncle Shucky, gave him a hug, and then told him about August still being in the cookhouse. One of the men reached out to Indie, but I couldn't hear what he said. She shook her head and approached me. "Are you okay, Tarek?"

I nodded my head even though my back was screaming from where I'd been whipped. Onyx's spell to ease the pain in my back must have worn off.

"His back is bleeding." Zach answered for me. "We need some bandages."

"Levi, "Shucky began, "get 'em to the cookhouse and then get them off this plantation. I don't want them to be here when we burn this muthafucka down."

"Burn it down?" Indigo looked at Shucky, then at Levi. "What do you mean? And where did these men come from?"

"The same way we did…by carriage. These were the men waiting back at the restaurant. Come on." Levi placed his arm protectively around my sister's shoulders and guided her towards the cookhouse a few hundred yards away.

"Come on, fellas! Let's do what we came to do!" Shucky yelled at the top of his lungs and bolted towards the main house.

At first, I wondered who he was talking to, and then I saw a surge of men appeared seemingly out of nowhere. It wasn't just the five men left behind. Shucky had managed to round up many of the men forced into hard labor on this plantation. It could not have been any less than twenty men…and they followed Shucky towards the main house. Some held lit torches that didn't extinguish due to the pouring rain. They raced past me and Zach. I didn't know who Levi was, but apparently, he must have been my uncle's second in command.

I heard fighting behind me; men yelling and some even screaming as the clash began. I looked around for any sign of Lady Onyx or Ms. Lulu. They were nowhere to be found.

When we burst into the cookhouse, Indie rushed to August and knelt beside her. Levi turned towards me, looked me up and down and then spoke in an unusually deep voice. "You must be Tarek." He looked over at Zach. "You his boyfriend?

Zach nodded hesitantly, not because he was ashamed of our relationship but because he had no idea who Levi was.

"We have to get off this plantation!" Levi said in an authoritative voice. "Who's coming?"

"I am." Indigo looked at August. "Have you changed your mind?"

"No. She shook her head. "I have to be here when they come back." She looked up at Indigo. "Send someone back for us."

"You'll never make it through the forest," Tess said without looking at us. "There're things out there; people that live out there and will show no mercy if theys to get a hold of you."

"How do you know this?" I didn't really want to know the answer.

An eternity seemed to pass before she spoke again.

"Two months ago, a girl named Darlene found herself on this plantation." Tess slowly turned around. "She couldn't have been no older than you," she said, pointing at my sister. "She disappeared into the woods. I guess she got tired of being the master of the house's concubine. She didn't want to pick fruits, vegetables…hell, she didn't even want to learn to cook here. So, one day, she just plain takes off! She makes a dash for it. Now she must have come from Atlanta because she acted like a wild horse that hadn't been broke in yet. She had a man, but they killed him long ago; fried him like an order of KFC by dipping him in a vat of oil. And then they set out to break her.

"So, one day she just runs. By the time the head of the household realizes she left, she had about a two-day head start. So, they set off after her. We seen them drag her body back with burn marks all over her a few days later."

"So, what are you saying? That there's no way off this place?" Indigo asked.

"That's exactly what I'm sayin', little girl!" Tess said hotly. "You ain't getting' off this plantation any more than the rest of us."

"Not if it was left up to people like you." Indie turned to me and Zach. "Come on, boys. Let's get off this godforsaken place."

"Little girl…"

"I'm not your little anything!" Indie snapped.

Tess put her hands on her hips, exhaling in exasperation. "You don't listen," she said in a low voice. "You don't listen."

"No, you don't listen!" Indigo raised her voice so that everyone in the kitchen stopped dead in their tracks. "Staying on this plantation is not an option for us! Maybe for you, but not for me and not for my brothers!"

"You think that white man is a brother to you?" She flapped a damp dishcloth at Zach. "You think he'll defend you should you find yourself surrounded by the patrollers or them gators? You think that he'll help you if, God forbid, you find them things in the woods we hear about?" She shook her head. "I'm staying my black ass right here!"

"As if you were going to do anything but." Indigo started towards the entryway and then doubled back. "What's the real reason why you're staying here serving these devil people? And don't give me any bull about things in the woods or gators or anything else!"

I made my way over to my sister-in-law and knelt painfully at her side. She didn't look like August anymore. Her natural hair that she had taken so much pride in was uncombed and matted, and she was wearing a dress that, under different circumstances, she would never be in. She looked up at me and burst into tears. We hugged, gripping each other tightly, but the next thought that came to me was, where was Drake? He must be out in the fields.

"Tarek…find my babies! The girls…they're missing."

Fear leapt up in my chest. My nieces were gone. How was that possible?

"Where did you last see them?"

"They took them." Her words came out in a voice that resonated more loss than hurt. "They took them like they was nothing."

I looked over at my sister and Zach. Levi stood in the doorway with an expression of urgency. I had to make my choice.

"Ya'll go," I said, wrapping my arms around August.

Zach looked at me with the same look of urgency. "Babe…" he started, and everyone turned their attention to him. "You can't stay here. We can get off this plantation and send help for everyone."

"I'm staying." My voice came out stern, harsher than I intended. "Go with my sister and send help."

"Now wait a minute!" Tess protested. "For you, this may be a place where you don't want to be but for me, this is my home."

"This is not your home," Indigo hissed at her. "This is a prison. Show of hands, who all is happy here?"

Only two or three people raised their hands.

Tess looked around the room, and then focused her attention on a woman seated on the floor in the corner. "Lean…ain't you happy here?" Tess demanded.

Everyone's attention turned to the woman on the floor. She raised her head, brushed her hair away from her face and nodded slowly. There was a certain familiarity in the way she nodded her head.

"Aunt Merline?" I released my sister-in-law, not believing what my eyes were showing me to be the plain truth.

"Lil T?" The woman raised herself to her feet.

"You can talk, Lean?" One of the girls spoke in a hushed tone.

"Aunt Merline!" I rushed to her, and we met in an embrace of tears. I knew right then that I couldn't leave even if Zach begged me. I swallowed the lump that had gathered in my throat. "I thought you were in Chicago."

Indigo made her way across the room and embraced Aunt Merline for what I assumed was the first time.

"I was on my way when they grabbed me," she said softly. "I had made up my mind to leave your Uncle Shucky and make a way for myself. I was catching a bus 'cause that was all I could afford. Figured I would go to Chicago and find myself an apartment when they caught me waitin' for the bus to take me to Atlanta."

"Who took you, Aunt Merline?" Indie asked, slowly releasing her.

"Someone related to the Carmichaels."

"We got to move, Indigo!" Levi looked out the door.

"He's right." I looked at Zach's grief-stricken face. "Go! Get out and send help for us!"

"But…"

"Please." I was on the verge of tears. "I have to stay with my family."

"I'm your family!" A tear slipped from one of his eyes and slid down his cheek.

"Go." I stood up and walked towards him, wrapping my arms around him. "Send help for us. I can't leave my sister-in-law here when my nieces are out there. What kind of uncle would I be? Surely you have to understand that." I hugged him tightly to me and then released him. "Take Indie and go!"

"We got to move!" Levi barked.

"Get out of here!"

"I love you, Tarek." Zach whispered in my ear. He turned reluctantly away from me, looked up at Levi and then nodded his head. "Indie, you comin'?" he called.

"Yes." She looked at Merline and then August. "We'll send someone for you. I promise."

"I know you will." I said. I mouthed the words, "I love you" to Zach and watched them as he, Levi and Indigo walked into the fine gray mist outside. The pouring rain looked like it was letting up.

"So that's your friend?" Tess asked, her voice dripping with sarcasm. "He ain't sending anyone for you, you know that don't you?"

"Well, it's a good thing that my sister went with him to make sure that he does, ain't that right, Mammy?"

"Boy, if you were my chile…"

"But I ain't your child, Tess!" I snapped. "And furthermore, don't come for me! You don't want none of this!"

"Who the fuck do you think you are, boy?" She turned to glare at the young girls that had gathered near the pots of boiling stew. The aroma reminded me of how hungry I was. "Don't ya'll have food to serve? Get up out my kitchen!"

The girls grabbed plates of food, covered them with lids and marched out into the mist. I inhaled, taking in the aroma of Tess's cooking and the damp grass outside. The mixture of the food and earth was intoxicating.

"So, since we have some time," I began while lowering myself slowly to the floor. "Why do you choose to stay, Tess? You never answered my sister when she asked you that,"

"She never asked me anything," Tess said slowly. "She wanted to know who was happy here? She never asked me why I stayed not that I didn't make mention to her earlier."

"I stand corrected." I looked down at the floor, and then up into her dark, round face. "Why do you stay?"

"It's safer for me here."

"How so?"

"Do you know how many young Black boys die in my old neighborhood as a result of gun violence?"

I shook my head.

"Two hundred fifty-three in just six months. When they come and got me, I was working as a waitress in a family-owned business that ran me ragged. I worked hard day and night and could still never make ends meet. Social Security barely paid my bills. But where could I go? What could I do? I had no family around to help me. When they came for me, I went willingly. Here, I'm fed. If I need medical attention, one of the women in the medical cabin can help me. I stand on my feet just as long, but now I don't have to worry about being put out my house because I couldn't make the rent this month.

"You talk to most of these girls, and they'll tell you stories close to mine. Out there, you struggle. In here, you don't. It's that simple."

"You're giving up your freedom."

"But for once in my life, I am safe. I don't have to fear any gang violence here. Don't have to worry about being shot to death in my sleep. Don't have to worry about cops grabbing me while I'm on my way to the grocery store saying I did something like vote when I shouldn't have."

"Living in fear isn't freedom."

"But that's just it, me and none of these girls feel like there's anything else out there for us."

"That's because they have you programmed to think that way."

"Well, you don't know what my survival was like when I was out and about in Darcy County."

An ATV stopped outside the door of the cookhouse. Everyone froze in their spots, their attention focused on the doorway. A heavy-set white man with a bald head came charging into the room.

"Get to your quarters!" He barked out orders as if he were in the military. "Tess, shut down lunch and then get to your quarters and lock up!"

Everyone looked at him as if he had lost his mind.

"Go, goddammit!" he shouted.

Everyone snapped out of their reverie and raced out of the cookhouse in all directions. Tess turned her back to us and shut off all the burners on the stove. I stood and extended my hand to August. She looked up at me, took my hand and slowly rose to her feet.

"Let's go to my bunk in the girls' cabin, Tarek," she said softly. "We can wait for any news there."

She moved on unsteady feet, leaning on my arm for support as we walked to the exit door on the opposite end of the cookhouse. Merline followed behind us.

"I want to come…that's if ya'll don't mind," she murmured.

"Of course not." I spoke with authority. "Family has got to stay together." I paused for a moment. "When we get out of here, you're coming with us, Aunt Merline.'"

"Before I take one step out of this cookhouse, answer me this…Shucky's here, ain't he?'"

Yes," I said without looking at her.

"Where is he?"

"Fighting."

"Where the fuck you think you're going, nigger?" The man's voice came out low and menacing.

I paused. August looked up with fear in her eyes. It never occurred to me to hide since I was the only man in the cookhouse. August's arms tightened around me.

"Answer me!" he shouted.

I looked at his face for the first time since he entered the room. He was well-muscled with the slight rise of a belly. The color in his cheeks was high.

"I…" I didn't know what to tell him, and prayed he wouldn't hit my back. "I came in here to hide, sir," I began slowly. "I saw the commotion outside and didn't want no parts of it."

The man took three steps towards me. I braced myself for what was coming next.

"Mr. Charlie, please don't hit this boy." Tess's voice came out unexpectedly.

I looked over at her, surprised she would speak up in my defense.

"He didn't know," she continued. "He's used to workin' the crops."

"What happened to his back?" the man asked.

"He was whipped, sir." She cast her eyes downward.

"What for?"

It dawned on me what Tess was trying to do.

"I backtalked," I murmured.

Charlie looked at all of us before speaking.

"Nigger, let go of that wench!" he said to me.

August's hands unraveled from around my waist.

He turned his attention to Tess. "If you ever speak again without being spoken to, I'll whip the black right off you!"

"Yes, sir," she whispered.

"I can't hear you, nigger!"

"I said yes, sir." Tess raised her voice, but only slightly.

"Boy, get to your cabin and stay the fuck there! The rest of you wenches get to your cabin and don't move until someone in authority tells you to!"

The women began moving towards the exit towards the opposite end of the cabin. I followed, not sure where to go once I left the cookhouse.

I wondered for a moment why Charlie or anyone else who ran this so-called plantation needed to be so cruel when it came to handling the people who were forced labor here. And then it occurred to me that they were simply acting like their ancestors did. They needed to dehumanize us because if they didn't recognize us as human, it would be easier to inflict pain on our bodies with impunity. They needed to take away any pride that we had. They considered us as property. We were beings without feelings or emotions. We had no rights here. We weren't even allowed to feel for each other. I had to keep reminding myself of that.

Once I got outside, I could see and hear some kind of commotion going on at the main house, but I was too far away to make out what it was. Fog lay close to the ground obscuring the vegetables underneath it. I looked around for the men's housing and couldn't figure out which cabin I should go to.

A blow to my shoulders caused me to crumble to my knees. The wounds on my back started bleeding as I looked to see who had hit me. Charlie kicked me in the face, and I fell flat to the wet ground.

"You think you were just gonna go to your cabin, boy?" Charlie stood over me as I tried to cover my head.

"We got feelings," I gasped, knowing that I would probably be whipped again.

"What did you say, boy?"

"You…treat us as if we got no feelings. But we do. We bleed." My words were coming out slurred by pain. "We hurt. We feel loss."

"I don't give a fuck!" Charlie spat at me. "Now get to your fuckin' cabin and stay there!"

"I don't know where the men's quarters are."

"Are…what?" he demanded.

"I don't know where the men's quarters are, sir."

This seemed to appease him. I knew I couldn't show any sort of intelligence. That would be an affront to his nature. The commotion coming from the house was starting to get louder and I could tell he wanted to head over there.

"Get up!" he snarled before yanking me cruelly to my feet. My legs felt like two strands of cooked noodles.

The commotion grew louder, and I realized it was moving towards us.

"Get to the cabin all the way down this path and then cut to your left!" Charlie ordered. "And if I don't find you there in fifteen, I'll go to the bitches' cabin and kill anyone that I think you care about…starting with the bitch you had your arms around. Now get!"

I rose to my feet slowly, one hand to my back, and stumbled forward, following the narrow path in front of me. Someone ran past me. I heard the crack of a rifle echoing in the air. In the next instant, strong arms grabbed hold of me.

"Come on, Lil T!" Shucky said in my ear. "We got to move!"

"My back!" I screamed.

His grip loosened. "Let's get to the men's cabin. They may split us up!"

"What happened at the house?" I said, lurching forward.

"They had something around it. Whatever it was, we couldn't break through."

"It's the witches," I mumbled.

"What?"

"Witches. They must be protecting the main house."

"I don't believe in that shit!"

"You better." I dropped to my knees, unable to go on.

Shucky pulled me up. "You bleedin'," he said gruffly. "Let's get you to the doctor's cabin."

He wrapped his arm around my waist gently and pulled me in the opposite direction. Swarms of men raced passed us heading in the direction of the men's cabin. I looked over my shoulder at the main house. I saw a weird yellowish glow coming off it.

"Where are those men going?" I asked.

"They're retreating." He glanced at me. "They can't get to the house. Can't break no windows. Can't get in through the basement. Shit, you can't even light the house on fire. Spare your strength. We're almost at the midwife's cabin."

It was starting to quiet down. Behind the steady whir of the ATV engines and men yelling, I could hear birds chirping. I wondered what they were doing. Clearly their plan hadn't worked. If they were going to attack the big house, they had to come up with another strategy.

"Don't you have to get back to the men that's out there fighting?" I said through gritted teeth.

Shucky nodded his head. "I'll tend to you first before I get to plan B."

"What's plan B?"

"You'll see." We stumbled through the door leading to what looked like the infirmary and my eyes fell on Kisha and Latrice.

"Tarek!" Latrice ran over to me and embraced me hard, sending fresh waves of pain up and down my back. I winced as I pulled away from her.

"The boy was whupped," Shucky said, looking around the room. "Where's the midwife?"

"Doreen's in the back."

"She needs to sew up, Lil T…"

"Tarek." I corrected.

"Tarek." Shucky looked at me like I was still twelve years old.

"What are you doing here?" I crossed the room and settled my weight on a makeshift but well-made cot.

Latrice sat down next to me, looking directly at Shucky.

"I ain't seen you for a long time, Uncle Shucky," she said, keeping a close eye on Kisha, who seemed to be sedated. "How'd you get here?"

"Same as you." He looked over at Kisha. "So, what happened to her?"

"She was raped," Latrice whispered. "And tortured."

"Shit," I murmured.

"Tell the midwife to take care of Lil T...Tarek." Shucky corrected himself while heading for the door.

"I'll tell her." Latrice watched Shucky walk out into the mist. "So let me see your back. I can at least clean you up before Ms. Doreen comes to tend to you."

I removed my shirt and dropped it on the bed.

"Oh my God...Tarek." Latrice burst into tears like she had been holding the anguish in all day. "Just a few days ago our lives were normal and now..."

"I know." I gritted my teeth.

"Hey! Who's this?" The voice came from behind us.

A woman walked through the door from another room. She was wiping her hands together rapidly and I could smell the antiseptic she had used on her hands.

"What we got here?" She didn't ask me my name.

"My cousin." Latrice glanced towards the bed where Kisha slept uneasily. "Please take care of him, Ms. Doreen. I must tend to my friend."

"Those wounds look nasty." Doreen gave Latrice a wistful smile. "Go tend to your friend. And chile, you can say girlfriend. I'm not small minded like some of these other fools 'round here."

Latrice gave her a quick grateful nod and returned to Kisha's side.

"Young man, you got to be careful with these white folks nowadays. You can't just go mouthin' off like you on the outside. In case you didn't notice, you in a different world now."

I hissed as she put some type of salve on my back. It stung at first, and then the pain slowly started to subside.

"This should take care of you but please watch your tongue with these folks." Doreen sounded grandmotherly. Her tone reminded me of the mothers that I remembered from my neighborhood when Indie, Drake and I were growing up. "What's your name baby?"

"Tarek."

"Tarek," she repeated. "Tarek, you got to be careful here. The salve that I put on your back should help it heal. You may have some scarring, but you'll be able to get back in the fields to do what you need to do."

"How did you get here?" My question came out low...almost a whisper.

"What do you mean?"

"I mean, how did you get here? When did you get here? Did they kidnap you?"

She looked at me with huge brown eyes. I could sense the sadness in them, but she didn't say anything for a full five minutes. "I was on my way home from bingo one night. It was about nine thirty and I was a block away from my home when she stopped me." Doreen paused, took a deep breath, and then continued. "I don't remember anything else after that. But once I got here, I was relegated to my own cabin that was furnished a lot better than my efficiency apartment in Darcy County."

Her eyes were faraway, like her mind had gone back to the night that she was abducted.

"They found out that I had my certificate of completion for nursing and made me the head of the infirmary. I learned how to be a doula…"

"What's a doula?"

"Basically, I'm a midwife." She took another deep breath. "Tarek, I've been here long enough to know that escaping is almost impossible. You see, the Carmichaels are not your ordinary slave owners."

"What do you mean?"

"They deal in black magic. Their magic is powerful but only in the confines of this plantation, and they are strongest when they combine their magic. At least that's what I've seen." She looked nervously around the room to make sure that no one else was listening. "They torture people, Tarek, which is why you need to mind your tongue. They would kill you if it would serve their purpose." She paused once again. "I've seen them dip their sacrifices in boiling oil. I heard it's supposed to appease whatever thing they worship. I heard it gives them power, but don't quote me on that."

I shook my head in disbelief. "How do you know this?"

"I've been around here for two years."

"And your family doesn't miss you?"

"I got a daughter somewhere in California that I haven't spoken to in twenty years. Other than that, I got no family." Doreen paused once again, took a deep breath, and continued. "They prey on people they think won't be missed. They get a lot of slaves from the border. Bring 'em right in, offer them a meal and a warm cot to sleep on and they're all in. By the time they realize they've been enslaved, it's too late. The overseers make sure of it."

"Okay, let's just say that I believe what you're telling me. My first question is, do you know of a way to get off this plantation?" I looked hard into Doreen's round face.

She tightened her head scarf and licked her lips. "There was a girl named Darlene that just took off because they broke her. Killed her man by sacrifice. They did things to her. Tarek, things that should never happen to any woman. They beat her…"

"You keep saying 'they'. Who is 'they'?"

"The overseers mostly." She stood up, smoothing her hands over her skirt. "I'll get you something for the pain."

"Wait! Ms. Doreen, has anyone ever successfully escaped?"

She shook her head slowly. "No, I'm afraid not."

"Why?"

She looked at me incredulously. "The overseers and the witches. Ain't that enough?"

I slowly nodded.

"Darlene was a stubborn one, that girl. She hated everything about this plantation, and she was bound and determined to leave. She tried to escape twice before the last time. Both times, they beat her…raped her…isolated her…strung her up by her wrists until she learned some respect. But they didn't break her, as much as they tried."

Doreen crossed the room and went out a side door. She reappeared a few moments later holding a small brown bottle. She opened it and shook out two tablets.

"Take these. It'll make you sleepy and take care of the pain."

I held out my hand and she dropped the pills onto my open palm.

"One more important thing…the witches have more power when they're united. Their power weakens when they're not together and it's reduced even more when they leave the plantation."

"So, they're powerless when they're not together."

Doreen shook her head. "They have some power. But the farther they get from this plantation, the weaker they become."

"How do you know?"

"I got eyes, Tarek. I'm very observant. That's how I stayed alive these last couple of years." She paused. "You need to lay down and get you some rest…allow those wounds on your back to heal. The salve will take care of most of the scarring as long as you don't rip them open. Can I get you anything else?"

I shook my head and stretched out on the cot.

"Ms. Doreen, do you know anything about two little girls and a man named Drake that went missing off this plantation?"

Doreen thought for a moment before sitting back down beside me. "They your kin?" she asked gently.

"Yes. My brother and my two nieces."

She looked around the room again and then spoke softly. "The little girls were shipped off to another plantation."

"Another plantation?"

"Yes. There are plantations in South Carolina, Florida, Georgia, Alabama, and Texas."

My heart sank.

"Do they all have…witches?" The word rolled off my tongue like a lifeless stone.

"No," she said. "But I don't know which ones do and which ones don't. I know they have a small coven in Alabama but that's about it."

I heard a commotion at the entry to the infirmary. Two men stood there, one propped up by the other, obviously wounded. Doreen rose quickly and crossed the room to them.

Damn! My nieces weren't on this plantation. They might not even be in the same state. And what about Drake? Doreen didn't have a chance to get to what happened to him, if she even knew. I had to find my nieces and I had to find my brother.

Drowsiness crept up on me with stealthy, dark fingers. What if I didn't find them? What would I tell August? I began to drift off into a restless sleep.

# Drake

When I woke up in the back of the van, my girls were still curled into one another, sound asleep. Miguel was nodding across from me. I had no idea where we were. I straightened as much as I could, found the door handle and stepped out onto the ground outside. Except for the chirping of crickets, it was completely silent. It was full dark and all I could smell was the thick scent of marsh. It looked like we were at the edge of someone's property, but the house was about two city blocks away and completely dark. We were safe…for now.

As I looked around, my thoughts returned to my wife. How was she? Was she okay? Up until now, I hadn't had much chance to think about August because my girls had my full attention. I couldn't rest until I got them to safety. August would do the same.

Where were we? Up until now, Miguel had overseen our travels. But I had to find August. Somehow, we had to get back to the original plantation in Georgia. But how was that possible, when I didn't even know where we were now? Did Miguel know any more than I did about where we were?

I didn't like not having a sense of control over my life. If it was just me, that would be one thing, but now the lives of my little girls rested on a stranger. I didn't like that either, even if that stranger had taken a beating for me.

A refreshing breeze blew gently through the surrounding trees. If I were a smoking man, I would have lit up a cigarette while I planned our next move. Finding out where we were seemed like the place to start. I just didn't know how to do that. I would have to leave my girls with Miguel, and I wasn't quite ready to do that.

Common sense told me that we would have to ditch the van eventually. But where would we find another set of wheels to get us to Georgia?

I stretched feeling my spine crack deliciously. I thought about everything that had happened to us in the past few days and still couldn't believe it. How had a simple carriage ride turned into enslavement? Where were my Aunts Macy and Pearl? I hadn't seen them since we left Carmichael's restaurant. I had been shipped somewhere by train, which told me that I was probably far from the original plantation. And if that were the case, how many plantations were there?

My thoughts were interrupted by the familiar click of a gun behind me.

"Who the fuck are you?"

How had I not heard anyone sneaking up behind me? I whirled and saw four Black men. Because it was full dark and there were no streetlights nearby, I couldn't see their faces clearly but they seemed to be between the ages ranging from mid-forties to late teens.

"You're on our property!" one of the men said. He held a twelve-gauge, sawed off shotgun menacingly by his side. "You got ten seconds to tell me who you are and then you get another five to get off our land."

Fear made me speechless. How was I going to convince these men that we were not the enemy? I looked him squarely in the eye. He appeared to be about forty-five, if not older. He may very well have been the father of the group. I raised my hands so he could see that I wasn't armed. Hopefully, this would prevent him from shooting me. And if he did shoot me, maybe he would spare my girls and Miguel if they thought that I was alone.

"My name is Drake Robeson." I began slowly. "I was abducted from a plantation in Georgia and shipped to another plantation by train."

"What plantation?" He cocked his weapon and aimed it at my chest.

My heart slammed against my rib cage.

"I wish I knew." I swallowed. "But I managed to escape. Me and my daughters and another captive in that place. We got a van somehow and we got off the plantation. We were driving for a while and needed to stop rest, but we also needed to be safe."

It then occurred to me that these men might send us back to the plantation we just left.

"You got chil'len?" the man with the shotgun asked me.

I nodded my head nervously.

"Anybody chasin' you?"

"I don't think so." I shook my head. I was going to get through this without getting shot. "We made it off the plantation and drove through the woods until we hit the first dirt road. We were looking for a road that would take us east."

"Where you headed?"

"Georgia. My wife is caught on a plantation there and now that I got my girls, I got to get her."

"Dad..." one of the younger armed men said. "He seems genuine."

"Just because he seems that way don't mean he is."

"Mr. Drake." Miguel's voice came from behind me. "You, okay?"

Miguel stood quietly just outside of the van. My girls were with him.

"I'm fine, Miguel. Thanks." I looked back at the men with the rifles and sawed-off shotguns. "This is my traveling partner, Miguel." Addressing the man that I assumed was the father of the bunch, or at least the man in charge, I said, "These are my two little girls and we're headed to Georgia."

The man paused and then reached into his pocket. He removed a beaten-up picture and held it out to me. "You see this girl?"

I studied the picture carefully and shook my head. "No. I never saw her."

He grunted and put the picture away, then set his shotgun down beside him.

"You probably hungry." He looked over my shoulder. "Them little girls could probably use a home cooked meal. Why don't you follow me to my home so we can break bread together and get you rested before we send you on your way."

I looked back at Miguel and my daughters. The girls rushed to me as if they had just found out it was okay to approach their father. I could see the slight smile on Miguel's face as he started to follow the two teens towards the darkened house. As we walked, I could see faint lights coming from the edges of the windows.

"My name's Archie Penton. I own this bit of land." His voice was low and gruff, and sounded like he needed to cut back on the cigarettes. Just as I thought this, he lit up a cigarette and took a deep satisfying drag. "Boys!" he said to his two teenaged sons. "Go to the house and tell your mother that we got some visitors. They gonna need a bed with fresh sheets and some hot food. Go on now."

Two of the boys broke into a mad dash to the house. Apparently, this man ruled his household, and his sons did as they were told.

"I appreciate this Mr. Penton." I said as we followed him through the field of neatly cut grass. "Could you tell me who it was in the picture?"

"Darlene. My daughter," he said without looking at me. "She and her boyfriend took off a year ago and I've been trying to find her. We think she's on one of these plantations. We just don't know which one."

"Well, just exactly how many of them are there?"

He paused for a moment and looked up at the sky. "Let's see…there's one each in South Carolina, Florida, Alabama, Mississippi, Louisiana, and Texas." He took a deep breath. "My baby girl could be in any of 'em."

"Sir, I mean no disrespect, but what makes you think she's on one of those plantations?" I asked in a low voice. "Is there a reason?"

"Where you from? Who you kin to?"

"The Robesons from Darcy County, Georgia."

Archie paused for a moment and then looked directly at me.

"Can't says I know your family," he said gruffly. "I thought I did."

"Mr. Penton, where are we exactly?"

"You're in Sumpter County, son."

"In what state?"

"You in Alabama. What part of Georgia are you headed back to? Darcy County?"

"Yes," I muttered softly. "We went on a carriage ride at the request of my aunts. We started off at Carmichael's restaurant and wound up on a plantation. Right now, I must get back to my wife and then get my family home."

"You got to cover some distance to get to Darcy County." He looked back at the van. "You can't use that vehicle to get you to Georgia. You gonna need something else."

My heart lurched inside of my church. Was this fellow going to help us get back to Darcy County? Archie stopped suddenly and looked me directly in the face.

"Son, do you know what you're dealing with?" he asked solemnly. "It's not just the slave masters that you have to contends with. That's only half of the problem. It's them witches that you got to worry about."

"Witches?" Madison perked up.

"Why, yes, little girl. Witches." Archie squatted, putting him at eye level with her. "Do you know what they are?"

"People that do magic. Sometimes it's for good and sometimes it's not."

Archie nodded and stood up, his knees cracking in protest. "That's right."

The house was solidly built. There were columns that lined the porch and shutters on each window that looked more for show than function. As we approached, I caught a glimpse of a tractor in the back, along with an old station wagon. A cool breeze caressed the side of my face just as my heartbeat started to slow.

I heard a commotion coming from inside, but it ceased the moment we stepped through the door and into the traditionally furnished living room. Two-toned brown and beige curtains hung on the windows and I could see the light-canceling shades that had been lowered.

A little girl of six or seven ran up to me with a wide grin. "Hello," she said happily. "My name is Emma. Mommy is almost finished making some food for ya'll."

I smiled wearily at her. She was the same age as Autumn. "Hello, Emma."

She turned towards Autumn with an even wider smile. "I have some dolls in my room. Do you wanna see?"

"No." Madison placed herself between the two girls.

"Baby girl, why?" I squatted down beside her. "It's okay. Maddie. I know you've been protecting your sister all along. But for now, sweetie, we're safe. So, it's okay for Autumn to play with Mr. Archie's daughter. I promise, she'll be back by your side in a little while."

Madison paused, giving what I said some serious thought, and then she smiled. Autumn looked up at me then at her sister. When Maddie smiled and nodded her head, Emma took Autumn by the hand and guided her to what I assumed to be her bedroom.

Emma was cute. If the situation was different, I imagine she and Autumn would have been good friends.

"I'm sorry," a female voice said from the kitchen doorway. She was an attractive woman; dark-skinned, with a headful of jet-black braids cascading to the center of her back. She looked at least ten years younger than Archie.

"Where are my manners?" She entered the living room, wiping her hands on a red checkered apron. "My name's Ora. I have some supper on the stove…leftovers from dinner. I hope that's okay."

"That's more than fine, Mrs. Penton." I looked at Madison. "What do you say Maddie?"

"Thank you," she said quietly.

Ora smiled at my daughter, then looked at Miguel. "What's your name, sweetie?"

"Miguel." His tone was meek. For the life of me I couldn't understand why.

"Well, come sit at the table and I'll get you some food."

"Thank you, baby." Archie planted a gentle kiss on her cheek. "Come sit down so we can break bread with one another." He nodded for Miguel and me to follow him to the dining room and we took our seats.

Something smelled wonderful and my stomach rumbled loudly in response. In a moment, Ora appeared from the kitchen with three bowls and a large circular container that she set down in the center of the wooden dining room table.

"Give me a moment while I heat up the biscuits for you," she said, and disappeared again through the doorway that leading to the kitchen.

"Archie, what can you tell me about the plantations…especially the ones in Georgia?" I asked quietly.

"I know a few things. Like they have ceremonies once a month. Them ceremonies include sacrificing someone to appease whatever them witches worship. From what I know, every time they sacrifice someone, it increases their power, but their power is restricted to their plantation. They are strongest when they're together in one of their rooms. Most times it's to protect their homestead."

"Shit," I murmured.

"The Georgia plantation seems to be the center of where the witches are. For the most part, they don't bother nobody…just don't fuck with them."

"Archie…language." Ora placed a plate of piping hot biscuits in front of us.

"Sorry, baby." He gave her a playful swat on the behind as she walked out of the room.

"I'm Archie's brother, Lamont." He was one of the men who had originally been with Archie when they discovered us on the property.

I quickly realized he wasn't one of Archie's sons and gave him a good hard look. He looked enough like Archie. "Hello."

"Archie, tell 'em how they sacrifice folk. They need to know that."

"They dip their sacrifice in burning oil," Archie said, as if he had seen it himself. "At least that's what I heard." He paused a moment. "I got a clunker in the back." Archie's voice came out gruff. "You can take that. It should get you to Georgia." He turned his attention to his brother. "Mont, get 'em the keys, will you?"

"Sure." He rose from the table and exited the room.

"You get some sleep now. Nobody's gonna bother you here. We'll get rid of that van so nobody can trace it to you. Another thing, stay clear of the woods once you get to Georgia."

"Why?"

"Because there are things in the woods. I don't know what they are because we haven't seen 'em in these parts…but they exist."

"What kind of things, Mr. Archie?" Miguel asked.

"Things nobody wants to know about. Things you don't ever wanna see."

# Indigo

We ran for what seemed like an eternity, slowing only when we approached a densely wooded area. There was no path to guide us through the growth; we either had to go around it or through it. I watched Levi as he looked right then left trying to decide which way we should go. The mist had evaporated, and the sun was starting to peek through clouds.

"What are we doing, Levi?" I asked, looking over at Zach. He looked lost…broken. "Tarek is going to be okay, Zach. Right now, he's depending on you to send help for him so even though you're hurting right now because you had to leave him behind, you must push on. Do you understand me?"

He nodded. I don't know how much my words changed his mood. I hope they did because we were going to have to go through the woods. The growth was dense, but not so dense that we couldn't claw our way through it. I looked behind me and saw two teen-aged girls just behind Zach. They must have followed us across the plantation from the cookhouse.

"Who are you?" I demanded.

They shrank away from me as if I were a slaveholder and not someone trying to get their freedom.

"I'm sorry," I said. "I shouldn't have yelled. Girls, what do they call you?"

"Cecee and Brenda," the taller of the girls said.

I looked them over and then turned to Levi. "What do we do?"

"We got to go through them woods if we have any chance of getting off this plantation." He turned his attention to me. "Indigo, where these girls come from?"

"I think they followed us when we took off from the cookhouse."

"Well, I'ma let you handle them. As far as I'm concerned, they just babies."

"They're grown women, Levi. Capable of making their own decisions." The girls looked fragile, and yet somehow, I knew they were strong. They had to be, if they survived a life of servitude on that plantation. "Girls, you got to keep up! Falling behind is not an option because we can't stop. Okay?"

They nodded their heads in agreement, but I could tell that they were both terrified.

"Looka here!" Levi began. "We gotta go through them woods. Keep pushing the brush aside with your hands and ignore anything that may fall on you. Don't make no noise and forgodsake, keep up! We gonna have to make our own way through since no one left a path to follow!"

"Let's go." Zach spoke for the first time since we left the plantation.

We started through the woods. My mind kept spinning back to a few days ago when we had just arrived in Georgia. How different our lives would be if we had never taken that carriage ride. And whatever happened to Aunt Pearl and Aunt Macy? I couldn't allow my mind to give too much thought to what might have happened to them.

Ms. Lulu looked across the table in the Meeting Room at the rest of her coven. Seated directly across from her was Lady Onyx. She filed her long, well-manicured nails and appeared annoyed.

The walls were painted dark blue, and the room was dominated by a wooden round table. Ms. Lulu was seated at the head of the table. People were in their designated seats approximately a foot apart. Three young girls, two Black and one Hispanic, served food from enormous trays they carried. Once they were finished, Ms. Lulu looked around the room, picked up a large wooden gavel and banged it on the table.

"The First Chapter of the Coven associated with the Carmichael Brand here in Darcy County, Georgia will come to order." She looked around the room. "We have business to tend to so let's get down to it, shall we? The first item on the agenda is the recent uprising of our field hands. They tried to overtake our plantation and burn our main house to the ground. Fortunately, we were able to fend this attempt by combining our powers to create an effective barrier around the homestead. It forced the insurgents to retreat which I imagine will be temporary. We were lucky. We all were here so we could defend our home."

A slender Black woman at the far end of the table raised a white paddle.

"The house recognizes Ms. Anita." Lulu pointed at her.

"So, what happens when they attempt to overthrow us again?"

"You know the rules, Anita. We can't stray too far from the homestead. Not now! The farther we go, the weaker we get. Unless you're like some people…" She cast a gaze at Lady Onyx. "Who decide they're going to use their powers for purely selfish reasons."

"I can use my powers for whatever I want!" Onyx snapped.

Ms. Lulu banged the gavel. "The house does not recognize Henry!"

"Whatever, bitch!" Onyx placed the file down and began drumming her nails on the tabletop. "You got something you want to say to me?"

Ms. Lulu pushed her glasses up on her nose and slowly stood, the color rising high in her cheeks. "You have been a pain in my ass ever since you joined our coven stead. I have half a mind to strip you of your powers…"

"On what grounds?" Onyx leapt to her feet. "And for future reference, you will refer to me as Lady Onyx, not Henry. Now if you got something to say, bitch, then say it!"

"We're not going to accomplish anything if we keep bickering," Anita said, looking back and forth at Lulu and Onyx.

"You both been squabbling for years." An older man with dirty blond hair spoke up. "I'm in agreement with Anita. If you can't squash this petty bickering, then shut the fuck up and let the people that want to be productive have their say! Am I understood?"

Ms. Lulu looked down at the table. "Yes, Mr. Carmichael."

Lady Onyx nodded, slowly lowering herself to her seat while gently twirling her long red hair in the fingers of her left hand.

"Good!" Cal Carmichael rose to his feet. "Now, to business at hand. How many slaves did we lose?"

"At least twelve that I could count, sir," said the man named Charlie.

"And what are we doing to replenish what we lost?" He looked around the table.

"We know who the leader is and we're working on getting him captured." Charlie looked around the table as if to see if it was okay to keep going. "He was a new one that we just acquired from the carriage ride."

Cal slammed his hand on the table, shouting, "House did not recognize you, Charlie!"

A young, dark-skinned woman with short cut hair raised her paddle. Cal looked at her and smiled. "Go ahead, Macelyn."

"It seems to me that the main person responsible for the uprising of our staff is the one that should be sacrificed. Everyone else will fall in line once he is sacrificed in front of all of them. There are five escapees at large and they are headed towards the outskirts of our plantation. The good news is that they're headed for the woods. If they can get through that, they'll still hit the gator pits before they reach the electric fence. I wouldn't worry about them too much.

"If we find that we have any traitors in our midst, they will be sacrificed, and their powers will be absorbed into the fold. That is what I must present to our coven. I yield back."

"Very well." Cal's eyes came rest on Onyx. "So, are we all on the same page?"

Lady Onyx nodded her head reluctantly.

"And Lulu? Are you with us?" He asked with a slight smile.

"I never left." Lulu adjusted her glasses again, looking at Macelyn. "And Macy, thank you for your observations. I'm sure that they were made for the betterment of the house."

"Always," Macelyn responded.

"We should arrange for another carriage expedition into early Darcy County so we can begin the replenishment process," Lulu said, looking around the table.

Another member raised her paddle as Cal Carmichael settled back into his seat.

"House recognizes Pearlene."

"Thank you," Pearl began. "My sister and I brought in the latest group of people to add to our staff. We need licensed professionals to tend to them, such as a doctor. One of us, perhaps the one with the strongest powers when they are off this campus, should bring in someone that can assist our midwife. I yield back."

"That is a good idea. Are you making a recommendation for the individual that should go out and bring a doctor into the fold?"

"Getting a doctor will not be easy," Pearl continued. "I recommend that Lady Onyx go into Atlanta as long as we can elevate her skill set."

"Excellent." Lulu looked around the table. "Does anyone second the suggestion?"

Anita raised her paddle.

"House recognizes Anita?"

"I second."

"Anyone else?" Lulu asked. "Everyone that agrees with Pearl, please raise your paddle."

Everyone except for Lady Onyx raised their paddles.

"And anyone that does not agree, raise your paddles."

No one raised their paddles.

Lulu slammed the gavel on the table. "Motion granted," Lulu said with a bitter smile, casting a long gaze at Onyx. "Thank you, Anita, Pearl, and Macy. Thank you."

"And one more thing…" Cal began, "There will be no more disrespect of anyone who presents themselves as anything other than what they believe themselves to be. That means there will be no more disrespect of any witch who presents as female when they were once male. There will be no talk of anyone who was once old and is now presenting as young. And lastly, we are a coven of multiple races. Let's present as such. Meeting adjourned."

As everyone rose from the table, Ms. Lulu approached Cal Carmichael with downcast eyes. "Mr. Cal," she began cautiously, "How is your appropriations of land in this area coming?"

"Very well." His wide grin revealed teeth that would benefit from a good dental cleaning. "I just took the Robeson farm and the Blake home up the road from it. We're in good shape. By this time next year, I should be the owner of ninety percent of Darcy County."

"That is good to hear." Lulu looked across the table. "Everyone, you are dismissed."

Onyx stood, sucked her teeth, and walked out without saying a word. The room soon emptied until the only two people that remained were Cal Carmichael and Ms. Lulu.

"You have something on your mind, Lulu?" Cal reached into his shirt pocket to retrieve a packet of cigarettes.

"Yes, sir," Lulu began. "I'm a little concerned about the last few groups of people that came in by carriage."

"What are your concerns?"

"Well, Pearl and Macy brought them to us, but they are proving to be problematic, as you saw by the people that tried to burn down our home. If we weren't all here to cast the incantation of protection, who knows what they would have done to the homestead."

"Go on."

"I am recommending that some type of disciplinary action be taken against Pearl and Macy. After all, they brought the insurgents to our plantation. They should be held responsible for all the chaos that occurred here…and it's still not over."

"What did you have in mind?"

"I think that they should be stripped of their powers until our plantation is rid of all of the insurgents that wished to harm us and interrupt our way of life."

"That's kind of extreme, don't you think?"

"Maybe, but it will set an example to prevent this from ever happening again."

Cal sat down, never taking his gaze off Lulu. "Do you really think that stripping Pearl and Macy of their powers will stop the slaves from trying to create some type of revolution to gain their freedom? For as long as we have a plantation and people are forced to be here against their will, there will always be the possibility of an insurrection.

"Now, while I understand your concerns, both Pearl and Macy have brought in more people than any of the rest of you."

"But…"

"I'm not finished, Lulu." Cal cut her off. "We got ten people out of the next to the last carriage ride. It was the very last ride that brought in the insurgents. That's not Pearl or Macy's fault. And it doesn't matter that one of the insurgents is a relative of either of them. We have enough protection around our plantation to keep people from escaping. We have the Warchucks in the woods plus the gator pond. If all else fails, there's the thin electric fence that surrounds the perimeter of the campus. You want to be useful? You find and stamp out the insurgents and if I find that by this time tomorrow it hasn't been done, I'll deal with you myself. Understood?"

"Yes, sir." Lulu's voice was barely above a whisper.

"Good." Cal stood up. "You're dismissed."

# Drake

"Daddy. Daddy."

I opened my eyes to see my youngest daughter standing beside my bed. "Hey Autumn." I stifled a yawn. "Are you okay?"

"Yes." She nodded, her eyes reminding me of August.

I smelled bacon and coffee. My stomach did an involuntary rumble which made my little one laugh.

"You hungry, daddy?"

I raised myself up onto my elbows and rubbed my eyes. "Yeah, baby girl. Daddy's hungry. What are you doing up?"

"I'm ready to go see Mommy. Are we gonna see her today?"

"I hope so." I pushed myself up and out of the bed. "Where is your sister?"

"I think she's eating breakfast. Ms. Ora said to let you sleep since she thinks you need it."

I planted my feet on the floor. Autumn hugged my legs, and I reached down and rubbed her back.

"Baby girl, why don't you go have breakfast? I'll be out in a minute."

"Okay." She gave me a warm smile before walking out of the room.

I wanted to get on the road as soon as possible, but before we went anywhere, I needed to comb that girl's hair. Archie and Ora were hospitable, and if it wasn't for them, we would still be lost on the backroads of Alabama. I grabbed my pants and pulled them on, then walked out into the hallway and almost ran into Lamont.

"Sorry about that, Lamont," I said quickly.

"Oh, no worries, my friend. Ora made breakfast. She didn't want to see you leave with an empty stomach. I think she may have even packed a lunch for you and the kids."

My heart filled with gratitude. "Thank you," I said. "And not just for breakfast. Thank you for not shooting us."

Lamont chuckled.

"Thank you for everything. Well, thank you, Ora, and Archie."

"It's nothing, Drake. We do to others as we want done to us. Archie's gonna give you the station wagon out back. I checked it this morning to make sure that it was in good running order. It should get you to Georgia without a problem."

"Thanks again, my friend."

"No problem." He headed towards the dining room. "I'm gonna have my second cup of coffee."

"What time is it?"

"Eleven-thirty…somewhere around there. See you in the dining room."

When I walked into the dining room, Ora was setting a plate of pancakes in the center of the table.

"Good morning, Drake." She smiled at me. "The girls are eating, and I have a cup of coffee for you when you're ready."

"I was ready yesterday, Ms. Ora." I sat down beside Madison who was working on her second pancake. "Did you thank Ms. Ora and Mr. Archie for breakfast?"

She nodded her head enthusiastically. Someone had braided her hair. I gave her a quick peck on the cheek just as Ora placed a piping hot cup of coffee in front of me.

"Thank you."

"My pleasure." She looked across the table at Archie. "More bacon or pancakes, baby?"

Archie shook his head. "No." He looked up at her and smiled. "But I'll take some sugar."

She approached him and bent over, planting a gentle kiss on his lips and then cast a smile at her two young teenaged sons.

"Boys? You good?"

The boys nodded and thanked their mother.

"Archie, thank you for sheltering my family. I appreciate you, my friend."

He gave me a half smile. "You got these little ones to take care of. I couldn't let you stay out in the cold. That's not how we do down here." He took another sip of his coffee. "Can I see you on the back porch for a minute?"

"Sure, Archie." I looked across the table at Miguel who was finishing up his breakfast. "Miguel, you may want to come out on the porch too."

We crossed the dining room and walked through the kitchen and out the yellow-painted back door. The porch faced an enormous tree lined back yard. I took a deep breath, taking in the fresh air while listening to the cicadas chirping in unison. I noticed the wood-paneled Chevy Kingswood parked in the yard. The car looked like it could hold me, my daughters, Miguel and possibly ten more people.

"I didn't want to talk to you in front of your girls, Drake. I didn't want to scare 'em," Archie began. "Lamont took care of the car. It's clean and will get you to where you need to go. We put a map in the car since it don't have a GPS. One of my boys took it for a test drive to make sure you won't have any problems. You have a full tank of gas." He handed me a set of keys. "You should get going if you want to get to Georgia before dark."

"You think that it'll take that long to get to Georgia?"

Archie nodded. "It'll take you the better part of six hours. You want to stick to the back roads and avoid the speed traps. If you're stopped…" He handed me a piece of paper. "There's my first and last name as well as my address. Just tell the PoPo that you my nephew and you should have no problem."

"How are we going to get your car back to you?"

"Don't worry about that, Drake. Just get your girls and Miguel to somewhere safe."

"Do you have another picture of your daughter?" I asked.

"Of course, I do," he said. "Why?"

"So we can keep an eye out for her when we get to the plantation. I'll look for her. I promise."

"I believe you, brother." He reached out and patted my shoulder. "I think Ora packed a lunch for you. Just drive carefully."

"Are the police that bad?"

"Just blend in…and to do that, you gotta do the speed limit."

"I got you. I appreciate you."

He smiled wistfully and walked back into the house.

"You ready for this?" I asked Miguel.

He nodded, and then we both followed Archie inside.

# Tarek

I was in bed with Zach. I could feel the warmth of the fireplace in our bedroom…except we didn't have a fireplace in our bedroom. He looked at me lovingly with those killer eyes. We were married and I felt…safe. I wasn't sure why I felt safe since there was no immediate threat present. I wrapped my arms around him and whispered in his ear.

"I love you."

"I love you too." His hands were around my waist, and we snuggled even closer. I felt the warmth of his muscular body. I took in the scent of his hair. "I'll always be here for you." he said softly. "But now it's time to move."

"What?"

"It's time to move."

And then the room disappeared like we were in a video game, and I was left standing alone in a field of tall yellow grass. Except something was in the grass with me and I didn't know where to run. "Zach?" I called but I didn't get an answer. "Zach?"

"Wake up, Tarek."

Opening my eyes, I was startled to be in a narrow cot instead of our bedroom. And then it all came back to me: where I was, what had happened.

"Tarek, get up boy!" I looked up into Doreen's round brown face, still feeling the effects of whatever was in the pills she gave me. "What's going on?"

Loud groans came from somewhere in the room.

"Tarek, we must move you out of here. Go out the back. There's a wagon out there that will take you to someplace safe."

"Wagon?"

"You don't think that the overseers would trust us with a motor vehicle, do you?"

I shook my head and instantly regretted it. My head was spinning. The room smelled like a bad combination of blood and alcohol. As I sat up in the bed and looked around, I could see why.

"Hurry Tarek!" Doreen turned to the man in the bed beside mine. I imagined she was telling him the same thing.

I stood on unsteady legs. The drugs made the room weirdly hazy. I really needed to sleep them off but there was no time. I stumbled across the room and out the back door. Sure enough, there was an old-fashioned wagon pulled by two horses. Latrice and Kisha were already inside, Kisha's head nestled on Latrice's lap. Latrice gave me a slight smile as I painfully climbed into the wagon.

"Where are we going?" I whispered to her.

"To a cabin to the south of the plantation to keep us out of harm's way when they attack the house again."

"Who is 'they'?"

"Shucky and them."

A young Black man climbed onto the seat of the carriage. Without saying a word, he lashed the horses and the wagon lurched forward. The horse's hooves clopped against the dirt and the wagon pitched slightly from left to right.

So Uncle Shucky was the leader of the attack on the house. I closed my eyes and prayed that he would be kept safe as well as victorious. I prayed that Zach and my sister would be okay. I prayed that my nieces would be kept safe until one of us found them. I prayed that Drake was okay. And I prayed for Lady Onyx.

Between the horse's rhythmic stride and the remainder of the painkiller that Doreen had given me, I fell into a light sleep and awakened later to my cousin shaking me.

"Wha…what?" I stretched; my back didn't like that movement.

"We're here." Latrice turned to aid her girlfriend. "We have to get in the cabin and lay low."

I climbed down out of the carriage. My back was starting to throb, and I thought it might be bleeding again. I was scared…but I was more afraid for Zach than myself. I hoped that he didn't have to go anywhere near the gator pits that we saw on the carriage ride into this godforsaken place.

My feet crunched on the gravel as I walked to the cabin. Latrice had both arms around Kisha's waist as they walked through the open door. I watched them go in and remained outside for a moment, watching the tall trees sway in the breeze.

# PLANTATION

My mind was still reeling over the fact that we were in the middle of a coven of witches on top of being involuntarily enslaved. I had to get back to a bed soon. Hopefully, there was one inside of the cabin. I thought of Zach once again and my heart ached. His face was etched in my mind and my heart. I hated not knowing where he was, if he was okay or if he needed me. I couldn't allow my mind to go there.

I entered the cabin and saw to my dismay that there were no beds anywhere. We would have to make ourselves comfortable on the floor. I watched as Latrice lowered Kisha to the ground.

"That bastard." Kisha said in a voice so small I almost didn't hear her.

"I know baby." Latrice sat down beside her.

"He took something from me, Latrice. I gotta get it back."

"I just want you to get better."

"I'll be better when he's six feet under!"

"Kisha, be careful. Keep it low. The walls have ears."

"I don't give a fuck!" Kisha snapped. "I won't be right until that mutherfucka's dead and gone!"

"And how do you propose to do that? You gotta focus your energies on healing and not revenge."

"Actually, we need to focus on getting off this plantation." I eased myself into their conversation. "We can always get back at them, but we have to survive this first."

Kisha fell silent. I could almost see the steam coming off the top of her head. Latrice cast a helpless gaze at me.

It was cool inside the cabin. Goosebumps rose on my arms.

Two young Black men burst in, causing a small yelp of surprise to escape from Latrice. I looked at them as they closed the door behind them.

"Sorry to scare you," one of them said, taking gulps of air.

"What's going on out there?" I asked.

"We couldn't get to the main house, so we're re-grouping and going for their crops. We're going to set 'em on fire. We'll burn this bitch down to the ground if it means that we'll get off this piece!"

"What are you burning?"

"Everything!" the second man exclaimed.

I looked at the darker of the two men exclaimed. He looked to be in his early thirties, at least ten or fifteen years younger than me.

"They're going to try to take the house again, but we gonna take their cars, trucks and ATVs."

"And how do you fight witches? Isn't that why you couldn't burn down the main house?" I asked.

"Witches?" Latrice's eyes widened.

Kisha looked at me in disbelief.

"That's why they couldn't burn down the house. Lady Onyx, Ms. Lulu…they're witches."

"You've got to be kidding me." Latrice looked as if she were trying to process what I was saying.

"I wish I were."

"They can't be everywhere at one time," the first man said as he fingered a small silver cross around his neck. "We can take the house when they try to put the fires out on their cars and shit."

"Well, every entity has to have a weakness." I wasn't sure if these men knew what they were up against.

"You right about that!" the second man said. "You right and we'll get 'em…even if I have to die to make it happen!"

# Indigo

It was cold inside the woods. We pulled and tugged at the vines, trying to clear a path, but it was hard without a machete. As a result, our progress was tediously slow. Levi struggled to pull down as many vines with his bare hands as he could. Zach was struggling, too; I could see it in his face. Most of it had to do with Tarek, but there was nothing that I could do about that.

My cell phone rang, and I reached into my skirt pocket and picked it up quickly before the call could be disconnected. "Hello! Hello!"

"Ms. Robeson? Ms. Robeson!" I heard Lucille Benton's soothing voice. "I've been trying to reach you for over twenty-four hours. Are you okay? It's not like you to…"

"Lucille, listen to me!"

Everyone stopped moving.

"I need you to call…hello? Hello? Are you there?"

"Ms. Rob…" The line went dead.

Of course, the call would drop. I was surprised that it had come through at all while we were in the woods in the middle of nowhere.

"I didn't know you had a phone, Indigo," Levi said as he took several deep breaths. He was winded from pulling at the vines.

"I didn't want anyone to know." I couldn't seem to bring his face into focus. The woods made it seem like dusk as opposed to midday. It was difficult for me to make out the details of everyone's faces around me.

"Shh!" Brenda put her index finger against her lips. "Be quiet!"

"What…why?" I asked.

"Just listen." Her eyes were as big as saucers.

We all stood perfectly still. I didn't know what we were listening for. And then I heard it. It was a low, distinctive clicking sound. I don't know how Brenda heard it over my brief phone call with Ms. Benton and my conversation with Levi.

"I think we needs to go back," Brenda said in a small voice.

"What?" Levi raised his voice. "Bitch, are you out your mind?"

I gave Levi a sharp, disapproving look.

"Take it down a notch, Levi!" His tone annoyed me. But more importantly, I wanted to know what was upsetting Brenda since she probably knew more about these woods than me.

"We need to go back!" she repeated, turning to head in the direction we just came from.

The clicking got louder, and suddenly, I didn't feel safe. A shiver ran up my spine and I turned to Zach. "I think we need to find another way off this plantation."

"Isn't this the only way to get off?" he asked. I could tell that he was just as unnerved as I was.

"This is ridiculous!" Levi shouted. "Let's keep moving! We're wasting time!"

"Let's go back!" Cecee turned and ran in the direction that we had come. Brenda followed behind her.

Zach and I turned and went after them. The clicking noise got louder. As we ran, I caught a glimpse of something shadowy in the bushes to my right.

We were running at a full gallop when something snatched Cecee. Even though she was in front of me, I didn't see who or what it was. It happened so quickly she didn't even have a chance to scream.

A low growl came from our left. Brenda screamed and tore off down the path we had just made.

"What the fuck was that?" Levi yelled, coming up behind me.

Something was in the woods…something deadly. We heard Cecee's blood-curdling screams finally. We heard Cecee's screams followed by grunts and the tearing of flesh. And then the screams turned into gurgling, wrestling and then dead silence. We continued our mad dash to get out of these woods. Zach was in front of me when something reached out, lightning-fast, grabbing and tearing at his arm. He screamed, stumbling over his feet, almost losing his footing and I shoved him so he could fall flat rather than into whatever was in the trees. I stopped running long enough to help him to his feet.

"Get the fuck off me!" Levi screamed from behind us.

I turned to see him swinging at something, but I couldn't make out what it was, only that it was a dark blur of a human form with mold on its arms, as if it had been submerged in water for a long period of time. And then it was gone.

Fear, icy and cold, gave wings to my feet. I was convinced that if we didn't get out of the woods, whatever was in there would kill us.

Levi screamed again. It was a guttural cry, and I was certain that whatever was in these woods was now attacking him.

"Levi…" I could see the terror in his eyes as he continued to run, almost tripping over me.

"Girl, keep running."

Once we hit the clearing, we continued to run for several feet before stopping to catch our breath. Whatever was in the woods stopped at the edge of the woods. I could still hear the clicking but it was growing fainter.

"What the fuck was that?" Levi demanded.

"We got to go back!" Brenda took deep gulps of air, looking terrified.

"Answer me!" Levi said. "What the hell was that?"

Blood flowed down his left arm. When he turned to look over his shoulder at the woods, I could see deep gashes in his back. Whatever had attacked him had claws.

"They the Warchucks." Brenda looked with caution at the trees. "I wasn't sure if they was real. I sees they are."

"But what are they?"

"It's rumored that the people that run the big house took a of people they had no more use for and put them in the woods. I don't know how they survived all this time. I heard that they survived offa the scraps from the big house." She took in another gulp of air. "I thought it was just a rumor…but it's real!"

"Levi, we need to stop the bleeding," I said to him.

He looked like he might need stitches, but only on his arm.

"I'm okay." Blood had dripped onto his pants leg in a steady stream. "We got to figure out another way to get off this plantation. Now let me think."

I cast a cautious glance back at the woods.

"Why don't you try your phone again?" Zach said as his breathing became normal.

I reached into my skirt pocket and pulled out my phone, dialing Lucille's number. I received the message that the number that I dialed could not be reached and to try my call again later.

"We better try to get around these woods." Levi looked around the clearing we were standing in. "We best keep moving."

"Levi, your arm." I was becoming concerned about his loss of blood.

"What do you suggest I do?" he snapped at me. "There ain't no hospital around here."

"Take off your shirt and let me tear off a piece so that we can stop the bleeding, otherwise you won't be good to none of us!"

That seemed to resonate with him and he took off his shirt. I gave his chiseled body a quick once over before taking the shirt from him and quickly tearing off two strips of cloth. I wrapped his arm as best as I could. Satisfied that I had stopped the bleeding, I searched his face for what would pass for gratitude.

He gave me a slight smile. "Thank you, Indigo."

"So which way do we go?" Zach asked.

"We follow the edge of the woods until we get to another clearing." Levi looked around us. "We don't have much time. Let's go!"

We started north in the hopes that the woods would break into another clearing. It was a long shot…but what other choices did we have?

None at all.

# Drake

For the most part, we drove in silence. I gripped the steering wheel tightly as we drove past a blur of pine trees. Ora had packed a generous lunch, more for the girls than for Miguel and me, and they munched on ham and cheese sandwiches and crackers in the back seat.

We had been on the road for three hours and so far no one stopped us. When I found Darcy County, I could go to the police and get some help in getting August off that plantation. Assuming that she was still there. I couldn't allow my mind to think that she wasn't.

According to the map, the road that we were on would take us to the Georgia border. Once we got to Georgia, we would make our way to 95 South, which would take us to the closest exit that led to Darcy County. From there, I was hoping that I could get some help. A part of me hoped the police would stop me once we got to Georgia. I thought that the likelihood of the Alabama police aiding me would be slim to none. The thought that I would be considered a runaway slave never entered my mind.

I continued on the two-lane highway, driving as quickly as I could. I kept my eyes squarely on the speedometer, starting to get anxious. I was doing sixty. I would have to bump it up to sixty-five so I would not look suspicious.

And then my head filled with thoughts of August. I kept thinking of when we met. I thought about the birth of our first child. I smiled to myself as I thought of how happy we were at that time.

I was worried about her. I couldn't let my girls see the concern in my face. My goal was to find my wife, hopefully safe, sound and in her right mind.

I prayed silently that she was okay, bargaining with God that He would return her to me.

"Daddy?" It was Madison.

"Yeah, Maddie?"

"Can we stop? Autumn has to go."

I nodded my head. "I'll stop at the next rest stop. Can you hold it until then?" I looked in the rear-view mirror at my girls in the spacious back seat.

Autumn nodded.

We drove on until we came to a strip of restaurants. I wheeled the monstrous station wagon into the parking lot of a Cracker Barrel, parking towards the rear of the building. I got out of the car and stretched, and then I saw something that made my blood run cold. A police cruiser had pulled into a spot two car lengths away from us.

I grabbed Autumn's hand and walked with Miguel in front of me and Madison to my right. The white police officer inside the cruiser didn't seem to notice us. I held onto my daughter's hand, trying to look inconspicuous. We entered the restaurant, bypassing racks of memorabilia to remind us that we visited Geme County, Alabama. I turned to Madison.

"Take your sister to the bathroom and be quick." I gave her a smile. "Can you do that for me, princess?"

Madison nodded, guiding her sister to the bathroom at the same time the police officer entered the store. Our gazes didn't meet.

I looked over at Miguel. He gave me a cautious glance. I motioned for him to go out to the car. Miguel promptly left the store and I waited for the girls to come out of the bathroom. It looked like the cop was stopping in for something to eat, at least that's what I hoped. And then another police officer entered the restaurant.

Ice cold sweat trickled down the small of my back. All the sudden, I wanted to be out of there and back on the road. I licked my lips and I pretended to peruse the sweatshirts which decorated a quarter of the store.

An older, gray-haired woman behind the counter watched me suspiciously. Great! I was on her radar. I didn't need any attention from anyone.

I looked at the entrance to the restrooms hoping my daughters would appear so we could get going. I looked back at the counter and saw that the woman was suddenly gone. That unnerved me even more.

Madison and Autumn appeared, and I breathed a sigh of relief. I looked down at my youngest. "Feel better?"

She nodded enthusiastically.

"Okay. Let's go out to the car. Miguel is waiting for us."

"Excuse me, sir?"

I looked around. It was the woman from the counter. She was looking at me through pale blue eyes with that same air of suspicion.

"Yes, ma'am?" I smiled and looked down at my girls. "Go on out to the car. I'll be right out."

"Do you have any merchandise that I can help you with?" she asked politely.

I gave her a disarming smile as one of the police officers made his way to where we were standing. And now he was watching us.

"No, ma'am." I shook my head. "My daughters had to use the rest room. They're all finished now so we'll just be on our way."

She gave me a cautionary smile as I started towards the door. All the while, the police officer continued to stare. Suddenly, the air inside the Cracker Barrel became stagnant. I needed to be in the parking lot taking in fresh air and getting on the road to get my daughters and Miguel to a safe place.

"Okay." She didn't sound convinced. "Thank you for stopping in to see us."

"Pleasure was all mine, ma'am." I headed for the door.

Once I hit the parking lot, it took everything in me not to run to the car. I walked at a slow, even pace. When I was inside the vehicle, I turned the ignition and put the car in reverse, driving out of the parking lot and heading east. My mind was reeling. How close had we come to being caught? In that moment, I had an idea of what a runaway slave felt when they were executing their escape. You constantly second-guessed yourself. Every decision was full of dread because you were afraid of making the wrong choice. Every time you stopped; it posed a different type of threat. You were always looking over your shoulder to make sure you weren't being followed. It was horrible. And yet, this was my life…for now.

My mind was on one thing: getting to my wife and getting my family away from that godforsaken plantation.

It was full dark by the time we pulled into the driveway of Aunt Pearl's home. I couldn't remember how to get to our rented condominium, and even if I did, I no longer had identification to prove I was Drake Robeson. My priority was to find shelter and a place where my girls could get some rest.

They were sound asleep in the back seat when I checked last. Miguel was seated awake and silent as I opened the driver's side door and stepped to the ground. Crickets chirped softly. I motioned to Miguel to stay where he was, mouthing that I was going to check out the house. If necessary, I would break in, hoping that Aunt Pearl didn't have an alarm system or if she did, that it wasn't turned on. I didn't know how I would explain to the police that I wasn't some random squatter who just happened to be on property that didn't belong to him.

I walked up the narrow driveway to Aunt Pearl's single family, three-bedroom home. She had neighbors on either side of her, but no one appeared to be there.

I crept around the back, very much aware of the silence around me. A dog barked incessantly in the distance as I approached her back door. I tried the handle to find it securely locked. I walked around the opposite side of the house where the bedrooms were. I tried the first window, and it slid open with ease. Hoisting myself onto the sill, I entered the house headfirst, landing on the floor of what I knew was Aunt Pearl's guest bedroom. I walked through the darkened house and opened the front door, bounding down the three concrete porch steps and approaching the car just as Miguel appeared from the passenger seat.

"Everything okay, Mr. Drake?" he asked.

I nodded, reaching into the back seat to retrieve my sleeping little girl. She instinctively wrapped her arms around my neck as I lifted her up and carried her inside. Miguel and Madison followed behind me.

"Daddy, is this Aunt Pearl's house?" Madison asked as I flicked on the dining room light.

"Yes, baby it is." I headed towards the kitchen. "You hungry? Miguel, you hungry? I'm going to check to see if there are any leftovers from dinner the other night."

"No. Can I watch some TV?" Madison approached the small, flat screened television that sat on a stand in the living room.

"Sure." I nodded. "Miguel, take the next room to the right. I'll look for some linens and put them on the bed so you can change."

"Thank you." He smiled and sat down on the sofa.

"So, what are your plans, Miguel?" I asked. "I mean, you wanted off the plantation and you're off it. So, what now?"

"Honestly, I don't know. I'll figure it out."

"Well, take tonight and think about it. Get some rest. If I can help you, I will."

"I know." He gave me a weak smile as I made my way to the kitchen.

After rummaging in the refrigerator, I managed to pull out some roast beef, turkey and macaroni and cheese. That should be enough for a quick meal.

My next thought was who I could trust to leave my girls with while I make my way to the plantation to get my wife. I couldn't take them back to the plantation...not after everything that we'd gone through to get off the one in Alabama. I'm sure that we had other relatives in the area, but none who I knew personally. There was always the possibility of leaving them with Miguel except I didn't know him that well despite the fact that he took a beating for me in Alabama; or at least he wasn't someone I knew well enough to trust with the lives of my little girls.

What was I going to do?

# Indigo

Levi had managed to build a small fire and we were huddled in a ball, trying to keep warm. I was still cold. Zach had shut down and wasn't saying much of anything, while Brenda was silent, watching the fire. We were on the outskirts of the plantation, far enough from the woods that we felt safe, but we knew that we were still on the property and therefore, still in mortal danger. We found a small grove of trees that seemed suitable for us to set up camp for the night.

We would search for a way to get off the plantation in the morning, but what we needed now more than anything was rest. I would have given anything to find a remote cabin so that we had shelter, but this would have to do. Levi would keep watch for anything should it decide to venture out from the woods.

I had no idea what those things were that had snatched Cecee. I couldn't get her screams out of my head…the sound being primal and guttural.

I pulled out my cell phone and pressed 911, hoping to get a response but all I got was the message that my call could not be completed. I folded the phone and put it away.

What were those things in the woods, anyway? Would they be bold enough to creep out of the woods to hunt us down? And were the slaveholders trying to hunt us too? There were too many entities that wanted us. I couldn't be sure if we were safe in this little grove of trees; they were hardly enough to shield us from anyone or anything that wanted to hunt us down.

And then my mind turned towards my little nieces. Where were they? Were they okay? Were they even alive? I couldn't bear to think of any outcome for them. And what about August? She must be losing her mind. I needed rest but I couldn't bring myself to close my eyes. And yet, somehow, I dozed.

# PLANTATION

Inside the big house, Onyx sat on the edge of the queen-sized bed in her room. She was alone and she didn't want to be. She felt isolated. What was happening here was wrong. She had initially joined the coven to become the woman she knew she always was. She understood who Cal Carmichael was and what he was trying to do. The coven was also aware of his wanting to purchase as much of Darcy County as he could, therefore enabling him to do whatever he wanted, which included subjugating unsuspecting people into slavery to serve the "New South."

When the coven was together, their powers were at their greatest; she knew that. If even one of them were not present, it weakened their strength. Plantations had been popping up in Florida, South Carolina, Louisiana, Texas, Georgia, and Alabama. There may have been more. Onyx wasn't sure. She knew they had been enslaving people for years, and for years it had never bothered her. But this last batch of people included children…children too young to be subjugated into slavery. She knew that children had been brought into slavery in the past and she knew that some of the rapes resulted in children born into servitude. Yet there was something about Madison and Autumn that played heavily on her heart. She had cast a spell of protection over the little girls who had come in the next to the last carriage ride. Her spell would help them if she stayed near or on this plantation.

She didn't understand why her powers were at their greatest when she was on the plantation. She should be able to use them wherever she wanted, and her strength should not be based on how close she was to this plantation, but those were the rules. Those rules didn't apply to everyone. Macy and Pearl had powers that extended well beyond the borders of the plantation. After all, they had seniority, but even with that seniority came certain limitations. In some ways it didn't matter that they had been part of this coven since the seventies.

Macy had turned her old, decrepit body into one that was younger and perhaps more vibrant than she had been when she was in her forties. Pearl had brought her own family in to sacrifice them to keep her powers high and permanent.

That was how the coven worked. Whoever brought in the most to be sacrificed or enslaved would reap the biggest reward. This would explain why her powers were minimal in comparison to Ms. Lulu's.

Lulu was the head of the coven and by unwritten rules, her powers were far greater. Onyx could go to battle with her, and she'd lose. That's how it was. But she no longer wanted to be part of this coven if it meant enslaving children. She just wanted to keep enough of her powers so she could change into Lady Onyx whenever she wanted. She did not want to have surgery to become a woman; she wanted the ability to change into the woman she envisioned herself as being. If her powers were strong enough, she could conjure up a following.

The enslavement had to be stopped, but Onyx needed the aid of others in the coven, and she didn't know who she could enlist to help. Several people had managed to escape over the years, but she wasn't sure where. She needed to leave the plantation. If she were gone, their ability to protect the main house would never be complete. They needed all the witches' powers to conjure up the spell of protection for the house. And it was clear to her that she had no desire to help them anymore.

She heard a commotion outside. Onyx approached the window and peered out carefully from behind a drawn curtain to see several male slaves running around the campus lighting the ATVs and other vehicles on fire. She took a step back. They would be summoning all the witches to protect the house. Now was her chance to escape. The slaves had created a diversion.

She crossed the room, cracked open the bedroom door and listened.

Nothing.

She opened the door all the way and slipped out into the hall. If she could make it to the side door, she could make her escape. She would have to do it as Henry.

She may have been able to escape while it was still dark outside, and if she made her escape, there was a chance she could keep her powers. It was a slim chance, but a chance all the same. Onyx crept down the stairway knowing that she would have to turn a corner and head towards the dining area before she could get to the outside door. She moved quietly down the stairs as the noise outside got louder and louder.

The insurrection must have been in full effect because she could clearly hear men shouting orders. It looked like they were lighting all the vehicles on fire. A small voice inside of her head started as a whisper and slowly began to increase in intensity, much like the beginnings of a regular headache.

"Get up to the Gathering Room on the third floor. We need you."
Onyx shook her head.

"Nope," she said to herself. "Not gonna happen."

She closed her eyes, muttered some barely audible words and a blue-gray cloud began to form at her feet, swirling slowly around her legs, encircling her torso and finally made its way around her shoulders and totally enshrouded her head. When the cloud dissipated, she was Henry again. In that moment, he raced down the hallway and darted out the house's side door.

The scene that greeted him was one of complete chaos as men with flaming torches raced across the campus lighting every car, ATV, and cart on fire.

Henry broke into a mad dash as he rushed across the campus to the garage where most of the ATVs were kept. If he could get to one, there was a chance that he could get off the plantation by taking the same route that the carriages came in on. Only the witches and the slaveholders knew where this route was.

He reached the garage and found that the uprising had not reached this building. Running to the closest ATV, he jumped on the seat and started the engine. It revved to life. He exhaled in relief. He put the ATV's gear into drive and the vehicle lurched forward into the dark Georgia night.

## Tarek

When I heard the first stirrings of the chaos that was going on towards the main house, I stood up. Kisha followed, raising herself slowly to her feet. Latrice did the same. All of us heard what was happening outside and we didn't feel comfortable with it. It was time for us to move. We had to get off this plantation by any means necessary. Even though my back hurt me tremendously, I knew that we had to go. But where could we run to? And could we send back help for August and Aunt Merline?

One thing was certain…we couldn't send back anyone if we were still here. "We have to get out of this place." I said as the noise outside got louder.

People yelling. There was a lot of profanity. At one point I thought I heard Uncle Shucky's voice. And then I heard gunfire.

"Where will we go, Tarek?" Latrice asked, "Do you even know?"

"I know that we can't stay here."

"You hear about what they did to some girl named Darlene?" I could see the terror on Latrice's face. "She was electrocuted. They got this entire compound surrounded by an electric fence."

"Do you have a better idea?" I was starting to get annoyed. "Because if you do, I want to hear it."

"It's not about getting out of this cabin; it's about knowing where you're going so that you can get off this plantation safely. None of us can afford to get hurt and we still gotta send back help for our people."

An explosion sounded in the distance. I didn't know what it was. I looked at my cousin.

"Let's go, Latrice. We can't stay here. We gotta go." I crossed the room with Latrice and Kisha close behind me. We pushed open the wooden door and ventured out hoping for the best but prepared for the worst.

Most of the chaotic activity was centered around the main house. I couldn't see if the insurgents had breached the house or not, but I could plainly see men trying to light the house on fire with torches. Others were lighting the cars and some of the ATVs on fire with mini explosives.

I had to give Shucky credit. If he was leading this insurrection, he was doing a good job. He had successfully rallied many of the enslaved men as insurgents. I could hear screaming, yelling and explosions. Latrice grabbed my right arm as we looked around, not sure where to go.

"This way!" I shouted, starting towards a part of the plantation that wasn't riddled with activity.

"Someone's coming!" Kisha yelled.

Shit! I didn't even have anything that I could use as a weapon. I wasn't sure what to do. There was no place we could run that would provide us with some shelter. We watched as the ATV approached us and slowed, coming to a full stop.

Henry yelled at us from the vehicle. "Hey ya'll! Tarek! That you?"

"Henry!" I was grateful that it was him. "What's going on?"

"World war three! Where're you headed?"

"Trying to make it off this plantation."

"I can take one of ya'll! I'm getting off this plantation right now!"

I looked at Kisha and Latrice.

"One of ya'll got to get off this plantation and send back help for the rest of us."

"How do we know this muthafucka ain't gonna turn us in?" Kisha asked, suspicion clear in her voice.

"Kisha, this is Lady Onyx," I said. "I'll explain later. One of you has got to get on the back of this bike and send some help back when you reach civilization."

"Latrice, you go!" Kisha said evenly. "Go!"

"Kisha, I can't leave you like this."

"Go and send some help. I'll stay with Tarek! I won't leave his side."

Latrice looked at me helplessly as if she expected me to talk Kisha out of her suggestion. I wouldn't participate. One of them had to get on this cycle and get out of here.

"Tricee, get on the bike!" I shouted. That seemed to do it. She climbed onto the back of the ATV reluctantly.

"Send back help, Tricee!" Kisha shouted as the ATV roared into life and took off.

"We got to get to the south end of the plantation!" I said, grabbing Kisha's hand. "Let's go! God only knows what the other witches are planning!"

I had no idea if I were wrong or right…but it got us moving.

Lulu paced back and forth, casting an occasional glare at the witches who remained in the Meeting Room. She did not have on her server uniform; instead, she was dressed in a dark, snug-fitting pants suit. Everyone sitting around the circular table was quiet, waiting for Lulu to say something.

"Where the hell is Henry?" she demanded, saying this more to herself than anyone else.

"We can't continue to hold off the uprising," Pearl said. "They're going to breach the house any minute now.

"Unless we cast a different spell," Macy suggested. "We can block all the windows and doors."

"Yes, but that will only give us ninety percent protection…" Lulu began.

"Which is better than no protection at all," Macy clapped back. "We'll deal with Henry when we find him. Let's assume that he's not coming. Have you looked outside?"

"I have!" Lulu snarled. "Why do you think I'm pissed that he ain't here? He knows that the house comes first."

"Well, it seems like he doesn't." Pearl waved her hand in a circular motion in front of her. "But I can find him."

The circle grew bright, reflecting Pearl's image, and then it became a window. She looked through the opening and saw Henry riding an ATV with a young, medium-skinned woman on the back.

"Looks like Henry's heading off the plantation." Pearl squinted to see if she could make out who the woman was. "He's still here but looks like he's hitting the trail where the carriages come in at." Pearl looked at Lulu. "Do you want to cast a spell to stop him?"

"No." Lulu shook her head. "Let's focus our efforts on defending the homestead. The gators will get him and whoever is on the back of the ATV."

The sound of glass breaking made them all whirl around.

"I'll check that out and put a stop to it." Anita leapt to her feet and rushed out of the room.

"Okay!" Lulu said, after Anita had left. "Cast the spell of protection." She took a deep breath and closed her eyes. "Spirits of darkness. Spirits of our coven. Protect our home. Spirits of darkness. Spirits of our coven. We command thee to protect our home from those that wish to do us harm."

Everyone began repeating Lulu's words. Each time they repeated the incantation, their voices grew louder until a dull glow appeared in the room, surrounding everyone.

"That should hold them off for a while," Lulu said with a little satisfaction in her voice. She looked directly at Pearl. "You feel up to handling our missing 'Henry' problem?"

Pearl smiled and rose to her feet. "I'd love to. I'll be back."

"Don't be too long," Lulu said. "I don't know how long this spell will hold up since we're only at eighty percent."

"Okay."

"Pearl, before you go, I have a question to ask you."

She paused in the doorway. "What is it?"

"How is it you were able to sacrifice your own family?" Lulu asked. "What was your mindset?"

Pearl turned slowly to face her. "It was easy," she said. "We needed to sacrifice someone to keep our powers. What better way to do it than to use people I haven't seen in a long time who try to call themselves family?"

"But family? Not that I care one way or the other, but your own family? With children?"

"What do you care who I sacrifice if it keeps the coven strong? I'll do whatever it takes."

"I see," Lulu murmured to herself.

"Does that answer your question?" Pearl asked coldly.

Lulu nodded. "Yes. Yes, it does."

# Drake

I woke up to a quiet, silent house. The girls and Miguel were still asleep. I don't know how long I slept, but it was time for me to get up and make breakfast for my daughters.

I swung my legs over the side of Pearl's queen-sized bed, stood up and stretched. I padded into the kitchen to see what I could rummage up for breakfast.

I found bacon and eggs and there was a container of grits in the pantry. This was enough to get us started. There was also some ham, cheese and bread which would make excellent sandwiches for the girls later in the day.

But what was I going to do with them once we ate? I couldn't take them with me. I couldn't risk subjecting them to the plantation…not after everything we went through to get away. Running the risk of them getting re-enslaved was not an option.

I looked around the kitchen and found coffee beans along with a grinder. At least Miguel and I could have a fresh cup of coffee. And speaking of Miguel, what was I going to do with him? I owed him my life. Had he not come along with the van, we might all still be enslaved.

In a few minutes, the aromas of bacon and fresh coffee filled the air. My oldest appeared from the room where Latrice used to sleep. She was yawning and rubbing the sleep out of her eyes.

"Hey, baby girl." I perked up. "How did you sleep?"

"Good. Is that breakfast for us?" Maddie asked.

I nodded with a smile. "I couldn't have my princesses start the day on an empty stomach."

"Are we going to get Mommy and then go home?"

I looked at her innocent little face. I didn't want to lie to her. I couldn't.

"I need to get you to a safe spot before I go get her. Then we'll all be going home."

She smiled, warming my heart. I took a few steps to her and then squatted just enough that I would be eye level with her. I formed my hands into the shape of a heart. "Love. Forever," I said softly.

She repeated my actions. "Love forever, daddy."

I gave her a quick hug then stood slowly. "Go get washed up and then wake your sister."

"What about Mr. Miguel?"

"I'm right here, honey," he said from the kitchen doorway.

"How long have you been up?" I asked.

"I smelled the coffee. I haven't smelled fresh coffee in a long time." He paused for a moment. "Well, not since we were at Miss Ora's house yesterday."

I removed the last pieces of bacon from the pan and placed them on a strip of paper towels to absorb the grease. "You hungry?" I asked.

"Starving, Mr. Drake."

"Go fix yourself a plate. Grab some coffee. Then we gotta talk."

"Okay." He began to put some eggs and bacon on a plate I had already taken out of the cupboard. I popped two pieces of rye bread into the toaster and crossed the small room to the fridge and pulled out a stick of butter.

My girls were pattering around the house…a clear sign they hadn't gone back to bed. What was I going to do about clothes for them? The only thing they had were those dirty floor-length dresses that were designed for someone in total servitude. Maybe Latrice had a couple of oversized tee shirts in her drawers.

"Mr. Drake, how are you going to get your wife off the plantation? Do you even know where you're going?"

"I'm going in the same way that my family went in a few days ago, only I'm going with heat."

"Heat?"

"The police."

Miguel went silent. After a moment, he spoke. His voice came out slow and quiet. "I can't go with you when you get the police."

"Why not?"

"I'm not here legally."

I thought for a moment and came up with the only viable solution. "Stay here, then." I was trying to be practical. "Stay here until we come back. I'll take the girls with me. You have food here. There's television…a warm bed, a shower. Stay here until I get back."

"I guess I can do that."

"You don't have a choice, my friend. But I owe you so much, Miguel. You kept me and my girls safe. God bless you for that."

"Every day, Mr. Drake."

I drove to Edison County with my girls in the back seat of the enormous station wagon. I didn't trust the police in Darcy County. I had no idea how much land Carmichael owned in the county. After all, if he had purchased our land, how many other pieces of property had he managed to get his hands on?

The day was sunny and beautiful, more suitable for a leisurely drive than the mission I found myself on. I was becoming anxious. I needed to find my wife and get our family out of Georgia, and I would do it by any means necessary.

It was a short drive to the police station and although I hated to do it, I intended to leave my daughters with the police while we drove back to Darcy County to retrieve my wife.

No one believed me…at first.

But then, miraculously, Sheriff Caroline Cuomo did. She was a fresh-faced, pretty woman with dirty-blonde hair pulled back into a tight ponytail. She listened patiently while the other officers were dismissive. It was something that I expected, but I was grateful that she listened and believed what I was saying. I told the tale of taking a carriage ride and winding up in pre-Civil War Darcy County, being enslaved and then separated from my family. I explained how I found my daughters and managed to escape from the plantation in Alabama. Now, all I wanted was to go back and free my wife from enslavement.

While I drove with them to Carmichael's Restaurant, I explained to the sheriff what my thoughts were as well as the facts of what happened. She listened, asked the right questions, and then fell into silence as we approached the restaurant. An officer sat in the passenger seat in full dark blue uniform while Sheriff Cuomo was in a tan uniform with a pistol holstered under her left arm pit.

My heartbeat quickened as we got out of the police cruiser and approached the front door of Carmichael's Restaurant. People were buzzing around inside the restaurant. I looked for a familiar face and my eyes fell on Ms. Lulu. She had on her waitress uniform again, only this time, she wore white crepe shoes, shoes sensible for someone who was on their feet all day. The sheriff approached her, motioning for me to stay back. I watched as they talked to one another in hushed tones.

Those few minutes felt like hours to me. All I wanted was to hold my wife in my arms again. God only knows what had happened to her once we were separated.

"Mr. Robeson," Sheriff Cuomo began as she approached me. "We're going for a ride."

"A ride?" I wasn't sure what she meant.

"Yes." She nodded as some of the patrons began to look at her. "We're taking a carriage ride into 1800s Darcy County."

# Indigo

We all seemed to wake up at the same time to stiff joints and aching bodies. The fire had died down sometime during the night. We were covered with a thin layer of dew and now we were all cold and shivering. As we got up, the sky turned robin's egg blue. I looked in the direction that we had fled yesterday expecting to see clouds billowing in the soft, late summer breeze. There wasn't a cloud in the sky. Maybe the uprising Shucky planned didn't work. There was simply no way of knowing for sure.

I checked on Levi. He looked tired. I imagine that he stayed up most if not all night watching over us to make sure we had no unexpected visitors while we slept. But we were determined to get off the plantation. None of us could forget what we saw yesterday…or what we thought we saw.

"Let's go," Levi said wearily. "We got a lot of ground to cover."

"How do you know?" Brenda snapped.

"What?"

"How do you know exactly how much ground to cover? Do you even knows where we going?"

"I know what we need to get away from! And unless you got a better idea, let's get going!"

"But if those things are in the woods, that means they exist. And if so, are we headed for the gator pits?"

"You got a choice, little girl! You can stick with us, or you can venture out on your own. How do you want it?"

Brenda closed her mouth. We all looked at one another. Even though we had just awakened, we were all tired of running. We were cold and hungry. But as we started walking, I wondered if Levi really knew where we were going or if he was just accustomed to being in charge.

Did I still trust him? That was a good question. Right now, I trusted him more than I trusted myself. And then I thought of the phone. I wondered if I could get a signal now that we weren't in the woods.

I pulled it out and dialed my office number. Surprisingly, it rang. I waited for Mrs. Benton to pick up and was bitterly disappointed when it went directly to voicemail. It was too early for her to be in the office.

"What happened?" Zach asked.

"It went through…but it went to voicemail."

I could see the disappointment on his face.

"Sorry," I murmured.

"What do you have to be sorry for? You have no control over who picks up and when. But Levi's right. We need to get moving."

We started towards the open field of lush, green grass. I shivered involuntarily as the mist hovering over the field like a lost ghost slowly evaporated. I kept my phone in my hand as we started across the field…a field that would've been beautiful under different circumstances. I had to wait a few hours before I could call Mrs. Benton again. As I was about to dial her number to leave a message in her voicemail, the phone rang. Everyone froze as I picked it up.

"Hello? Hello?"

"Ms. Robeson!" I had never been so glad to hear Mrs. Benton's voice as I was at that moment. "I've been trying to reach you for days now! Are you okay?"

"So far. Are you in the office now?"

"No. I had all calls re-routed to my home line in case you called. Where are you? Are you still in Georgia?"

"Yes…but listen to me. I need you to call Jason Ribbler. His number is in my electronic rolodex."

"Jason…from the FBI Jason?"

"Yes…and please call Councilman Andy DelVecchio and tell him that my family and I are trapped on a plantation here in Georgia. Have him work with Jason to start a search for us beginning at Carmichael's Restaurant in Darcy County. You got that?"

"Yes, but Ms. Robeson, what's going on?"

"It's too time consuming to explain. Just have them work together. My family is being held against their will."

"Oh, goodness! I'll get right on it."

Then the phone went dead in my hand. I wasn't sure if she had hung up or if the signal was dropped. It didn't matter. Help was coming and that was all that mattered.

"Indie, what's the verdict? Is help finally coming" Zach asked.

"Yes. Finally." I turned to Levi. "I was able to get a hold of someone on my work phone. Help is coming."

"But it ain't here yet. Let's keep moving. We can't stay here. Now come on, let's…" Levi's voice trailed off as he tilted his head slightly to his left. I wasn't sure what he was doing.

"Levi, what…" I began.

He put his index finger to his lips. "Wait. Listen."

I couldn't hear anything at first. And then I heard it. The sound was faint, but I could hear it growing. Ice water trickled down the small of my back at the sound of motorized vehicles and dogs barking in the distance.

"We got to move…now!" Levi ordered.

Cal Carmichael sat at the head of the circular table glaring angrily at the remaining members of the coven. "Where is Onyx?"

All six people seated at the table looked at one another, but no one spoke.

"I know where Lulu is. Now where is Onyx?" The color in Cal's face rose. "Where is she?"

"Sir, we don't know," Anita said in a meek voice. "Last we saw, she walked out of yesterday's meeting."

"I believe she left, Mr. Carmichael," Macy said.

"That drops our power to seventy percent! That's enough for anyone to breach our home. We can't let that happen!" He looked around the room, casting an icy, crystal blue stare at each witch. "Go fetch that bitch August out of the women's cabin. Bring her to the pit and prepare the consecration oil. We need another sacrifice to help bring our powers up to speed."

"August?" Macy spoke up. "Why August?"

"Why not?" Cal asked with a cold smile.

"It's just that…well, she's my nephew's wife."

"And?"

"That's it."

"I don't see why her being your nephew's wife should factor into anything we do. After all, wasn't it you and Pearl who decided to sacrifice your own family to keep your powers? Didn't you want to be young again instead of locked inside that broken-down, decrepit body you were encased in, Macy? Was the tradeoff worth it?"

Pearl chuckled to herself.

"And you!" He turned his gaze on Pearl. "Weren't you the one that sacrificed your own daughter because you said she would be better off dead than a lesbian?"

No one said a word at the table.

"Get that bitch August and bring her to the pit!"

The carriage had been moving for approximately fifteen minutes when an ATV whizzed past us, going in the other direction. I couldn't make out who was on it, and it really didn't matter. My priority was getting my wife out of that hellhole, and I was grateful to have Sheriff Cuomo by my side. We rode for an additional ten minutes before coming to a halt in what looked like the center of mid-1800s Darcy County.

As soon as we came to a halt, I bolted out of the door and raced across the ground. I looked around, not sure of where I was. I called my wife's name. "August!"

"Mr. Robeson!" The sheriff called as she followed behind me. "Do you know where you are?"

I looked around, wildly hoping that I would find something that would resonate with me. Nothing looked familiar. I had been taken unconscious from the carriage and all I remembered was waking up inside of a box and riding for an hour until I found myself on an auction block, where I was bought, along with a few other men, and shipped off to Alabama.

"August!" I shouted again.

Some of the people appeared to be paid actors and actresses. They looked at me.

"Mr. Robeson!" Sheriff Cuomo yelled.

I turned to face her. "We have to find my wife!"

"And I will help you do that, but we have to do it right!" she said. "Now come with me so I can question some of these actors. Maybe they'll know where to find your wife!"

She approached a woman wearing a long dress and a bonnet. She was white, and even from where I was standing, I could see that she had enormous blue eyes. Sheriff Cuomo said something to her that I couldn't hear. They talked for what seemed like hours but had been only a few minutes.

When she returned, she told me to follow her. "Drake, can you tell me what exactly happened to you and your family when you got here?"

I explained to her about the carriage ride, how it came to be, why my family and I found ourselves in Darcy County and how we all managed to get separated. As we walked, I told her that I found my daughters at the same plantation that I had been sent to and how we managed to escape and make it back to Georgia. She told me that we had to walk at least a mile to the place where the women were sent for the rest of the day.

She believed me. As it turns out, the woman with the big blue eyes told her that behind this charade of late 1800s Darcy County was where the real slave quarters were hidden, about a mile west of where the makeshift Darcy County was built. Short of flagging down someone in a horse drawn cart to take us there, the only way to get there would be on foot.

The sheriff tried to radio for backup and found that she was out of range. That's when we realized that we were on our own. We had no idea how big the plantation was…but we knew that it would take us minimally a half an hour to get to where we needed to be.

The sun rode high in the sky and the humidity started to build. We began to sweat as we made our way to the slave quarters.

And that's when we heard the commotion. People were running roughshod over the property. Out of the corner of my eye, I saw the sheriff unlatch her gun from the holster strapped to her side.

The first gunshots rang out and the sheriff shoved me brutally to the ground. She squatted down beside me, prepared to cover me in case bullets started raining over our heads.

"Wait here," she said. "Owens, come with me. Stay low. Mr. Robeson, stay put!"

I watched the two officers creep slowly into the chaos that surrounded the plantation's main house. It looked as if people were trying to break in. More gunfire erupted and despite all the madness around me, all I could think about was getting to August.

I waited for a lull in the gunfire before jumping to my feet to find the sleeping quarters on my own. My feelings overtook me, and I ran in the direction of some cabins that I could see in the distance. As I ran, gunfire erupted once again. Bullets whizzed past me. I screamed, preparing myself to be hit, but nothing happened...to me. Out of the corner of my eye, I saw the sheriff fall to the ground. Two seconds later, the accompanying police officer dropped as well...both mortally wounded.

I raced to where she had fallen, grabbed her gun, and then ran towards the cabins in the distance.

Charlie kicked in the wooden door of the cabin that housed the female slaves. The women stopped moving, their conversations ending abruptly.

"August, over here! Now!" he shouted.

Everyone looked at August with fear in their eyes.

"I said get the fuck over here now!"

August had been sitting on the edge of her cot and now she stood tentatively. Tess looked over at her from the next cot. She mouthed the words, "Go to him."

August crossed the room until she was face to face with Charlie. "Where are my children?" she asked.

"You don't have any children here."

"I have two daughters...Autumn and Madison Robeson. They're incredibly smart and..."

He slapped her with the back of his hand, causing her nose to bleed and stunning her into silence. Grabbing her roughly by the arm, he snarled, "Now shut the fuck up and come with me."

He pulled her out of the cabin and into the chaos of the afternoon. Gunshots could be heard with bullets ricocheting around them.

"Where are you taking me?" August asked.

He whirled on her, his face bright red with anger. "You don't get to ask any questions from me, you understand, you nigger bitch?"

"What kind of a man are you that you have to dehumanize other people to make yourself feel good?"

He punched her in the face, and she fell to the ground.

"Get the fuck up!" he shouted. "You ain't nuthin'! Don't you know that?"

August rose slowly to her feet. "I want my children and I want to leave!"

"That ain't gonna happen!" He grabbed her arm again and pulled her towards an opening behind the main house.

"Where are you taking me?" August cried out.

"You gonna be sacrificed, gal!" And then he began to laugh.

My heart was slamming against my ribcage as I stumbled into the first cabin. It was filled with women. They looked at me as if I were from another planet.

"August!" I looked wildly around the room.

"She ain't here." She was a large woman wearing a kerchief and a long skirt.

"Where is she?"

"They just took her outta here," she said. "We don't know why."

"What direction did they take her in?"

"Out the door. Maybe 'round the back of the big house."

I turned to leave.

"They may be takin' her to be sacrificed."

"Shit." I rushed out of the cabin.

The women followed me and then scattered in different directions while I made a beeline to the back of the main house which was three cabin lengths away. I saw a man pulling on a woman: an overseer pulling on a slave.

August! It was my wife who was fighting against the man.

"August!" I ran towards her.

"Drake? Drake? Oh my God, Drake!" She pulled away from the man.

The man tugged at August viciously, causing her to lose her footing and fall. He pulled her arm to get her to her feet.

Something inside of me snapped. I saw blood red and although I had never touched a firearm in my life, I raised the sheriff's gun and pointed it at him.

"August!" I called out. "Come here, baby."

"Who the fuck are you, nigger?" he asked, never relinquishing his hold. "Oh, is this your bitch?"

"I've never taken a life but if you don't let go of her, I'm gonna hurt you." I cocked the gun and aimed it at him. "I'm not playin', dude. You got three seconds to let go of my wife!"

"Really? What you gonna do? Shoot me?"

"Like you've never been shot before!"

"Try it nigger! Go ahead and…"

I squeezed the trigger, aiming for his arm. The bullet struck his shoulder. Blood spurted like a geyser as he fell back. August screamed, stumbled away and then rushed towards me. When she fell into my chest, I instinctively wrapped my arms around her. She cried and for a moment, so did I.

"Drake, we can't leave! The girls…"

"I got the girls, baby! They're safe! Police station in Edison! Now let's get out of here."

August looked at me disbelievingly, and then whispered in my ear. "Let's get off this godforsaken place."

"Let's go baby. I got you."

Bodies had fallen in the uprising. Guns were firing and the odor of cordite filled the air. We smelled burning flesh mixed with the sour smell of ignited gasoline. Through all the chaos we spotted an ATV with its engine idling. That was a sign from God!

"Baby, let's go! Come on!"

We rushed towards the vehicle, looked around to see if its owner would show up, and then climbed on. I revved the engine once and we took off, not sure of where we were going only that we had to get out of there.

I looked back at the main house. There were licks of flame coming out of the first-floor windows. Someone must have made it inside and was truly burning the place to the ground.

"We have to get your Aunt Merline." August said in my ear.

"Aunt Merline?"

"She's alive and well on this plantation!"

"Let me get you out of this place…then I'll deal with that."

And as we rode across the campus, I spotted a road that appeared as if it would lead us out and off this plantation. I took it and hoped to God that I would never see this place again.

# Tarek

It was hot and muggy as the sound of the cicadas buzzing in the woods reverberated across the trees above. We stood on the edge of what appeared to be dense woods. I had no idea how to get to the civilization that I hoped existed on the other side.

I looked over at Kisha. We had been walking for most of the day and I sometimes felt like we were walking in circles. We were exhausted. We were hot and dehydrated. The sun beat severely on our shoulders for most of the day. There was no way of knowing what time it was, but we had to find shelter before dark.

"How're you doing?" I asked as we sat on the grass at the edge of the woods.

"Tired." She looked at me. "Do you think we'll ever get out of here?"

"Yes." I nodded. "But we need to get through these woods to whatever's on the other side."

"Do we have to go through the woods?"

"If we want to get off this plantation…yeah. We gotta go through it."

She paused, looking at the dense growth before us with apprehension. "Let's go."

And that's when we heard the sound we had been hoping to hear ever since we decided to escape from this godforsaken place. Helicopters beat above us like dragonflies, some flying towards the main house, others towards other areas of the campus.

We raced out into the open so that they could see us. And with the last ounce of our strength, we waved and shouted. Kisha burst into tears when she realized that one of the choppers had spotted us and was now hovering, ropes extended, with uniformed men jettisoning down to us.

My legs crumpled beneath me, and I fell to the ground. We were finally getting off this plantation.

# Indigo

They came! Mrs. Benton came through. She called the Congressman and my contact at the FBI and got us help. And as we were lifted to safety, I collapsed into Levi's arms. My tears burst out of me like water held back by a dam which had now crumbled. I began to pray. I prayed for my brother Drake. I prayed for my nieces. I prayed for my aunts. I prayed they were all safe and out of harm's way. I prayed for my Uncle Shucky, hoping that he would make it to safety. I prayed for Ida and Wilson.

"You okay now, Indie." Levi said gruffly, wrapping his arms around me.

My tears fell, coming hard and fast as I buried my face in the remains of his shirt. It was over. Oh my God, it was over.

Pearl, Macy, and Anita stood in the back yard beside the vat holding the sacrificial oil. They looked at the men who had fallen, their bodies scattered on the campus grounds like toy soldiers. They watched as the main house went up in flames.

Cal Carmichael was nowhere to be seen. Where he disappeared to was anyone's guess.

"We have to do something," Pearl said as the choppers beat incessantly overhead.

"One last spell," Macy said. "Join hands and we can conjure up a disguise. I'll go back to my old form. I won't like it, but I'll do it. Who would suspect an old woman being a part of the slaveholders on this plantation? Ya'll need to come up with a look that won't be associated with this house. Now is the time to be a victim...not an oppressor."

Pearl and Anita nodded, and the three women joined hands. The words came slow and inaudible, and then the frequency and speed increased until blue smoke enshrouded Macy and Anita's feet and swirled around their bodies. When the smoke dissipated, Macy was old again, her body shriveled. Pearl had chosen to appear as her original self. But something was wrong. She could feel it.

Anita was hunched over, standing on wobbly legs. She had aged by thirty years, appearing to be in her eighties. Pearl wrapped her arms protectively around both women as the choppers descended around them.

Shucky appeared from the house, his clothing torn, and his face soot-stained. He descended the steps and collapsed to his knees in the front yard. And then he saw her. "Merl!"

At first, she didn't hear him. Maybe she didn't want to. Then she turned slowly to the source of his voice.

Shucky raised himself to his feet and approached her. She stood, looking at him in disbelief.

"You've been here…all this time?" he asked softly.

"And I've been happy," she said in an exhausted voice.

He allowed the words to sink in. "Was bein' with me that bad?"

She looked away, and then stared back at him with defiance burning in her eyes. "It was that bad. Being beaten almost daily whenever you drank. Silencing me so that I could never say anything. You were a horrible man." She turned and walked away.

Shucky looked around. He had successfully taken down this plantation with the help of the many migrants and people who had been enslaved. He should have been elated. Instead, bitterness started in his core and spread throughout his body. His wife preferred to be a slave than to be with him. "Ain't that some shit?" he muttered, shaking his head. Then he followed her.

"I was on my way to Chicago when they took me. At first, I was afraid." The words tumbled from Merline's mouth in a torrential flood. "You made life hell for me. I was a prisoner in my own home. Every day, I never knew when the demon in you would come out. And every day, it did."

"But Merl, Imma changed man." He looked behind him at the burning main house. "I'm sorry, baby. I never meant to hurt you."

"Sorry don't make it right." She looked down at the ground, trembling as the tears began to fall. "Sometimes, some black mens don't realize what they do to their womens until it's too late." She looked directly into his eyes. "I'm glad you changed, Shuckland, but there ain't no you and me anymore. Not now…not ever."

She turned and began to walk towards the cookhouse.

"Where will you go?" Shucky asked.

"I don't know. But you don't got to worry about me no more."

Shucky watched in disbelief as she walked away, her form shrinking slowly as she headed towards the cookhouse. There would be no reunion. There would be no reconciliation. He always thought if he found Merline, things would be different.

For the first time in almost a year, he wanted a drink.

# Drake

We rode along a dirt path I had never seen before. I knew that we weren't on the same path that brought us into this land of enslavement. But as long as it wasn't taking us back to the main house, I was happy.

We pressed on for another fifteen minutes before we hit a dead end, but there was a footpath ahead of us. The ATV wouldn't fit but we could walk it. Climbing down from the bike, I took August's hand. We looked at each other, and then, knowing that we were on the same page, began to walk down the path together.

It rose and fell in low, sloping dips. We went carefully, walking for about a half an hour before we reached a clearing that I didn't want to see. It wasn't so much the clearing as what was in the clearing. We had seen them when we came through on the carriage…gators sunning themselves on rocks and sandy coves beside a wide body of water.

"Baby…we're gonna have to tread lightly as we pass these gators. Are you with me?"

"You lead…I'll follow," August said softly.

She held onto my hand as we walked on a path so narrow that at times, we had to question if we were on a path at all. Each step was slow and deliberate as the ground beneath us crumbled.

Sweat began to accumulate in our palms as we continued, knowing that each step would lead to an almost certain death if we fell into the gator pit.

We kept going, holding hands tightly…and up until that last step, I thought we were going to make it. August got clear and I took the final step that would take us away from the gator pit when the ground beneath my feet gave way. I slid down a steep embankment and into the sandy clearing. Hearing August's voice, I looked wildly around for her. I looked up and there she was, at the top of the embankment where I had just slipped and fallen. I struggled to find a rock or a tree root that would give me the necessary footing to get to the top of the embankment and back to her.

There was nothing.

"Drake…"

"It's gonna be all right, baby!" I shouted.

I really believed that until I heard the loud grunt followed by a hiss, and something grabbed my right foot. I felt myself being pulled towards the water.

August screamed my name and dropped to her knees at the edge of the embankment.

Suddenly I was in the water, turning and splashing, water going up my nose. I called out to her, only for my voice to be drowned out by more water. I struggled as the huge gator pulled me under the water, its razor-sharp teeth cutting into my calf. I was losing strength as I fought to bring my head above water. I fought until there wasn't any fight left in me.

At least my wife was off the plantation and my kids were safe.

But what about the rest of my family? What about Aunt Pearl and Macy? What about Tarek?

# Epilogue

The fire burned out of control for hours. Fire trucks couldn't reach the main house to put out the flames. The other survivors of the uprising had been taken to safety by the armed forces which had rescued the family.

Anita, Macy, and Pearl were among those who were rescued. And Macy was right; no one suspected these elderly women being a part of the coup or residents of the skeletal remains of the main house. A third of the crops had been torched but there was no one left to finish the harvest, so the vegetables and fruits were left to rot or grow wild.

Henry made his way to the parking lot of Carmichaels Restaurant, where he was greeted by police. Latrice looked around in bewilderment as she climbed off the ATV. They seemed to be lost in a sea of spectators, emergency crews, and uniformed police officers and state troopers.

"So, what now?" Henry asked.

She looked around helplessly. "It looks like they're still bringing people out of the property. Maybe I'll get reunited with August and Merline. I'm gonna wait here."

"You sure?"

Latrice nodded. "I'm sure. I want to see if Tarek and Kisha made it to safety. What about you?"

"I have enough power left to cast one last spell. I'm gonna be Lady Onyx forever. I already have the clothes and wigs. If I lose my powers for good, at least I'll be who I want to be."

Sirens warbled in the distance as another ambulance pulled up into the massive parking lot.

"Good luck to you, Onyx." Latrice reached out and hugged Henry.

He hugged her back. "You too, baby. It's gonna be dark soon. Find some shelter and get some rest. We've all been through enough to last us a life…"

"We found another one!" a male voice shouted.

Latrice turned in time to see August stumbling out of the woods.

"I gotta go, Onyx!" She rushed to August, excusing herself as she pushed people aside. As she reached her, tears began to fall. "August! August!"

August burst into tears as she raced into Latrice's arms. The two embraced as they collapsed to the ground.

"Drake…Drake is…gone!" August said through sobs.

"No!" Latrice burst into fresh tears.

"I've…I've got to get to my babies. They're at a police station in Edison County."

"We need to get personal effects from inside the restaurant. Your truck should still be parked in the lot. Then we can pick up the girls."

"Should be. No reason for anyone to move it. Let's go. And I want to get on the road tomorrow. We're never coming back down here again!"

Latrice wiped tears from her eyes as they headed into the restaurant. She hoped her cell phone was still there.

Once inside, August sat down at an unoccupied table. She began to rock suddenly as more silent tears rolled down her face. Latrice sat beside her, wrapping her arms around her as she braced herself for what was coming next.

"Drake…" August threw her head back, the sobs becoming uncontrollable. She wailed, finally allowing her grief to overtake her.

Many of the survivors of the Carmichael Plantation had been whisked away to a facility where they would be reunited with their families, interviewed, and given hot meals and medical treatment. When Tarek, Zach, and Indigo were reunited, there was an overflow of tears and hugs. Questions were asked about Drake, August, and the girls. Similar questions were asked about Macy and Pearl. As the facility began to fill with more people who had been imprisoned against their will, those answers slowly came to light.

Cal Carmichael blamed his father, John, for the creation of the plantation system, but fled secretly when it became evident that he played an active role in imprisoning people to work the fields. Although the other plantations remained in existence, no one seemed to be willing to talk about the travesty of justice surrounding the imprisonment of those that remained.

The fight still rages to close the remaining plantations…a fight currently being waged by the ACLU.

Miguel eventually left Pearl's home, knowing he couldn't stay there longer than a few days. His undocumented status forced him to travel to Queens, where he would be reunited with his own family. He had no money, and searched the house until he found forty dollars. That was enough to get him started.

The hardest part was not knowing what happened to Drake and the little girls. Perhaps he would never know. Drake had helped him so much. Miguel would never forget the man who had fiercely protected his daughters and himself. With a heavy heart, he left a note for Drake on the dining table, apologizing for taking the money, and saying that once he got settled, he would repay him and his family.

He owed Drake so much. It didn't matter how long it would take, he would pay them back. Right now, he had another journey ahead of him, and as he traveled, he hoped that Drake and his family were okay. The hard life on the plantations had changed everyone…himself included.